FAR SHORE

THE AFTER SERIES
BOOK 3

TRACI L. SLATTON

parvati
press

This book is a work of fiction. Names, characters, places and incidents are either the product of the author's imagination or are used fictitiously. Any resemblance to actual persons, living or dead, or to actual events or locales is entirely coincidental.

Far Shore

Cover designed by Gwyn Kennedy Snider
http://www.gkscreative.com

Cover art: Copyright © iStock 3727828, Mystery; iStock 10710992, Couples, iStock 158620, squiggle4b; iStock 19409679, tropical butterflies

Published by Parvati Press
http://www.parvatipress.com

Visit the author website:
http://www.tracilslatton.com

ISBN 978-0-9890232-8-3 (eBook)
ISBN 978-0-9890232-7-6 (Paperback)

Library of Congress Control Number: 2013917682

BOOKS BY TRACI L. SLATTON

IMMORTAL

THE BOTTICELLI AFFAIR

FALLEN

COLD LIGHT

FAR SHORE

DANCING IN THE TABERNACLE
(poetry)

PIERCING TIME & SPACE

THE ART OF LIFE
con Sabin Howard

THE LOVE OF MY (OTHER) LIFE

PRAISE FOR *FALLEN* AND *COLD LIGHT*
BOOKS 1 AND 2 OF THE AFTER SERIES

 This series continues to haunt me. I fell in love with the characters in the first installment, **Fallen**. Within this story [**Cold Light**], the characters have changed for the better. The tension was high throughout the story. As the reader joins in the adventure, they continue to wonder if Emma will be in time to save her daughter, if she will give into the overwhelming love and desire between her and Arthur and if the mist will catch them The surprises were thrilling and sprinkled within the story adding fun to an already compelling plot. The ending is left open allowing for the possibility of third installment. For which this reader, hopes is more than a possibility. I have loved both books in this series.

HC Harju, *Night Owl Reviews*

 Slatton displays exceptional storytelling abilities in **Cold Light** by weaving fragments together at the end in a way that was delightfully unforeseen. And her poetic prose spirit the reader away into complete submersion. She also leaves a few mysteries behind to make you ache for the third book.

Rebecca Skane, *Seacoast Online*

 It [**Fallen**] is well-written, and I love the sci-fi aspects of it, the paranormal activities. It makes for a great read. . . . This book is incredible. It puts life into perspective for me. . . . It's not for the faint of heart. It is for women who want to hear their voice

and are as comfortable chopping wood, as wearing make-up. As the world changes, I like to read about women who make their own decisions, have opinions, and possess inner courage and strength. We older women worked long and hard to fight against antifeminist media and men. We want all of us to have choices; our sons and daughters, grandsons and granddaughters.

I love the main character, Emma Strong; knows her own mind, down-to-earth, smart, talented, powerful, not unlike the author! I highly recommend it!

Jennifer Jilks, *Country Cottage Reflections*

 **Cold Light** picks up over a year after **Fallen** left off. Emma has made it back to the Safe Zone in Edmonton, Alberta with Haywood and the girls, and quickly brings the reader up to date on how it happened. Even though my heart broke at the end of **Fallen** when she left Arthur, I understood her reasons . . . an excellent story that I wouldn't hesitate to re-read in the future. New characters are introduced early, and many of them are easy to like and amazingly relatable considering the circumstances of. My favorite early on was Gaff but edged over to Kangee by the end. Emma is still the survivor, Arthur is still the leader, Gaff is the resourceful kid, Kangee is the enigmatic mystery; the rest have their own unique attributes as well. Ms. Slatton did an excellent job creating believable characters and situations based in a hard to imagine post-apocalyptic world.

Daysieanne, *My Book Addiction Reviews*

 I read **Fallen**, loved it. I read **Cold Light**, loved it. Now I must wait for what will seem like an eternity for the last of this amazing trilogy? . . . **Cold Light** leaves us with another heart-wrenching, cliffhanger ending. I cannot WAIT for the last book. I must know what happens. I NEED to know. Grrrr.

If you haven't started reading **Fallen** yet, do it *NOW*. Then read **Cold Light**. I believe you will be as spellbound as I am by these marvelous reads.

Julie, *Books Complete Me*

 I have long awaited this second book, **Cold Light**, after the way **Fallen** ended. I was NOT disappointed! Emma's daughter has been kidnapped by a rogue group and she goes on a suicide mission to get her back. I was very excited to be reunited with a few of the cast from **Fallen** and am still in anxious need of book three now to see how this all wraps up.

Emma is one strong and determined woman but Arthur is just as determined. I am torn on which way I want Emma to go because with the one man her husband she has the strong history and children but she shares something with Arthur that I don't think she and her husband ever really had or ever will.

I can't say much more without a spoiler comment but I will say I didn't really like the way **Cold Light** ended. I would not want to be in Emma's shoes and have to make the choices she is being forced to but it's time . . . there can be only one victor in this war.

Jennifer, *Gimme The Scoop Reviews*

 There are a lot of twists and turns . . . . **Cold Light** is a book of survival, fighting all the odds and trying to rebuild what has been lost. It is a love story between Emma and Arthur, only will Emma make the right choice? Does she live with a man she doesn't love for her children's sake while living in misery without the man she loves? This is a situation that many people have faced throughout history.

The book is a cliffhanger, as was book one, and I am one of those people who hate that and almost always give a poor rating because of it. The reason I didn't in this case is because the story is just too absorbing, the characters are amazing and the author's description of post-apocalyptic Earth is fascinating. I read at least a book a day. Often times when an author leaves you hanging at the end, by the time the next book comes out, you don't remember all the details of the book you just read. That is not the case with Ms. Slatton she brings the reader up to date on what happened prior so I know I will not be floundering about wondering what happened before. I can't wait for the next book in the series.

Linda Tonis, *The Paranormal Romance Guild*

 This book [**Cold Light**] in one sentence: A haunting, heart-wrenching, action-packed emotional roller coaster of a read that will leave an impression on you long after your finish the book.

To say that I love this book or this series would be an understatement. Traci Slatton has done an impeccable job with what I thought would be an impossible hurdle for her two main characters to overcome after the ending of **Fallen**. Not only did she do the impossible, but she made me love the characters and the new additions to the book even more.

Evelyn Amaro, *Paromantasy Blog*

 The After trilogy is a post-apocalyptic romance story that is as heart-breaking as it is realistic. Earlier this year, I dove into Slatton's **Fallen,** quickly immersing myself in a world that sucks you in and characters that keep you enthralled in their very existence. As I began reading **Cold Light**, I immediately felt like I was home again. The way of life for the survivors of the mists really keeps you cheering the characters on. I couldn't imagine living in the After world. It's disturbing on so many levels. I have to admit that some of the survivors really do make the best of their situation, revealing a spark of hope amongst the darkness. . . .

Slatton once again has created a brilliant post-apocalyptic world that will have you on the edge of your seat. I couldn't read it fast enough. The *After* trilogy is, by far, one of the most exciting reads I've read all month. I'm dying to find out how Slatton will end the trilogy. The worst thing about **Cold Light** is that it ended leaving me wanting more of the After.

Jennifer, *Fictitious Musings*

 Slatton's ability to weave a tale that is filled with adventure, loss and love is unmatched. Her writing makes it so easy for you to fall in love with the characters so much so that you find yourself riding a roller-coaster of emotions. One minute you are mad, then your lips curl into a smile, and sometimes you cannot help but reach for a tissue.

The Mists are changing, and our favorite Russian cut-throat is back in **Cold Light**. But don't get me started on the ending. I only hope that the final installment comes out quickly, and things work out the way I want them to. (I am totally on team Arthur!!)

An exceptional series that will keep you reading and ignoring your family. So grab **Fallen** and **Cold Light**, grab a bottle of wine, head to your favorite reading spot and be ready to spend the next four to eight or so hours falling in love with this series.

A MUST have series!

Annette Marie Guerriero Nishimoto,
Gothic Mom's Book Reviews

 Emma's courage is only matched by her determination to find her daughter. But her heart is torn between the man whom she married and the man to whom she has fallen in love.

. . . Arthur's relentless pursuit of Emma is both heartbreaking and remarkable given the circumstances of the day. Finding a woman like Emma is a once in a lifetime occurrence, but his love has forced many of his friends into life-threatening situations. But like family, they argue and fight, and in the end, the survival of one means the survival of them all.

Cold Light is an amazing look at one person's passion to find someone they love- Arthur's pursuit of Emma and Emma's hunt for Beth. The storyline is slow to evolve as Traci takes the reader on a cold, dark and deadly trek across the snow covered fields of Alberta, but once Emma reaches a survival Outpost, the interaction of the characters quickly uncovers a series of plot twists and anxiety ridden re-introductions to the colorful characters from the series first book. Arthur's reunion with Emma is heart-wrenching and painful knowing he has travelled thousands of mile and 18 months to find the only woman he will ever love.

The character development continues as each of Arthur's family members seeks to find a place to where they belong. And survival 101 after an apocalyptic nightmare can also mean finding someone to love for all of the right and wrong reasons.

Sandy, ***The Reading Café***

 Traci Slatton nails it with her follow up to **Fallen**. In **Cold Light** Emma is faced with hard decision after hard decision—and we're not talking about decisions on simply where to live or who to be with. We're talking life and death decisions in a place that is just simply not pretty.

The end of **Fallen** leaves of with the reuniting of Emma with her family. She leaves behind someone she's grown attached to and does what is right and honorable. But now her life in Europe has followed her to Canada—in more ways than one.

What I appreciate about the After trilogy is how the world can be so bleak, but yet there is so much hope in the story. There's love, and thoughtfulness, and honor in a place where those just don't seem like they'd exist anymore. And what I love even more is how honest Traci's writing is. She doesn't hesitate to do what needs to be done to move the story forward. When writing a story like **Cold Light** (or it's previous book), there are hard things which need to be done to give the story credibility. You cannot write about bad people and have them not do bad things. This is not a young adult dystopian or post-apocalyptic story—this is hardcore, knuckle-whitening stuff and it kept me riveted from page one.

Lydia, *The Lost Entwife*

 **Fallen** is another captivating story about the end of civilization as we know it. . . . Knee-gripping suspense and a host of great characters bring the post-apocalyptic world to horrifying life in **Fallen**. . . . I eagerly anticipate the next installment.

Margaret Marr, **Nights and Weekends Reviews**

Slatton is a fantastic storyteller. . . . **Fallen** awakens emotion and captivates with the turn of each page. . . . From every angle, **Fallen** is a captivating adventure with just enough romance to keep you enthralled and begging for more."

Jennifer, *Fictitious Musings*

Fallen is an exhilarating post apocalyptic thriller that contains superb twists and spins, which keep the reader wondering what next. The fast-paced story line grips the reader early on with the vivid description of a world gone mad and never slows down. . . . An exciting end of the world thriller.

Amazon Hall of Fame Reviewer Harriet Klausner
for *Alternative Worlds Reviews*

Excellent book [**Fallen**], I mean Unbelievable! So I tracked down the author because I was dying to know when the next one came out. . . .

Taking Time for Mommy Blogspot

The reader is forced to consider previously stable definitions of time, obedience, psychic powers, science, and most importantly, love. Powers exist, perhaps, that enhance long-ignored mental skills but is the power of memory too strong to allow for new ways of relating and the freedom to explore same without guilt and ignoring the instinctive inclinations of the heart?

Many, many questions arise as one reads this story [**Fallen**] that defies what can be falsely read as a simplistic story/plot. Traci L. Slatton is a writer to watch closely, including in whatever sequels follow this unique, well-written sci-fi novel!

Viviane, *Crystal Book Reviews*

 This is so not a world I want to live in—a mysterious mist that kills, rogue bands of survivors who round up women and children for far more nefarious purposes than you could imagine, dwindling food supplies . . .

I like Emma. She's strong, she's resolute, and she's fearless in standing up for those who can't help themselves—almost to the point of getting herself killed . . .

The plot is simple (survive), the story is moving. I enjoyed reading **Fallen**, and the realization at the end makes me antsy to find out what happens in the sequel to this first-in-a-trilogy.

Drey, *Drey's Library*

By the end of the book [**Fallen**], I wanted to know more about everyone. What will they do? How long can they survive? Will they find happiness? The book ends with a very emotional cliffhanger. This is the first of a trilogy, and I can't wait to find out what happens."

As I Turn the Pages Blogspot

 Slatton's natural storytelling ability takes over and the reader finds themselves engrossed in another well envisioned story world. . . . Slatton has once again allowed her ability with words to develop a post apocalyptic world that draws the reader in, and allows them to work towards the struggle of survival right along side the characters. The characters are compelling and real. . . . They have weaknesses, and compulsions that are both horrifying and ennobling. Slatton has developed characters that have the courage to face a failing world, while at the same time demonstrating not only everything that is right about mankind, but everything that is wrong, as well. . . . I look forward to the future installments of this trilogy.

Lisa, *The Book Worm's Library*

 In the post apocalyptic world of **Fallen**, survivors are tormented by a mysterious mist that can disintegrates animate and inanimate objects alike. Many have also developed psychic powers, like Emma's ability to heal. Emma was in Europe with her young daughter when the mists descended and the apocalypse began. As they travel to find a safe haven, more children joined their group and Emma protects them from both the mists and the roving bands of marauders. When they come across Arthur and his men searching for provisions in a dead town, Emma strikes up a deal. . . . Slowly, they fall in love, but Emma is torn between her new feelings and the husband she left behind overseas. When Arthur's devastating secret is revealed to her, she doubts the strength of her feelings for him.

Fallen has a very vivid world populated with interesting characters.

Laura Lehman, *Bella Online, The Voice of Women*

 What would you do if your daughter was stolen by Raiders? This is a story [**Cold Light**] that will stir every parental emotion in you and then take you for a ride. Emma's daughter was taken by raiders and there is nothing she will not do to get her back. The books plot and pace was stunning with its action packed story line and the dangers lurking around every corner. But she is not alone, she has loyal companions along the way. The world building is set in a post apocalyptic world. The characters were creatively built and I love how much they were relatable. Over all a great addition to the 1st book in this series.

Melissa, *Were Vamps Romance*

The second exciting "After" post-apocalyptic thriller moves forward on two fronts: Emma's relationships and the anticipated suicidal Armageddon Mists war as Traci L. Slatton deftly blends both subplots into a superb dystopian tale through her quality cast. The triangle participants fear the repercussions on the young at a time when nightmares are prevalent yet none of them can leave. Readers will wonder who will quote Dickens' A Tale of Two Cities: 'It is a far, far better thing that I do, than I have ever done; it is a far, far better rest that I go to, than I have ever known."

Amazon Hall of Fame Reviewer Harriet Klausner
for *Alternative Worlds Reviews*

I haven't read the first book in the *After* Trilogy, but after reading **Cold Light** I have already ordered it on my kindle and will be reading it within the next few days. The way Traci L. Slatton has created the After world is amazingly real to a reader. I can picture it easily in my mind without even trying too hard. The characters in the book are very easy to relate to as well. The way people have to live now really hits home and makes me wonder if I would even be able to do that. Life without phones and computers and even tvs… kinda scary. As I previously stated I haven't read the first book but the way the author fills us in at different places in the book tells some of what I missed in the book. I didn't feel lost at all.

Jen's Corner Spot

 **Cold Light** is absolutely thrilling, even better than **Fallen**, but a bit shorter. I burned through the book in a couple of days and it left me longing for the conclusion to the story.

Once again, I love the characters in Slatton's story, as well as the intense and horrifying storyline. This is post-apocalyptic storytelling at its best. I'm a sucker for disaster movies and stories of post apocalyptic survival and I can visualize Slatton's stories as if they are a movie in my head. That's what great storytelling is all about. Highly recommended.

Game Vortex

 I've fallen for Fallen . . . Let me just throw this out there: I love dystopian books. . . .

A few other things you might want to know about me is 1) I love science fiction, 2) I love the conflict of man against nature gone wrong, and 3) I love a hearty romance thrown in there for good measure. Fallen had all of these ingredients, and more.

Full of action, adventure and a very intelligent read, I absolutely loved this story. . . . **Fallen** ends in a place where you know there will be a sequel, and this was fine by me, because I wasn't ready to let go of this world Traci L. Slatton had created so beautifully.

L. V. Lewis

 If you'd read **Fallen**, there is no way you can forgo **Cold Light**. I read this immediately after reading **Fallen**, but am just now getting to review. However, don't let that lead you to believe that this book isn't as stellar as the first. In fact, this book is more action-packed and the stakes have gone even higher than Emma and her family just avoiding the mists that can consume them. This is a do-or-die, life-and-death story that leaves you guessing at every turn—How is Emma going to get out of these newest pickles? Read **Cold Light** and find out.

This is a dystopian romance for the mature set, (Hunger Games and/or Divergent on steroids). Don't ignore this wonderful series.

I give **Cold Light** Five out of Five Stars!

L. V. Lewis

 From page one I was riveted to this bleak world where hope and honor can still exist. Yes, there was evil, greed, fear, bad people taking advantage of others, but love, strength and the will to live still existed, too. The author told an amazing story, brutally well. **Cold Light** is Book 2 in the *After* Series, following the book **Fallen**.

Tome Tender

Fallen is well written with twists that keep you reading. Traci L. Slatton does a good job describing the scenes, you feel like you're there with them. The characters were well-rounded, having good and bad sides, which helped make them feel real.

This is a solid, enjoyable story for fans of the post-apocalyptic and/or dystopian genres."

To Read Perchance to Dream Reviews

 **Fallen** definitely had my attention from page one. It is an intense post-apocalyptic action/romance that's so well written you feel like the mists exist; (and you will probably avoid fog after reading). Being a fan of the survival-horror genre, I didn't know how a "survival-romance" would mesh, but Traci Slatton made it work. Her writing style is really descriptive and has a great flow to it; one minute your heart is racing, and the next minute you can't help but smile. The characters, Emma especially, had an authentic quality to them. They weren't just cookie-cutter characters, but 3-dimensional, and the dialogue fit them perfectly. As for the plot, it was very well developed, fast-paced, twisty, unique, and you won't see the ending coming. I personally can't wait for the next book in the trilogy!

Allizabeth Collins, ***The Paperback
Pursuer Blogspot***

 I was pulled into **Fallen** from the first few pages. Traci L. Slatton's apocalyptic world seems eerily possible. . . . **Fallen** is billed as the first of a trilogy. . . . This is not a girly romance. Slatton has written an apocalyptic novel with a romance built in— like most good stories should have. **Fallen** is excellent. I'll have to watch for the sequel.

Jandy's Reading Room

For my readers, with my warmest gratitude,

and my best wishes for joy

FAR
SHORE

1 I STOOD IN AN EXULTATION OF BLUE AND ORANGE butterflies, in a rolling landscape where leafy trees reached longingly into a blue sky filled with soft, white flakes. It was summer, and it was snowing.

Multitudes of people moved around, carelessly laughing, murmuring, and stamping. Everywhere the world was as it had been three years ago: buildings powered by electricity, streetlights, paved streets thrumming with cars and trucks, dogs and cats. Most surprisingly of all were the inorganic things like cell phones and air conditioners and fire hydrants and street signs. They were so easy and plentiful, the ordinary manufactured stuffs with which the world had run itself Before.

There was no sign of the encroaching mists that had devoured most of those things for their metallic components, along with billions of human beings—no sign of the devastation and loss of the mists' apocalypse.

My heart was whole, so I knew I was dreaming. It wasn't the merging of seasons in an irrational landscape that tipped me off. Rather, it was the feeling of not being shattered.

With this realization came a sense of how precious the glimpse into times past really was. I kept very, very still and looked around, engraving the images on my mind. I wanted to retain them, to remember what life had once been like. *At least I know what was Before,* I thought, *but will my two daughters remember this lost world, with all its precious, silly artifacts? Or will*

21

they grow up knowing only the struggle, danger, and loss that challenged survivors every day? How can I possibly make a better world for them out of the dust of the past, when the mists still ravage the planet and swathes of survivors go mad and become bloodthirsty raiders?

In the distance, behind a verdant tree encased in ice, stood three figures. The first moved toward me. He must have floated, because he was suddenly sitting, cross-legged, right in front of me. He was a wise man, a Rastafarian who emanated peace and knowing, like a Buddha. "How will you do it, Emma?" he asked, beaming at me. His black skin was very smooth and soft, and his voice was deep and musical.

"Do what?" I wondered.

He laughed and waved his hand; just like that, a cairn of stones grew up beside me. "How will you do it?" he asked again in that sing-songy voice. "Will you trust yourself? Will you remember to do that?"

Before I could respond, a girl approached. She was scrawny, with stringy blonde hair. "Emma," she said, smiling.

"Newt!" I cried. I leapt toward her and hugged her, squeezing and squeezing, as if I couldn't bear to ever let her go. Her lithe, warm body felt solid and good in my arms, causing a hot spring of joy to burst in my chest. "Newt, I . . . oh how I've missed you! I-I'm so glad to see you," I declared between sobs.

"I'm right here," she said, her voice softened by its familiar British twang. "Always."

"Are you okay?" I asked.

"All good," she said. She pushed herself a few centimeters away, just enough to show me that she was whole and unscathed.

My heart ached. The last time I'd seen her, in the south of France, she was being consumed, cell by cell, organ by organ, by the mists that had murdered billions of people and destroyed civilization and left behind madness and psychic gifts. *The mists. They had hurt her terribly.* I had killed her with a knife thrown into her throat, just to spare her more agony.

"I'm sorry for what happened to you." I clutched her tightly. "I'm so, so sorry, but I—"

"You couldn't stop it, Emma," she said. "Some things are meant to be. They're like . . . oh, landmarks in time. But other things can be changed."

"What things?" I asked. I couldn't help but feel amused and relieved at the same time. Newt was still Newt. Even beyond death, she was herself, piquant and whimsical, full of ellipses. She had been given precognition by the mists, as so many of us had been endowed with psychic powers hitherto disbelieved.

The mists affected the human bio-mind, the part of the human brain endowed with extrasensory perception. The mists made us all psychic, gave us gifts, made us mad. Worst of all, they ate us.

The gifts the mists had given me was a wondrous one, healing with my hands. But any gift from the mists came with a steep price to pay. *Am I doomed to madness, sooner or later?* I wondered.

Newt wavered for a moment, as if she'd vanish. Her flickering was a remnant of the time Before, when a computer or television pixilated.

"Wait!" I cried. I couldn't lose her again, at least not so soon. She was one of the precious ones, the orphaned children whom I'd shepherded south from Paris after the Day of the mists' global incursion. We'd finally found shelter and safety in a camp. I'd also found love there, only to discover sorrow in the end, before my husband came to get me and I left with him.

Newt solidified and grabbed my arm. Her skinny fingers tightened on my flesh. "Emma, you must do something. You must change it. I've seen. You must. Give whatever it takes, whatever is necessary to save him. They're coming, so give whatever it takes. Now. Don't wait. Give . . . just give it all. Remember." Then she was gone.

I walked through snow and summer light and winged creatures, wondering what I had to change. *What now?*

A man appeared, and when he approached, my heart sang. He was tall, with black hair and gray eyes. His features were even and symmetrical, with a perfection of form unseen in the everyday world, as if the ancient gods had sculpted him. He stood before me, his eyes effervescing. "Emma," he said, then put his warm hands on my shoulders.

I felt a fleeting body-sense of awful pain. When it passed, all I felt was the joy of his presence. "Arthur."

"Emma, I love you," he said. He pulled me into him roughly, laughing as he had a thousand times before. He kissed me, and I responded as I always had. His mouth was on my throat. He was hungry for me.

"Arthur . . ." I moaned; I was hungry for him too.

"I want you," he said urgently, lifting me up and pushing me backward against something.

A tree? A wall?

His hand roamed up inside my skirt, along my thigh. He was inexorable, demanding all I had to give.

I wanted to dissolve completely, from the inside out. It was all that was left of me, that exquisite annihilation. I was sugar in hot water, melting away and exulting. "Arthur, I—"

His tongue found mine as he found my warmth and wetness. He pushed himself deep inside me.

Then, suddenly, the flakes that were drifting like pale feathers landed on my eyelids, and my hips were churning. I had fallen off the cliff into bliss.

"Emma!" a voice wailed, shattering the dream. The last throes of ecstasy ceased.

"What?" I gulped, groggy and disconcerted. *Where am I? Wh-what's going on?*

"You're dreaming about him again," said Haywood wearily. My husband sat upright in the dark. "I can't take this, Emma."

It took me a few moments to recall where I was. I blinked in the dark, made out the black outlines of the footboard of the bed, a chest of drawers against the far wall. *Our bedroom, in our new home in the Canadian town of Carstairs, given to us by Deputy Mayor Carl.*

We'd lived here for the past month, after Haywood, Beth, and I had arrived directly from the raiders' camp in Scotts Bluff. Haywood had needed medical attention, and none of us could stomach Edmonton after the city had turned its back on the people kidnapped in the raid, one of whom was Beth.

Carl was happy to welcome us to his town. He personally rode up to Edmonton and retrieved my little daughter, Mandy, my mother-in-law, Renee, and Sally, our ward.

Recall seeped in bit by bit. Between Edmonton and the raiders' camp, I was with my other family: Arthur and my beloved comrades from Europe.

"I can't go on this way," Haywood whispered raggedly. "I feel you in your sleep, dreaming of him. You're in ecstasy." The white sclera of his eyes floated like phantoms in the murk. He was staring at me, hard.

"I saved *you*. I left him."

"You've never really left him, and you never will." Haywood turned away from me and curled around our daughter Beth, who was lying on his other side.

Beth sighed in her sleep.

I lay back down. I was sorry for the pain I'd caused my husband, a man I loved. But he was on the mend after our ordeal of retrieving Beth from the raiders who had stolen her out of Edmonton, the heart of the Safe Zone, a place where mists never encroached. Moreover, I was with Haywood, not Arthur. Still I knew my husband lying beside me was right. I would never be able to separate myself from Arthur, however far away he was. We were interwoven in a way that transcended logic and obligation.

. . .

"MORNING, EMMA," said Renee, smiling as she poured me a cup of tea. "Is Haywood coming down?"

Beth had preceded me downstairs, and she and Mandy were already sitting at the kitchen table, leafing through an old copy of *National Geographic.* Even if the magazine would never again be published, I was glad they could look at that one issue, a small snapshot or two of what life had once been like, what the world had once been. They'd retain images if not memories.

I carried my cup over and sat between them. I placed the cup on the table and reached one hand to squeeze Mandy's arm and the other to squeeze Beth's. *My girls, both of them, safe and well and close to me,* my heart sang. Looking at them, I knew all over again that it had been worth all the pain and sacrifice. I took a deep breath. "Haywood will be down in a few minutes."

"Your hair looks better, Mommy," Mandy said. She leaned over and laid her head on my upper arm. She had missed me terribly when I'd left Edmonton to retrieve her sister from the raiders who had kidnapped her.

"Yeah. The dye is washing out, and your blonde roots are growing in," Beth said. She scanned my face, her eyes narrowing with thought. She was the observant one. She noticed the sadness weighing on my features, and she didn't like it one bit.

"It's not so turd brown anymore." Mandy giggled. A lilting arpeggio of music trilled in the kitchen, underscoring her words, and she grinned widely. She had recently discovered that she could cause music to play in the air around her, an ability granted to her by the mists.

"We talked about this, Mandy, love. You're supposed to refrain from doing that," I chided gently, tweaking her nose. "We can't let anyone find out you can do it."

"Don't worry, Mommy. Everyone already knows Mandy's crazy," Beth teased.

"Mommy, Beth shouldn't call me names!" Mandy cried.

When she leaned over to pinch her sister, I gripped her wrist and prevented it. "Girls," I admonished with a sigh, "how did my hair cause you two to bicker?"

"Well, it's because your hair looks so bad. I could trim it up for you, so it's not so shaggy," Renee offered, wearing a good-humored smile as she skidded her hand playfully across the top of my head. "You let the French gal butcher it good, the bad haircut disguise."

"Did the trick, right? Got me into the raiders' camp without being recognized," I said dryly.

"We still don't recognize you," Renee teased.

The girls laughed, and another riff of music rippled through the air. We all looked at Mandy, and a reproach lay on the tip of my tongue, but Sally bustled into the kitchen.

Sally drew herself up with great dignity. Before, she had always been mute, with vague blue eyes and spells of motionlessness. In contrast, her eyes were now sharp and clear. "They're coming. Will you go with them?" she asked, her voice whispery and fragile, like a child's. It was soft but shocked us all. During the year she'd lived with us, first in Edmonton and now in Carstairs, she'd never uttered a single word.

I rose from the table. "Sally?"

"They're coming," she repeated. "Will you go with them?" Then she smiled shyly, as if pleased with her newfound vocal ability.

Mandy, Beth, Renee, and I rushed over and hugged her, congratulating her on her ability to speak after all those silent months. Few survivors ever overcame the mists' depredations on their minds, but somehow, she had.

Sally giggled, then struggled to push herself back so she could look at me. Her fine, small-featured face took on a serious mien. "Emma, will you go with them?" she asked again.

"Them who?" I asked carefully.

"No, she won't," Haywood said, limping into the kitchen.

Renee trotted to the counter to pour him some tea.

Haywood pulled out the chair next to Mandy's and thumped down heavily into it. "If she leaves here, she leaves forever."

"Why would I leave?" I wondered uneasily, suddenly recalling Newt's words from the dream: *"Give whatever it takes . . . Give it all. Remember."*

"They're coming," Sally repeated, this time staring at the door.

We all turned to follow her line of sight, but when no one knocked, we turned back to Sally.

"They're coming," she insisted. "Is there tea?"

"Emma cannot leave," Haywood said in a gravelly, determined voice. His hand trembled as he raised his cup to his mouth. He wasn't whole yet after his ordeal in the raiders' camp. He'd been kept in a cage and was beaten by Alexei, the Russian sociopath who ran the camp. Haywood had suffered horribly. Maybe he'd never be whole again.

I knew I wouldn't.

• • •

AN HOUR LATER, the prophesied knock sounded at the door. I was getting Mandy ready to take to school. Beth didn't want to leave home yet, and after her time in the raiders' camp, we weren't going to force the issue. Mandy, on the other hand, had made friends and enjoyed the schoolhouse.

Again, I reminded her not to play celestial music, that her mist-given ability had to remain secret. "We don't know how they'll react if they know you can do that," I said, buttoning her jacket. "We're still new here."

"Yoo-hoo!" Carl opened the back door, poked his head into the kitchen and waved. He gave me a sharp look.

"Come in," I invited, wondering what was up.

"I've brought . . . some friends of yours," he said. He stepped in and turned to gesture at those who followed.

Theo, Charles Nwokocha, and Brendan! I was yelling and leaping to hug them.

Mandy, Beth, and Sally shrieked and rushed to embrace Brendan, who had lived with us in Edmonton and who had followed me when I'd set out on foot to retrieve Beth. Theo and Nwokocha were two of my dear friends from Arthur's camp in France, and they'd journeyed with Arthur to Canada to find me.

"Every parting gives a foretaste of death, every reunion a hint of the resurrection," murmured Brendan, practically smothered by Sally and the two girls. He was only as tall as Mandy after all, an African-American dwarf. In the Before, he'd worked as a professor of literature. He fought free of the clenching arms. "Sally, when did you start speaking?"

Theo and Nwokocha said nothing and simply stood with their arms around me, mine interwoven with theirs. I knew from their stillness that it was bad, that they had come for me because someone was in trouble. They needed my gift.

"Jeannie need you," Theo said softly. Kind Theo, who had claimed he was my brother, back in France when I saved his brother Pyotr. He'd had my back in every fight, and I knew he'd have my back all the way to the gates of hell and beyond.

My eyes slicked over with emotion. Jeannie, who was pregnant; Jeannie the invincible warrior woman with the gorgeous head of Nefertiti; Jeannie was in trouble.

"Would you like a meal and a shower?" I croaked, remembering all too well how welcome those things were when traveling hard and fast on a mission.

"Thank you, but there's no time. We need to ride out as soon as possible," Nwokocha said tightly. "She may not make it."

Squirming free of littler ones, Brendan touched my arm in greeting.

I stepped back and bent to kiss his forehead.

He was still wearing a patch over one eye, a souvenir from his injury before we were marched out to hang in Outpost City, when we tried to steal horses so we could ride after the raiders who had taken Beth. His good eye remained luminous and soulful. He gripped my arm and squeezed, and for a moment, we were both too choked up to speak.

How I'd missed him! There's an unbreakable bond with someone who has stood next to you in a noose, both of you waiting to be hanged. Finally, I managed to clear my throat and turn back to Theo and Nwokocha. "She lose the baby?"

Nwokocha shook his head. "No. She's in pain but says she still feels him kick. She's febrile and can barely eat. We need you, Emma. She's been calling for you."

"I'll pack my things." I moved toward the staircase. I could be ready to go in less than a quarter of an hour.

"No!" Haywood shouted, startling us all. He stood at the stairwell, blocking my ascent with his body. His thin face was ragged with anger and desperation, and his cheek was knotted and red where it had been broken. "No, Emma. This stops here and now. You can't leave. You need to cut ties with these . . . people. I forbid you to go!"

"But Jeannie, our mate, need Emma, her healing hands," Theo said earnestly. He stepped closer to Haywood. "Jeannie have baby inside. Emma our last hope."

"No!" Haywood repeated. "Emma, these people are *not* your family. I am. We are, the girls, my mother, and me. We're here, and *we're* yours. You don't owe these travelers anything. You owe *us*. You belong to *us*. We're finally all together, the way it's supposed to be. Beth is back and safe,

I survived being captured and beaten by Alexei, and you and Mandy survived Europe and the mists. After everything we've all been through to be together since the apocalypse, you can't possibly want to leave now."

"Mr. Anderson, we beg you to reconsider. We only need your Emma for a while, and we promise to bring her back to you," Nwokocha said in a pleading, soothing tone. "Emma's unique healing abilities are our only hope. Jeannie and her baby will surely die without her, and—"

"That isn't our problem," Haywood said wildly. "Emma, let go of these people!"

"Surely there are doctors who can help her," Rence said, moving to stand beside her son. Like him, she was tall and lean. Her hair was still auburn, though his had turned white during his recuperation from incarceration at the raiders' camp.

"The necessary medical technology doesn't exist anymore," Nwokocha said. He fixed an insistent stare on Haywood. "We need Emma. *Jeannie* needs Emma."

"If she leaves here, it's only because of Arthur, and she can't help him," Haywood shouted.

I jumped. "Arthur? What do you mean, I can't help him? What happened to Arthur?"

No one spoke. Haywood glared at Nwokocha, as if willing him not to tell me.

"Arthur was captured by Alexei during the battle after you left with Beth and Haywood," Nwokocha finally said, averting his gaze. "We've been unable to rescue him. We don't have the manpower to launch a frontal attack, and Jeannie's condition has commanded our attention. We haven't been able to formulate a plan for entering Alexei's camp and freeing Arthur by stealth. Latest intel indicates that he's alive but wounded."

I must have looked sick. Everything inside me withered. Arthur was a prisoner of a dangerous sociopath who held a grudge against him. The two men shared a bitter history. Alexei's wife had been killed by the mists, and he blamed Arthur for that. Alexei had kidnapped me from Arthur's camp in France to heal his dying son and also because he wanted vengeance for his wife's death. The feud between the two men was so fierce that Alexei had left Europe to pursue Arthur through North America.

Alexei would torture Arthur mercilessly, if Alexei held Arthur prisoner.

"That's what I mean!" Haywood pointed at my terror-stricken face. "It's always about Arthur. He might be your lover, but I'm your husband, these are your daughters, and we've suffered enough because of the enmity between Alexei and Arthur. We're just pawns in their battle, Emma. You don't owe them anything. You don't owe Arthur anything."

I owe Arthur everything. I took a deep breath to steady myself. *First Jeannie, then Arthur.* "Right now, it's about Jeannie. She saved my life a dozen times, and I can't abandon her in her time of need. I just can't. I owe her, whether you like it or not."

"You owe us!" he repeated hotly. "You can't abandon us."

"Jeannie shot me down out of a hangman's noose," I said. "I'd be dead if it weren't for her sharpshooting."

"As would I," Brendan acknowledged, then sighed.

Haywood set his jaw. "If you leave now, don't bother coming back." He paused, then painfully stood erect. He was, after all, still healing from the blows he'd taken from Alexei's fists during his final hours at the raiders' camp. "Emma," he said, "it's me or him. The choice is yours, but you have to make it right now, right this minute. If you walk out that door with these people, you are choosing him, and I will never let you back into this home. I will be done with you and will go on without you—forever. Go with them, and you'll leave me a widower and your daughters motherless."

The tension in the room was thick, sharp, and cold, like

a hanging icicle. Beth and Mandy looked distressed. Beth, whose sweet face looked suddenly haggard, was the sensitive one. Mandy didn't seem to be falling apart as much; she was stronger, having survived the mists' incursion in Europe with me. As I gazed at my daughters, both of them precious to me, then darted my eyes back to my friends who had gone through hell with me and saved my life time and time again, I wondered, *How can Haywood throw such an ultimatum on me? How could he be so cruel as to force me to choose? How can I leave my little girls, my home, forever?*

Carl shuffled his feet and looked grim. "Seems you folks have some talkin' to do. Meanwhile, I'll take your friends over to my place for a meal, Emma."

"Thank you for your gracious offer of hospitality, but we don't have time to sit for a meal," Nwokocha said, his dark face sorrowful. "We must return to Jeannie as soon as possible, with or without Emma."

"Pack food in bag to go?" Theo asked.

"Think about what you're giving up, Emma," Haywood insisted. "You walk out that door, and you'll never see me or the girls again." He crossed his arms over his chest.

I had known Haywood since I was a girl, and I'd never seen him look so determined. "Haywood, I have to—"

"Emma, this has to be over, once and for all." He squared off to me.

Did I know what I was doing, what the implications were of my choice in that pivotal moment in my kitchen? I think, somehow, I did. Not with Haywood's mist-given prescience, but with the intuition of my heart, which would not be denied.

I took a deep breath and pushed past my husband.

2 I RODE WITH THEO. MY FACE, DAMP WITH
tears, was pressed into his back. We were headed
to Outpost City, the last refuge of the lost and
the mad—*back* to Outpost City, I should say,
because I'd been there two months ago, en route to rescuing
Beth.

I dreaded my return to that town, where the good citizens
had tried to hang me for attempted horse theft. Arthur and
his crew had rescued me by starting a stampede and explod-
ing some buildings. Now, I couldn't imagine the reception I'd
get. I only hoped the ragged, multicolored mop on top of my
head would keep me from being recognized.

Over and over in my mind, I replayed the last few minutes
in my kitchen. I'd kissed Mandy and Beth and whispered into
their ears that I loved them, promising that I'd be back, in
spite of what their father had said.

Mandy nodded at me solemnly. She had lived with me in
France, in Arthur's camp. She understood the bond I had
with Jeannie. And with Arthur. She was aware of how much
we all meant to each other and therefore she accepted the
lengths to which I must go on my friends' behalf. She played a
solemn, hymn-like tune very softly, close to our heads.

I shushed her with a finger to my lips. "No music, remember," I mouthed.

Mandy nodded again.

Beth cried silently and refused to look at me as I darted

past Haywood to run upstairs for my gear. I knew she was still raw from all she had endured at the raiders' camp, but I also knew how lucky she was; Alexei had shown her preferential treatment because she was my daughter. She'd been sheltered from his cruelty.

Most importantly, Beth was alive. Jeannie's baby, on the other hand, might not be so lucky without my intervention. I would never forgive myself if I didn't at least try to save the baby.

When I came back down, changed into my traveling clothes and with my gun and knife packed into my backpack, Brendan told me he would stay behind, because he needed rest and recuperation.

He had lived with us before the move to Carstairs; he had, in his own way, become part of our family. He knew he would always have a home with us. I'd looked into his weary, wounded face and nodded.

Haywood stood still as if rooted to his spot by the stairs. Aghast, he stared at me in disbelief, without saying another word.

At the door, I'd turned to him, hoping, pleading for some softening.

But Haywood had closed his eyes and collapsed in on himself. That was my last image of him. It hurt. I knew he was hurt, too. It broke my heart that he had challenged me, that he had made an ultimatum.

I had proven myself to Haywood. I had saved him from Alexei's camp and left Arthur behind—to be imprisoned. Of course, I'd never fathomed that Arthur could be taken prisoner. Really, it was unthinkable. Now that I knew, though, I had to help him. Had to. It wasn't a matter of choice, it was an absolute. Didn't Haywood see that?

The horse trotted with an unsteady gait, either because it wasn't well schooled, because its hooves were sore, or because the beast was tired. I bounced along on its rump behind Theo and clung tighter to him to stay seated. *For Jeannie*, I told myself. Then, because I wasn't going to lie to myself, I admitted, *And for Arthur*. There was no way I could stand by and do nothing while Arthur was being held in Alexei's camp of horrors. Not while there was still breath in my body. No matter what I had to sacrifice.

• • •

IT WAS A week's ride to Outpost City, eight days if the horses didn't cooperate. The first day, we rode past Airdrie, into the empty land near Chestermere, far enough north and east of Calgary to avoid interested parties. We made camp in an abandoned storage facility that had been picked clean of everything by the Royal Forces.

It was spring, and there'd been rain, and the ground was slushy with cold mud. We walked around the storage building, looking for a place to tie up the horses. In the back, behind the structure, we discovered a tall, pyramid-shaped pile of stones. They were tightly fit together, delicately balanced and interwoven, a marvel of engineering. When I bent close to examine the structure, I saw names etched into each one.

"We see those all places," Theo said somberly.

"Cairns?" I clarified, remembering my dream.

Theo nodded. "Names of dead."

"An ancient practice made new again," Nwokocha murmured, "an old and universal rite of memory."

"How else people remember loved ones?" Theo asked.

Nwokocha shrugged and nodded, and his dark eyes dimmed. Later, as we rested in the shelter of the abandoned warehouse, he laboriously worked a rock over with his knife, carving letters into it. He grunted and perspired, entirely absorbed in the task. When he was finished, he curled up into himself, clutching the rock close.

I wondered who he was commemorating, as I hadn't even seen him take the rock from the ground, but he was inaccessible, and I couldn't bear to ask him.

That night, I dreamt of falling gray rocks. Boulders rolled past me, leaving dust clouds in their wake. Out of the floating dust walked a tall, blond man who was missing an arm: Alexei. He continued walking in my direction, until he was standing right in front of me, so near I could smell the salted meat of his last meal on his breath. His blue eyes blazed out of his rough-hewn face. Slowly, laboring with his one arm, he peeled off his shirt, revealing a chest mottled with red slashes. "You did this to me," he said, his words thickened with his Russian accent. He held up the golden pelt of a cougar. "You sent your cat to hurt me!"

Then there was pain, terrible pain. I woke screaming and clutching my eye; in my dream, it had been burning, melting, liquefying.

Theo scrambled over to lie next to me. He wrapped himself around me, trying to comfort me.

Still pressing his stone to his chest, Nwokocha watched me with heavy-lidded eyes until the nightmare passed entirely and I sighed with relief.

The next morning, on our way out, Nwokocha stopped by the pile and found a space where his rock would fit. I could have sworn the cairn exhaled and shifted to draw in Nwokocha's stone, but after his hand retreated back to his chest, the cairn looked exactly as it had before. There was one more name in the mix, but no one would have known it.

• • •

THE NEXT DAYS consisted of a muddy slog through unsettled spring weather. Periods of rain alternated with stretches of cold gloom. We were granted one afternoon of bright, sharp sun. We rode hard and spoke seldom, for Jeannie was always on our minds. We knew that every minute we weren't riding to see her was a minute that delayed whatever help I could offer. We ate dried jerky that Carl had packed for us, and we shot ptarmigan and grouse. At dusk one day, Theo caught some walleye, which he pan-fried to perfection.

For me, the nightmares continued. Alexei strode like a colossus into my dream world. He was huge and rugged, all lethal sinew and muscle. Sometimes he made accusations, and at other times, he was stoic and silent, brooding and threatening all at once. Always there were body-senses, flashes of sharp or burning pain. I often woke up crying and screaming, and I grew so hoarse from it that I had to whisper. I wondered if madness was taking me, and I trembled to think of Alexei invading my consciousness.

Nwokocha and Theo took to sleeping with makeshift earplugs.

· · ·

ON THE MORNING of the third day, it was cold enough that our breath frosted over. We had made camp near the ruins of the village of Ralston, in a ramshackle building with a windmill.

Theo made a fire out of some fallen fence posts. I stood beside him as he worked, staring out over the endless flatlands and then up into the huge, empty sky.

I was anxious about returning to the scene of my near execution, but my anxiety was tempered by the fact that Outpost City prided itself on living in the present. Its citizens had lost too much to be tangled up with memory. As long as I didn't flaunt my identity and my spectacular escape from hanging, I'd probably pass through unscathed.

Out of nowhere, a woman walked toward us. She was sturdy, with a long, black braid and a pink Juicy Couture tracksuit under her unzipped parka.

"Kangee!" Theo cried, jumping up and joyfully clapping his hands.

"Hi, Theo," she called, but she fixed her gaze on me. "Hello, Emma."

"Kangee!" I rasped. I clasped both her hands and squeezed, making sure she was really there, in the flesh.

The mists had bestowed many psychic gifts. I'd been given healing power; Haywood saw the future; Mandy could play celestial music; and Kangee could travel in odd ways Sometimes I thought she bi-located, that it was possible for her to be in two places at once. Other times, her walk whisked her over miles and miles of terrain. She had an unconcerned ease about her abilities, as if she'd had them all her life, even before the mists. I wasn't ever sure if she was even tangibly present when she appeared out of nowhere like that. But this time, her hands were solid and warm in mine, and I was happy to see her. The sweet smile on her broad Sioux face reminded me of the times we'd shared.

"How is Jeannie?" I asked.

Kangee frowned. "That's why I came. You have to hurry."

"We ride through night," Theo decided.

"Use the south gate of Outpost City, the new gate. The guards are new too." Kangee grinned at me. "They won't know you."

I scrunched up my face with worry. "I've been so focused on Jeannie that I haven't even thought about getting in "

"You'll get in," Kangee said. "If there's a problem, it will be getting back out. But I think your hair will disguise you. Everyone remembers your long blonde hair."

Nwokocha exited the building and stood beside me. "How are the others faring?" he asked in his polite, controlled way.

Kangee exchanged a look with him. "Robert is worried sick and won't eat. Susie is doing a lot of the practical stuff. Donny is taking care of everyone. Laurette is running the show. I think she misses you."

The notion softened Nwokocha, and he smiled for the first time since placing his stone in the cairn. "I'm sure she does."

"Good news: Gaff and Marco escaped the raiders' camp right after you did. They've been wandering, but they finally reached Outpost City and found us," Kangee went on. "They're both a little messed up. Marco is mad."

"They escaped? What about Arthur?" I asked breathlessly.

Kangee shook her head. "That Russian has him."

"Have you seen him?" I pressed.

"Only once. They know what I can do, so they watch out for me. That Russian . . . what's his name? Alexei? He somehow knew I was coming. I can't hide from him. He's got powerful vision." Kangee shuddered.

"When did you see Arthur? How was he?" I demanded.

"Six weeks ago. Pretty bad." Kangee's black eyes glittered. "Now's not the time for you to worry about him. Jeannie's in trouble. Riding through the night won't be quick enough. Theo and Nwokocha can ride. You have to come sooner if you hope to help her."

"But how can I travel faster . . ." I started, then sighed. I pressed my hand to my throat, willing my voice to strengthen. "You want me to travel . . . with you?"

"Yes. I can carry you on my back," Kangee said. "We talked about it to get your daughter Beth out of the raiders' camp."

"You think you can carry me?" I was doubtful. "What if you drop me?"

"Let's hope I don't, because we'll be between worlds." Kangee crooked her finger at me, then turned and stooped. "Climb on."

I was hesitant. "What do you mean, between worlds?"

"Between worlds," she repeated. "Don't know if you'd make it back to ours, but you're strong, even if you're skinny, so I know you'll hold on tight."

"I don't know," I answered, feeling more than a little anxiety about Kangee's strange mode of travel. *Between worlds?*

Does that mean through the veil, where the dead linger? Do I dare
pass through there, even for Jeannie? What if the veil is a net and
catches me so I can never return?

"Hop on. Not wait," Theo said, gesturing. "Go help Jeannie. We bring bag and horse to south gate."

"I wonder what they'll do to me if they recognize me
there," I muttered. "And as for this between the worlds business, is it like being dead?"

"That haircut will keep them from recognizing you."
Nwokocha gripped my shoulder and smiled for the second
time since we'd set out from Carstairs. "And between worlds,
Em, is quite an opportunity, something few get to see. Pay
attention and tell us what it's like, what you see." His lean
dark face took on a wistful cast. "*Who* you see."

"Between worlds is part of nature, as much as plants and
animals and the sun and stars," Kangee said. "You don't have
to fear it. Just respect it. Come on. Let's go help Jeannie."

There was no preventing the trip, and I was eager to help
Jeannie, so I climbed on Kangee's back. I wrapped my legs
tightly around her waist and my arms around her shoulders,
weaving my fingers together so my hands couldn't be sepa-
rated; the last thing I wanted was to be stranded between
worlds. I muttered some imprecations, then asked, "Are you
sure you can carry me, Kangee?"

"I've carried seals that weighed more than you do." She
straightened and gripped my calves firmly, then started
walking.

At first, it was ordinary. Her feet thumped against the
ground, the percussion rippling up through my spine. Then,
all of the sudden, the world smeared into red streaks. That
was followed by emptiness. For some span of time, I myself
was a slight thickening of something in a vast nothingness.
Around me swam nebulous almost non-existent scrims of
vibration. In the spaciousness of it, there was a sense of playful
intelligence. That was the only way I could think to describe

it. It fwas also peaceful in a way that nourishes you where you don't even realize you're starving.

Suddenly, shockingly, there were rainbow streaks. The land rose up hard against us. Kangee trotted fast to accommodate the shift, her legs windmilling furiously as she stumbled to slow down.

"Wow!" I exclaimed, uplifted and exalted as I slid down from Kangee's back. "That was amazing! Is it always like that?"

"Sometimes," she said. "Sometimes it's different."

I realized that my throat was whole again, my voice normal. "Kangee, there's magic in that place. My voice is healed."

"Like the magic you do with your hands, I guess." She shrugged nonchalantly but looked pleased when she pointed. "The south gate."

Still giddy but trying to settle myself, I took in my surroundings. The hilly prairie had fuzzed over with the pale green grasses and shrubs of spring. Directly in front of us, a half-kilometer away, a tall barbed wire fence delineated a town that was less a community than it was an ugly collection of unsightly lumps and bumps clumping into the dirt, forming a haphazard maze.

Outpost City. I felt myself go cold with nausea. I'd been marched out of that town's north gate to die. I had stood with a noose around my neck, listening to soldiers divvy up my gear, and I'd peed myself out of fear. Outpost City boasted only two laws. First, everybody worked. Second, stealing a horse, or trying to, was a hanging offense. That's the law I'd run afoul of.

To the east, outside the horse ranch, some kind of orchard project had been started, with trees planted in orderly rows. To the west, there was farmland. To the south, there was a glistening blue lake.

"Why not drop me off inside?" I asked.

Kangee shook her head. "I can go in myself that way, but

I didn't want to risk losing you when I slowed down. It's crowded in there. I have to be careful." She held up her hand. "I'll let them know you're coming."

"Where will I find Jeannie?" I asked. A tremor of anxiety passed through me. *Am I really going to do this? Can I really walk back in there and give them another opportunity to hang me?* I found myself stroking my throat and chest, a feeble attempt at self-soothing.

"The badlands, Norm's place," Kangee said. "Don't worry. You'll pass through the gate. There are new guards, and you've got that crappy hairdo. All will be well." With that, she whirled and walked and vanished.

I had to walk the usual way, which turned out to be a good thing, as it gave my nostrils a chance to acclimate to the vile stench of waste. Outpost City had only a rudimentary sewer system. I hadn't noticed the stink two months ago, in the frigid depths of winter. Now, with some days almost as hot as summer and the ice in the pit toilets melted, I couldn't miss it.

3

AS IT TURNED OUT, KANGEE WAS RIGHT: I wasn't recognized at the gate, which consisted of a swath of barbed wire rolled back to create on opening. When the rookie guards pointed guns at me from their posts atop wooden crates, I waved and then held still for them to look me over.

"Name?" a guard on the ground barked.

"Angie," I called back, wondering about their supply of bullets. New bullets weren't being made anywhere. Two months earlier, Arthur had taught our group how to use a bow and arrow.

"Okay, Angie," the guard said. He snapped his fingers.

The other guards snapped up their rifles and rotated on their crates to survey the plain, revealing that they had big recurve bows strapped on their backs. *So the military in Outpost City is turning to other weapons,* I realized. *That means bullets will make for more valuable currency.* I made a mental note. Currency was everything in Outpost City.

I kept my head down as I walked through the gate of the place I'd sworn never to set foot in again. Such was the nature of promises in the After.

The city was even more thickly populated than it had been a few months ago. It was a true melting pot, filled to overflowing with men, women, and children of all races and ages. Everyone was armed with guns, knives, spears, or bows. I even saw machetes and swords. Some folks wore daft expressions;

Outpost City wasn't scrupulous in its sanity requirement. That's why so many survivors ended up there. They'd either been rejected in other cities or knew they would be, with the curious, canny knowing of the insane.

Dogs, goats, ducks, and chickens also roamed the muddy pathways that served as streets, weaving among throngs of people. Dogs and goats nosed hands and pockets for food, while the poultry clucked and pecked. The smell of it all—animals, people, trash, and defecation—was overwhelming. I distracted myself by gazing at some of the structures. Most were shanties of one sort or another, but there were brick and wooden houses and even big buildings made of poured concrete. I presumed those sturdier dwellings must have been constructed almost immediately in the After, when there was still gasoline to fuel trucks.

The south gate opened near the Badlands, the part of town that was even seedier than the rest of Outpost City. I turned west to make my way to Norm's.

Amy, Norm's wife, whom I'd met at the raiders' camp when I'd freed Beth, saw me first. She happened to be looking out the front window of Norm's bakery and spied me at precisely the same moment when I noticed her red curls. Our faces lit up simultaneously with recognition, and she raced out the door to hug me.

"Come in!" she sang, squeezing me. "Come in, come in!" She didn't say my name but looked around carefully, then threw her arm around my shoulders to hustle me inside the bakery.

The yeasty, sugary scent of bread and cake enveloped me like a lush, warm wrap of the softest fur.

Norm was standing at the counter, grinning. "You must be here for your friends, miss . . ." He came out from behind the counter and laid his hand on my shoulder.

"Angie," I said, my heart lifting. It was always good to meet friends again, especially now, during these precarious end times, when so many had died. Those who remained were ever more precious to each other. I clarified, "I'm Angie."

He nodded and glanced around to see how closely his customers were watching us. He lowered his voice and leaned to speak close to my ear. "Sure glad to see you, Angie. I owe you a debt of gratitude for getting my Amy back to me. Means the world to me. I can never repay you."

"Glad to help," I said. "Maybe you'd better take me to my friends now."

He nodded and gestured for one of the girls behind the counter to throw him a sweet roll. It was still warm when he pressed it into my hands. Amy hugged me again before Norm gripped my arm and led me hastily out of the store.

Farther down the mud street, he said grimly, "There're folks here who want your blood."

"Figured as much," I said, around the honeyed morsel in my mouth, such a sweet treat in such a dismal place.

"Theo and Charles Nwokocha told me they were riding out to get you, but I didn't believe they'd convince you to come back here."

"My family and friends mean everything to me," I said. My mind flashed to Haywood and the girls, and my chest burned with an ache like a shriek. I quickly quashed it. I had to do this. I had to help Jeannie. Then I had to try to rescue Arthur. I didn't have a choice. Even for my daughters, whom I loved more than my own life, I couldn't stay safely at home while Jeannie was sick and Arthur was captured and being tortured. Alexei's face rose before me. When the body pain of my nightmares pulsed through my tissues, I shivered.

"I understand. Amy means everything to me."

Norm led me around a sharp bend in the street, then down a narrow walkway between buildings. We stopped at a large, brightly colored building that looked like giant red and blue kids' building blocks stacked together.

Norm tapped on the back door. "Synthetic composite

panels with an insulating foam core," he said when he saw my curious gaze wandering over the building.

"How'd you build it?" I wondered. "Did you find it?"

"I was one of the first people here in the After, even before the barbed wire went up," he said. "There were some modular pre-fab units on display on the border of the Hat. No one claimed them during the chaos, so I did. I disassembled them, piled them on horse-drawn wagons, and brought them here. I knew Outpost City was on its way to being a real town. I lost everything when the mists came, so I decided to start over here, where things are as ugly as I felt inside." He ran his hand along the beam. "I lost everything, family, business . . . just everything. Almost didn't want to live myself, ya know?"

I felt an empathic softening; so many had lost so much. I was one of the lucky ones. Before I could respond, the door opened.

"Em!" Robert said fiercely. "Not a moment too soon!" He grabbed me and dragged me through the first and second cubes and up some stairs into a second-level cube, where my friends Laurette and Susie were standing beside a bed.

"Emma! Delighted to see you, as always," Laurette said in her brisk French accent. She had been with us at Arthur's camp in France and had then accompanied him to Canada, when he'd come for me. She'd chopped off my long, blonde locks and then dyed my hair brown to disguise me so I could enter the raiders' camp unrecognized. She was, in some ways, as close as a sister.

Despite her greeting, she didn't look delighted. Her pixie face, framed by its ever-chic coiffure, was drawn, and her voice didn't lighten. It had to be very bad with Jeannie.

Laurette kissed my cheeks crisply. "I suppose Charles is not with you, since Kangee brought you."

"That's right." I turned to hug Susie, but gently, because she was sensitive to touch. She had joined us en route to rescuing Beth, when the mists attacked. She had been a slave to a group of men who had treated her badly. To free her, we'd each had to kill one. Since then, she'd been a warrior, one of us.

"I'm glad you're here, Emma," Susie said quietly. Then she turned and stalked out of the room.

Laurette and I watched her tall, slim frame disappear. Laurette shrugged and moved away from the bed so I could approach.

Jeannie lay there, barely conscious. She was terribly thin and wasted away, except for her round, hugely bloated belly. Her glossy, dark skin was dull and shrunken in around her skull; beads of sweat stood on her forehead, cheeks, and neck. Her hair was matted against her head.

"Oh, Jeannie," I murmured, heartsick. I hoped I could help her. I touched her arm gently. It felt like a stick beneath my fingers.

Her eyelids fluttered. "Em-Emma." Her cracked voice was little more than a whisper. "I-I knew you'd come."

Laurette leaned in around me to spoon some water into Jeannie's mouth.

"Can ye help her? Can ye help my babby?" Robert demanded. Under the stress of his concern, his Irish lilt made his words almost unrecognizable.

"She can," Jeannie assured him, struggling to smile.

Laurette made a skeptical noise. "I certainly hope so."

"Get me a stool," I said. "I need to sit. This is going to take a while." I took off my coat and threw it on a chair.

Robert bustled away to get a stool. "Here you go," he said, scooting it into position. He gripped my shoulder and then backed away.

I seated myself atop the stool and laid both hands on Jeannie: one on her shoulder, the other on her hip. Immediately, my hands tingled. That sensation was always the first sign of the healing gift that had come upon me after the mists had scoured the world clean of people and buildings. I hadn't asked for the healing gift; it had been dumped on me, yet I tried to use it to help whenever I could.

My hands felt as if they were swelling and filling with warm, bubbly water. My breathing slowed and deepened, and my focus narrowed and intensified, like a laser. Sounds and images around me fell away. All that was left was me and Jeannie. Then the tingling spilled out of my hands and flowed into her. As I kept slowing myself and concentrating, the flow seeped ever deeper into her flesh and bones, into the very cells of her being.

Jeannie was worse off than I had first perceived. The life force in her was low, barely stuttering. I had no idea how she would sustain herself through labor and delivery.

But the baby inside her was well, with a strong, pulsing heart. Its life energy was throaty and scarlet, robust with life. Its body was perfect and healthy. This child wanted to live.

Sometimes, in the midst of a healing, I found myself talking to the inner being of the person on whose body my hands lay, channeling words as well as the juicy river of healing energy.

"Don't give up," my mind said to Jeannie. *"Don't resign yourself. Your baby is strong. Your husband loves you. You must fight to hang on."*

"Don't want to," came the anguished cry. It was unspoken but reverberated through my head like a distant chime.

"You must," said the words. *"It is your duty, your honor to live."*

"So much suffering," was the response.

I realized then that beautiful Jeannie was much more heartsick than I'd ever imagined. I would never have guessed that her tough warrior woman façade could conceal such tenderness. The words flowing through me asked, *"Who do you miss?"*

The answer came as a torrent of images, faces from Jeannie's past. There was a tall black man, an athlete of great personal dignity, whose beautifully modeled face resembled Jeannie's; he had to be her father. Then came a soft, round, loving, proud woman who could only be her mother. Other faces also wafted by, some who had to be part of the same family and some who must have been friends.

I held the energy steady in its current and simply witnessed the procession of lost loved ones. Sometimes the faces repeated. The images were accompanied by deep feelings of grief, but I sensed that the grief wasn't merely personal and attached to those individuals who were part of Jeannie's inner world. Rather, the grief had a larger dimension: It belonged to everyone, to the whole body of humanity. It was overwhelming, full of profound emptiness, and it was all I could do to hold the valence.

I wasn't sure how long it lasted, but at a certain point, the parade stopped. A sacred circle of remembered people remained. Those people held gray stones in their hands, resembling the ones in the cairns that dotted the landscape.

I seized the image as a tool for Jeannie's healing. "*Build the cairn here and now, within her, so she heals!*" I said to the sacred circle of lost loved ones. "*She must live. Her baby must live!*"

Something intricate and beautiful happened next. It can barely be described with words: The people within Jeannie obeyed me and built a cairn inside her innermost sanctum. They built it with love and sorrow and hope. It was the most sacred thing I had ever experienced.

The current of energy moved through me for a dozen hours. I kept my hands on Jeannie and allowed the flow. When it finally stopped, I stood and stretched painfully. I backed up and saw Robert crying.

Even Laurette had damp eyes. "I do not know what you have done, but it is beautiful beyond measure," Laurette said.

"My Jeannie and my babby will live," Robert murmured in a tone of fiery reverence.

I could barely make it to the toilet with my bladder crying out for relief. Oddly enough, I wasn't at all sleepy, even though I hadn't rested in two days.

• • •

JEANNIE WAS UP and walking around and eating everything we put in front of her. She even sipped Outpost Ale.

"Are you sure it's okay for you to drink that?" I asked, having declined a glass. "It's a lot like lighter fluid, only less tasty and more toxic."

"It'll make the little guy strong," she assured me.

"It might ruin his sense of taste, since it reeks of sewage," I pointed out.

"It's good for him, and I feel good," she told us as we sat around Norm's dining table, enjoying a plentiful meal. She laid her hand on me. "Weak but good. I knew you'd come through, Em."

"Don't thank the hammer when the carpenter builds something beautiful," I murmured. I was happy to have been of service—beyond happy—and I was thrilled to have helped my dear friend, but I knew I couldn't take credit for it. The healing energy that flowed through me was not mine. It only used me to do its work.

"You undersell yourself, Emmy," Robert said, draping an arm around my shoulder and smooching my cheek, leaving behind a greasy smudge of lamb chop fat.

"Ugh! You're worse than my kids," I said, scrubbing at my face with my wrist. For a moment, my heart wrung out, as Beth's and Mandy's faces rose within me.

"Robert worse than kids," Theo said, wearing a grin that pulled me back into the present. He and Nwokocha had arrived an hour ago, tired and hungry from riding around the clock.

"Well, I'll be lavishing myself on me babby soon enough, and you'll all miss me bold ways and me strong back in a fight," Robert said. He beamed at Jeannie, then at me, and then at everyone at the table. His expression turned to a grimace, though, when he looked at Susie, who was staring at him fiercely. "Mind yourself, darling. I'm only slagging."

"The baby will need to be protected." Susie scowled. "It's no joking matter."

"All will protect baby," Theo assured her.

Laurette raised her eyebrows, then turned to Jeannie. "You will go soon, I think."

Jeannie was sucking marrow out of a bone but asked, "How did you know? I'm having little contractions—not real ones, but those Braxton-Hicks, I think they're called. They don't hurt."

"You have dropped since Emma laid hands on you," Laurette said. "You're carrying lower."

"I went soon after I dropped, both times," I said. "Though the doctor always said that isn't really a sign."

"Doctors! Pssh. What do they know? In the Before, they were bought and sold by insurance and pharmaceutical companies. They let themselves be crippled that way. Now they are weak and ineffectual without their fancy equipment and gadgets," Laurette said scornfully.

Nwokocha stroked her arm.

She mellowed immediately and leaned toward him with a coquettish mien.

Robert rolled his eyes. "Try to keep it down tonight, would ya? The rest of us need our beauty sleep."

"It doesn't matter how long you sleep, Robert. You will never be beautiful," Laurette said, sniffing.

"You're a beautiful bird, love," I said, winking at Robert. "I'd scuttle you, and I wouldn't even have to be polluted to like it." I was quoting what Robert had once said to me.

He winked back and nodded, remembering.

"'Ave a go at 'im if that's your fancy," Jeannie said, grinning and exaggerating her Scouse accent for effect. "But remember, if you tap that, Arthur kill that, and me baby's without a dar!"

Chuckles sounded around the table, and I smiled. It was good to see a smile on Jeannie's face again. Then, in the next second, we all sobered. *Arthur.* He was still being held captive in the raiders' camp while we were laughing around the dinner table.

"We have to go after him," I said quietly. "Not just because we love him, but because he may be the only person who can destroy the mists."

"I agree. We, as humanity, cannot allow him to die," Nwokocha said.

"I can't do anything until me Jeannie pops," Robert said tensely.

"I in," Theo said.

"As am I," Nwokocha said.

A ferocious smile spread over Susie's young face, which, with its heart shape and dusting of freckles, should have known only angelic expressions. She stroked her long blonde hair over her shoulder. "An opportunity to kill raiders? Wouldn't miss it!"

"I will go. That will ensure our success," Laurette said, casting a teasing look at me. "Surely I will be the one who makes a successful plan for rescuing him."

"If you're talking about rescuing Arthur, your plan had better have a miracle built into it!" called a voice from the door. A brown leather cap appeared first, followed by the rest of him. Skinny and pale, dressed in a ragged coat three sizes too large, Gaff, the teenage pickpocket with whom I'd become acquainted during my first stay in Outpost City, stepped inside. He grinned with his usual insouciance. "Emma! Did you miss me?"

"Not much," I said, "but I suppose it's good to see you. What took you so long? Where have you been?"

"The usual. Scouting for saleable intel." He was holding a rope in his hands, and when he stepped inside Norm's cube home, he yanked on it. "Come on, now."

Marco, with his hands bound and his head hanging low, reluctantly trotted in behind Gaff.

"Marco!" I said in dismay.

Marco's head rose. His face was blank and innocent like that of a very young child. His eyes were cloudy as they scrolled back and forth around the room, before ultimately resting on me. He said nothing and just gazed uncomprehendingly at me.

"He's not well," Robert said softly.

"Oh, Marco," I murmured. I rose and went to him, then reached out to hug him.

"I wouldn't do that," Gaff warned.

Marco's teeth snapped at my arm just as it landed on his shoulder.

I jerked back. "Marco, don't you remember me?" I cried, wondering how he could have possibly forgotten. He was one of the innermost circle. He had traveled with Mandy and me in France after the Day, when I'd led a band of children south in search of safety and finally ended up at Arthur's camp. Marco, the laughing Italian boy had been as dear to me as a son and as close to the other children as a brother. Now he'd grown into a young man, gangly and taller than me.

Marco didn't answer. He gazed steadily at me without a shred of recognition.

"At least he's alive," Gaff said softly. "Is dinner ready? I'm hungry. I've been roaming up in the better part of town, and I didn't wanna pay their prices."

"Aye, come sit," Robert said.

"Em, can't you help our boy?" Jeannie asked. "There's magic in your hands."

I shook my head. "I've never been able to heal madness. I don't know why. It just doesn't work."

"The mists bring the madness, so maybe the mists have to cure it," Gaff said.

"Emma, please say you'll try," Jeannie persisted.

"Of course. For Marco," I said miserably, knowing it would be to no avail. The madness was impervious to healing energy, just as it was probably impervious to God.

• • •

AN HOUR LATER, I had my hands on Marco. The tingling energy was flowing, but it wasn't making one damn bit of difference. He was secured to a bed in a third-story room in Norm's crazy cube house, but he kept tearing at the ropes and lunging at me, ready to bite and strike me. He'd have killed me if he could have.

I kept my hands on his shoulder and arm and let the healing tingles swirl into him. It saddened me to see sweet Marco so unhinged. I remembered how he was in France, at the camp near where Valensole once stood, in the Before. Merry Marco, with his dark curls and laughing eyes, had always been ready to play soccer or to tease Felix or to carry a gun and strut around as if he were a big man. Now, he was nearly a man, but he was mad as a hatter.

If he hadn't left France to help Arthur find me, Marco would still be sane. And I had no idea if he would recover while the mists roamed the Earth, consuming metals and shadowing men's minds with insanity.

Finally, the tingles spent themselves. Feeling defeated and a bit useless and guilty, I descended to the dining room on the first floor, where the others sat around the table. Kargee had joined them and waved at me from over a plate of food, which she was devouring with great concentration.

Donny sat beside her, and I leaned down to kiss his cheek in greeting, glad to see his kind, pockmarked face. He was a portly black man with the kind of gravitas that seeped into every room he was in and made it calmer. He'd be a soothing presence around Jeannie and Marco.

"Any luck?" Robert asked.

I shook my head and seated myself.

"You'll try again," Jeannie said in a soothing voice.

"Not now," I said. "Now it's time to set out for Arthur. We can't leave him there. He's too important. You're feeling better, so we don't have to worry about you, but we all know that Alexei is hurting Arthur."

"It's a matter of time before that fiend kills him," Robert noted grimly.

I nodded. "And with him, probably our last chance to get rid of the mists once and for all. We have to go, and the sooner, the better."

"We can ride out in the morning," Susie said, brightening.

"Ride out? Haven't they confiscated the horses?" I asked.

"We left the nags with some friends outside of town," Robert said. "Paid them well to stable them for us. The horses will be waiting for you."

"Why Outpost City?" I asked. "There were other places, and this town is as dangerous for you as for me. They know you set off the stampede. Someone might remember."

"They have the best medical doctor here," Robert said, throwing his arm around Jeannie's shoulders. "Jeannie was so bad off that we had to take the risk. Memory is short here." He winked at me. "They let you walk right in, and you're public enemy number one."

"I've given the plan to rescue Arthur considerable thought," Nwokocha said, folding his arms and resting them on the table. "There are several travails. The mists have grown bolder and less predictable outside the Safe Zone, and we will not have Arthur with us to dissolve them as we travel. If we even make it to the raiders' camp at Scotts Bluff, Alexei has no doubt posted sentries in the surrounding community, specifically to watch for us."

"He knows we'll attempt to rescue Arthur," I acknowledged. "Plus, he sees in advance."

"Mist-given precognition?" Nwokocha queried.

I nodded grimly. "Not just precognition. He can interact with other minds." I recalled how he invaded my nightmares, as if he'd pushed his way into my mind without invitation, and a realization dawned on me that he meant to do so. He was purposefully sending himself to me. *He wants to make contact with me. Maybe he wants more than contact. Probably. Almost certainly,* I realized.

"He has a strong mind," Kangee said. She wiped her mouth with the back of her hand. "But maybe we can use that against him."

All of us sat up straighter, and Robert tilted his head. "How so, missy?"

"I think she means me," Donny said softly.

We all looked at him, and I nodded encouragement.

"Recently, I've realized that I can join my mind with others," Donny said. He passed his hand in front of his face, shielding his eyes. "It's a soft thing. I can't do much, other than influence the other mind a little bit. The weaker the mind, the more I can affect it."

"That is a useful gift," Laurette said.

Donny smiled. "I'd rather be able to travel like my wife. I hope this gift isn't a symptom of madness coming on. So many lose their minds after the gifts show up."

"You'll be all right," Kangee said. "Your mind is good."

"You might be able to psychically influence Alexei so he doesn't see us approaching," I said.

"Maybe but not for long," Donny warned. "Kangee says his mind is strong and determined."

"Maybe we'll only need a little while," I said slowly. "Maybe we can make do with just a little bit of obscuring." From Alexei's nightly visits to me and our conversations in the dream space, I was starting to understand what would be required to rescue Arthur: me.

4

WE WALKED OUT THE SOUTH GATE I HAD entered through. I didn't even want to wait to sleep. I figured I could sleep en route to Scotts Bluff, the collection of steep cliffs on the south side of the North Platte River and the last known location of the raiders' camp. Alexei had liked the defensibility of the location. He was always thinking ahead to conflict and danger, something he'd learned to do in the Before, when he was a black market provider of everything from weapons to drugs to information.

We packed backpacks with food and weapons, strapped bows on our backs, and rolled blankets that we tied onto our packs. Then we left in groups, so as not to attract attention. I walked out with Donny, Theo, and Laurette. The guards looked us over but didn't stop us, and we kept walking south. Susie, Gaff, and Nwokocha strolled out a few hours later. Kangee was coming by herself, in her own way. We all knew she'd come and go as she saw fit. Robert stayed behind to take care of Jeannie and Marco.

We gathered at an abandoned farmhouse a few kilometers outside of Outpost City. The horses were stabled in Cypress Hills Provincial Park, eighty kilometers south and east of the Hat, which was twenty kilometers due south of Outpost City. It would require twenty-four hours of foot travel to reach the horses. Mostly, we'd follow the old Buffalo

Trail, AB 41. Somewhere along the way, we'd have to make camp and sleep, unless I could convince the others to march straight through. I was reluctant to yield to the nightmares that dogged me, as sleep always felt like I was surrendering to Alexei. I was also so intent on reaching Arthur at the very earliest moment possible that I didn't want to stop for a minute, even to rest or eat.

The others must have sensed my determination, because they were uncharacteristically quiet. Even Laurette didn't complain at all.

• • •

CYPRESS HILLS ROSE in a gorgeous, rolling plateau above the prairie. It was rugged, mountain-like terrain, with lush pine forests and an astonishing variety of birds and animals, all framed by the vast bright spring sky. We hiked toward Reesor Lake, looking for a village that had been erected in the After.

I was glad when we finally spied the settlement in the distance. It consisted of plain, log-cabin-style buildings set back from the lake and grouped around a large, rectangular field of grass.

"They know we're here. They're sending scouts," Donny announced. He made a low rumbling noise in his throat as he rubbed his temples. "I can feel them."

"Friendly scouts, as before?" Laurette asked.

"Why wait to find out or depend on Donny's psychic sense?" Susie asked, eagerly nocking an arrow into her bow. "We need to be prepared, in case the village has been raided. They could be hostile now. We might have to fight them to get the horses back."

"I hope not," I murmured. "I don't want to waste time fighting for the horses."

"I don't think they're hostile. They're good people, and we paid them well," Donny said; nevertheless, he had taken out his gun, a Glock .22.

I had learned more about guns since the Day than I'd ever considered knowing, Before, and I knew that was a law enforcement pistol. That made me wonder if he'd once been a cop, before the world had fallen apart.

Donny noticed my gaze and smiled with nostalgia. "I was a police detective a million years ago, in the Before. I carried this piece for twenty-five years and would've retired with it."

"Ah, our yesterdays. I was a linguist," Nwokocha said, releasing a nostalgic sigh. "I spent my days lecturing in universities and writing papers in libraries. Libraries! Ha!" He had a gun, too, and he was checking it over. "I miss libraries—the smell of books, the muted noises, people whispering. Even with computers supplanting card catalogs, there was such a lush, tactile experience in a library. Will this world ever know a library again, or will they exist only as fond memories of a less barbarous time?"

"I was engineer in my country." Theo wore a small, proud smile. "Cool stuff."

"All I did in the Before was go to high school," Susie chirped. "I was worried about what my friends were texting about me and who would take me to the prom. I had no idea that someday I'd be thinking about a bunch of raiders raping and killing me. That stuff only happened in the movies. I can barely remember that time now. It seems so far away, after all that's happened to me."

"I was in high school too. I lived with my family, who I haven't seen since the mists went through Medicine Hat," Gaff said sourly. "This is the After, and we all have tough-luck stories. At least we're alive."

Susie scanned him up and down, then tossed her head dismissively. "I know you weren't one of the cool kids. You had to be some kind of outsider, a nerd or something, one of those scary, smart kids no one wanted to talk to. I bet you were in the Math League. Ugh."

"I was!" Gaff bridled, then chortled. "Whatever. If it makes you happy, think whatever you want about me Obviously, you're still caught up in some imaginary status game that was silly to begin with. Now, cliques—all that talk of cheerleaders, jocks, and geeks and Goths—doesn't matter at all. Now, all that matters is how resourceful you can be. I've always managed to eat, and no one's raped me."

Susie gasped with indignation and pointed her arrow at Gaff. "Why, you—"

I placed my hand on her bow and pushed it away. "Enough, you two. Knock it off. The Before is gone, so let's not carry petty high school rivalries into the After. We have enough to worry about without that."

Susie would have argued, but her words were quickly hushed when she caught sight of two men and a woman approaching on horseback.

Nwokocha walked out ahead of us with his hands raised in the air. "Hey, we've returned. Is Mike around? He'll vouch for us."

"Charlie Nwokocha, is that you?" called one of the men. "We've been waitin' for you folks. How's Jeannie?"

• • •

I WAS THROWING a tantrum—a full-scale, five-alarm, ten-point-zero-on-the-Richter-scale tantrum.

"Must sleep, Emmy. You too. Walk all day and night. Sleep now," Theo said.

"NO!" I yelled, beating my fists in the air and stomping my feet for emphasis.

Mike, our crew, and some of the settlers were sitting at a table in the communal dining room, a high, wood-beamed space in a community hall they'd erected for the settlement.

They'd shown us our horses, which were all healthy and well kempt. They'd fed us. Then they'd offered us rooms for the night.

"Emma, you are being unreasonable," Nwokocha said in a tone of mild reproof, as harsh as he ever got. He sighed and cocked his head and looked as if he wanted someone to volunteer to spank me.

But I didn't care if I was being unreasonable. I didn't want to rest. I wanted to get on the road to Scotts Bluff. Every minute we delayed was a minute during which Alexei might murder Arthur. I had to rescue Arthur. I burned with that intention.

"Emma, this is enough, you are being emotional and crazy, which is exactly why you need sleep!" Laurette rose and wagged her finger at me.

"We have to keep moving," I insisted. "We've been fed, and we rested enough during dinner. Let's ride out. We can grab a few hours of rest around dawn. Let's keep moving. Time is short!"

Gaff and Susie exchanged a glance, then rose simultaneously and flanked me.

"Emma, even if you can keep going—and that's a big if— we can't," Gaff said, sounding far older than his sixteen years. "We're at the limit of what we can do, for now."

"We're safe here," Susie added from my other side. "We can get a good night's sleep and set out bright and early in the morning, when our energy is restored."

"You don't want to wear us out now," Gaff continued. "That wouldn't be wise. We'll need to be awake and aware when we confront the raiders. Whatever plan we devise for getting Arthur outta there, we're gonna need to be sharp."

They each seized one of my arms, and I realized, belatedly, that they meant to subdue me. Both kids were preternaturally strong, probably out of necessity.

"Stop this right now!" I cried, struggling in their grip. "Release me!"

"Please, Emmy, be good," Theo begged. "Go sleep, like nice angel. Please."

"Do not make us knock you out," Laurette said in a tone of pure exasperation. "We will if we must. But, please, it is so undignified. Look at our hosts. What will our kind hosts they think of us? How will this help us rescue Arthur?"

"The longer we delay, the greater the chance that he gets killed," I said urgently.

"Emma, that's enough," Nwokocha said flatly. He made a motion with one hand, and Susie and Gaff hauled me toward the stairs.

I thought about shaking loose and getting a horse and going to get Arthur for myself. *The others will just catch up to me later,* I told myself.

"Don't, Emma," Gaff said softly while tightening his grip on my arm. "You're acting as crazy as Marco. Don't be this way."

I wanted to retort, but when my eyes met his, he looked so deflated, so emptied of his usual sass, that I quieted myself. I allowed myself be led to a loft above the hall, where some cots and sleeping bags were scattered about. A small, circular window let in a milky wash of starlight, illuminating the place just enough for us to make out the furnishings. Gaff and Susie released me, and I flounced over to a cot.

"Stay in bed. Don't make us tie you down," Susie said earnestly. She then knelt on one of the sleeping bags and tucked herself in. She was snoring even before she was fully ensconced. She let out a deep whuffle.

Gaff and I shared a grin. "That's better," he approved. He chose a sleeping bag near my cot. "You'll feel better in the morning, Emma. You'll see."

It was only a few moments before he, too, was breathing

with rhythmic sibilance. The others came upstairs quietly, selected sleeping places, and lay down. I sat upright, but they didn't look at me; finally and reluctantly, I surrendered.

• • •

I WAS ALONE in a room with sunlight streaming through tall glass windows. It was Paris; I could see by the wrought-iron gate on the balcony.

It was a small apartment with a gleaming wooden floor, and I was painting. In my hand was a Number 2 flat, its bristles covered with lush yellow acrylic paint. *What kind of yellow is that?* I thought. *It's so beautiful.* It was confusing that the half-finished painting in front of me was an impressionist landscape, completely unlike my style, but I didn't let that distract me. I let the brush fly over the canvas.

There was a knock at the door.

"One moment!" I called. I put the brush down and slipped off the old shirt that served as my smock. It was Haywood's shirt, a short-sleeved, cotton poplin aviator shirt with long tails, one I hadn't seen since the Before. My hands ran over the soft fabric, which was spattered with spots in many colors. How I had loved to paint. How I had loved that shirt and my brushes and my canvases and even the smell of paint thinner. Would I ever paint again?

The knock sounded again, louder and more intense.

"Okay, okay," I said. But when I opened the door, I froze.

It was Arthur standing in the door, so tall that everything behind him vanished.

I moved aside, and he stepped in. I didn't quite know what to say. *What is he doing here?*

He was standing so close that my heart skipped a beat, then thundered. He was so beautiful, with his blazing gray eyes and the perfect symmetry of his features, as if he'd been created in an ideal realm of perfect forms and set down on Earth to prove that such a realm truly existed.

Oh, but he created the mists, I remembered. *He isn't perfect.* He had meant to end war and suffering, and instead he had unleashed the apocalypse.

Arthur didn't say anything. He just looked at me for a long time, his face alive with wonder and love. He put his palm on the side of my face and caressed my cheekbone.

"Wh-what are you doing here?" I asked, trembling.

"I came to be with you," he murmured, his hands resting lightly on my hips. "I want you."

I let him draw me close. "And I want you, Arthur. Always."

"You're keeping me alive." He nuzzled my cheek, then my neck. "I feel you all the time."

I felt myself arching to fit into his chest and arms, my sternum lifting and my hips pushing against his. My arms wove around his shoulders. He was erect, and the feel of him on my belly was so luscious that I gasped.

"Give yourself to me, Emma—all of you," he said. His voice was deep and uneven. He trembled slightly against me, a tiny, barely perceptible motion.

"I am yours," I said, my hips churning against him.

His warm, strong hand slid up under my shirt to cup my breast. My nipples pricked with sensation, with desire. He groaned and squeezed.

"More," I whispered. My skin was warm and alive, and everything in that circle of pleasure between my knees and my navel throbbed with fire. I wanted Arthur as I'd never wanted any other man. I wanted him to penetrate all of me, every orifice, every cell membrane, every ripple of my consciousness. Everything that was me attenuated, and what remained was a marvelous, sinuous receptivity.

He neared, and his body morphed into a sparkling web of light. The web held the generic shape of man, but it shimmered and pulsed with sparks, a living template.

I was surprised into total stillness, like a sculpture. "Arthur?"

The web fell across me, as if merging into my very being. Before it could weave itself into me, a hand peeled it back, like parting a curtain. The web shimmered out of existence like a firefly winking out.

It was Alexei and he laughed. He put his remaining hand on his hip, and boomed with mirth, "Do you think you can escape me?"

"Alexei, what do you want?" I cried. "Why are you coming to me in my dreams?"

"I talk to you this way, Emma. I want what I have always wanted," he said.

"And that is?"

"Justice. And you." He reached his amputated arm toward me. His blue eyes stared into mine, and he was cold but filled with heat. "It is not right. Arthur took my wife, the mother of my son. Arthur destroyed the whole world. 'Eye for eye,' God says. If God will not take justice, I must."

—The pain started. Deep, agonizing slashes through my flesh that hacked chips out of my bones. Burning ropes of fire that plunged into my chest and abdomen. There was such pain. Everywhere, there was pain.

I was sitting up, and Laurette and Theo were shaking me.

"Emma? Emma!" Theo said, tightly gripping my shoulders. "Wake!"

"You were dreaming," Laurette said. "My God, what kind of dream did you have?"

"Oh," I rasped, my throat sore from screaming. I came to in the murky loft with my friends all staring at me. "I'm sorry. I've been having nightmares. I just . . . I can't control them," I spoke in a gritty whisper because my voice was gone again.

"Okay, Emmy?" Theo asked.

I nodded and waved for them to leave me be. "Go back

to sleep," I choked out. I rose from the cot, intending to get some water from the hall downstairs.

"We're up," Nwokocha said. "Might as well pack and ride out." He sounded peevish, and I couldn't blame him; it wasn't even dawn yet.

"I'll wait downstairs for you. Rest some more," I urged in a whisper.

"We are awake," Laurette announced, standing to stretch and yawn. "Tonight I will make you some herbal tea, and you will sleep soundly. This is unacceptable."

The others rose too, but I beat them downstairs, looking for water to soothe my throat. I went to the counter where a jug was sitting out.

Susie came right up behind me and stood at my elbow. "I awoke before the others," she said in a low voice. "I heard you moaning. It sounded like more than a nightmare."

I poured the water into an earthenware mug and gulped it down, even though it tasted musty. "The dream didn't start as a nightmare."

"You were dreaming about Arthur first?" she said. She held out another mug, and I filled it for her. She took a deep swig, made a face, then giggled. "Makes me miss Outpost Ale."

I shuddered. "Ew. Nothing could make me miss that. This is the nectar of the gods by comparison."

She shrugged. "The question is, were you dreaming of Arthur when it got bad? Because if you were, that means he's in trouble."

"I-I don't know," I said softly. "I hate the dreams. I'd rather skip sleeping altogether and be tired. Besides, all I can think about is getting Arthur out of the raiders' camp, away from Alexei."

"He would risk his life to rescue you or any of us," Susie agreed.

I would have said more, but the others finally joined us, huddling around the jug, drinking water, and discussing options for breakfast. We could scrounge for what was left from last night, or look through the stores in the kitchen, or head out to hunt for deer or wild turkey, which were abundant. The lake was also stocked with trout, which, Theo promised, would be so delicious when he fried them that we would want to dance with joy.

· · ·

WE MADE IT past Havre, Montana, to the rolling grasslands, pine and fir woods, and aspen groves of Beaver Creek Park. There, we encountered mists.

At least it had once been Montana; official land divisions made little sense in the After. The important distinctions were Safe Zones, where the mists did not encroach, and Wastelands, where the mists frequented, demolishing buildings and consuming people. We were far out of the Edmonton Safe Zone, which stretched north from Medicine Hat to the Great Slave Lake and east from Kamloops to Saskatoon. There were a few other Safe Zones in the world: the South Island of New Zealand, the islands off the coast of Washington state, a broad swath of Uruguay, part of Iran, and a strip of Eastern India—all original Safe Zones from the Day.

I had discovered that Edmonton was home to one of Arthur's original aides, a man who had helped him invent the mists. I'd always thought the other Safe Zones must, similarly, represent homes to others who worked in Arthur's lab, the people who worked most closely with the mists. Their experiences had somehow been transferred into or imprinted on the mists in the early days, when the mists were being engineered.

Now, most of France was a new Safe Zone, at least according to Arthur. He had cleared the mists from France using the power of the mists themselves, powers they had bestowed, wittingly or not, upon him. He could disperse the mists. He could also call them. But his gifts were localized, too specific to the area he was in for him to affect the Earth at large.

If he could have done so, he would have long ago driven the mists away for good, something Arthur had told me within the first half-hour of meeting me. But he hadn't been able to, and now we faced a wall of mists that was four stories high, a broiling white cloud bank exuding the sickly odor of lilacs and sulfur, stretching across the land for at least a kilometer. It was about half a kilometer away from us, but we knew how quickly the mists could advance.

Like a zoo going mad, animals—elk, deer, wild turkeys, rabbits, bobcats, and every other local species—raced ahead of the mists, and birds flew up in advance and wheeled about, looking for safe passage. The animal movement created a churning in the Earth, spinning grass and dust up all around the walls of mist.

"We must retreat!" Nwokocha said. He reined in his horse and stared, aghast, at the mists.

The rest of us closed in around him. The horses made a tight, restless circle, snorting and stamping and prancing with anxiety. They, like all of us, felt the danger.

"We have to warn Havre," Donny said. "That city has suffered enough. They've been hit six times since the Day, losing people, buildings, and livestock every time."

"We don't have time to go back, and Havre has watchers," I said. "They'll alert the town. We have to stay on track to rescue Arthur. We can go around the mists."

"No! They will follow and pursue," Nwokocha said. "There have been many reports of that recently. The mists are growing more aggressive. They appear to have grown more intelligent than they were at first, when their destruction was random."

"We can drive them away as long as we all stay together and ride in synchronized timing. The beat of the horse hooves will be rhythmic enough to disperse the mists," I argued.

"It is true that the mists are sensitive to the particular rhythm of a horse running," Laurette said, "but we cannot be sure. Sometimes it doesn't work."

"We have to try," I urged. "Let's ride toward the mists as a group and try to drive this embankment away. If it doesn't work, we'll gallop back to Havre."

"Should still warn Havre," Donny said. "They have a new percussive deployment system, so they'll want to be ready. Like I said, they've lost a lot, and they've been good to us, feeding us and our horses without asking for anything in return."

"Donny makes a good case," Nwokocha said. "Havre was hospitable. We have to reciprocate with this information about the approaching mists. It's the right thing to do."

"Intel? That's my game," said Gaff. He fixed his leather cap on his blond head at a jaunty angle. He stretched his arms overhead and clasped his hands, palms out, then cracked his knuckles. Then he gathered his reins close. "I'll ride back to last outpost we saw, warn them, then turn around and ride fast to meet up with you."

"We'll follow the old Beaver Creek Road, then head southeast," Nwokocha said.

"We'll take the east fork," Donny added, "unless we can't pass through the mists."

"If that happens, we'll ride back toward you," Nwokocha clarified.

"Got it!" Gaff nodded, kicked his horse, and turned at a canter, rocketing back the way we'd come.

Nwokocha checked his stirrups and the buckle on his saddlebags. "People, please ensure that your saddlebags are secure. We don't want to displace our provisions. Emma," he said, casing a wry look at me, "we're all eager to help Arthur, but if we can't drive off the mists, we will turn back . . . or go around."

"Understood," I said. I checked my saddlebags, then stared

at the mists, willing them to vanish. It was ludicrous to imagine that my will would affect them at all; they were agents of destruction, meant to save humanity from the ravages of war, and instead, delivering the harshest fury of war, wiping out people and civilization. Only Arthur's will could affect the mists. Arthur's will and percussive sound, like the galloping of horse hooves, which sometimes influenced the mists, causing them to lift above the Earth and scatter.

Arthur had saved my daughter Mandy from the mists that way, the day I'd met him. "You almost lost her," he'd said. I would never forget how his gray eyes had played over me as he'd spoken those words. In the way every moment contains the seeds of all the moments that follow it, did I know then what we would become to each other?

"How close before turn?" Theo asked, jolting me back to the present.

"Let's say . . . fifty meters," Nwokocha said. "That should suffice. At that point, we'll know if the mists are responding or if we must retreat."

"I don't like this," Susie said unhappily. "There's no telling if it will work, and if we get too close, the mists might affect our minds. Remember what happened when I met you guys? That giant embankment made everyone suicidal and homicidal. The guys I was with killed my friend and would have killed me."

"This mist formation isn't nearly as big," I said "It's not deep, and it's moving slowly."

"We're still risking madness," Susie argued. "Everyone says the mists are getting stronger, that they're evolving."

"Susie, we will make this attempt, and it will be brief," Nwokocha said crisply. "Ride next to me, and I will personally make sure you get away if it doesn't work."

"Must help Arthur," Theo said quietly. "Must get through."

"Everyone ready?" Nwokocha asked.

"Yes!" we all cried.

"Yeah!" Nwokocha screamed, racing forward.

We massed our horses around his, and the six of us rode in a peloton, straight toward the mists. My horse, a dappled gray gelding who was old and wise enough to know the value of discretion, kept trying to veer away. It was all I could do, with my poor riding skill, to keep him on track with the others.

The mist wall was fast approaching, and the smell of the mist formation intensified: nectar and sulfur. As we neared the white wall, its internal structure grew visible. Within the pulsing white clouds was a curving maze of white lines. That, in itself, was troubling. The mists had never before presented that way; they had always been inchoate gaseous forms. They were definitely evolving, and that could only make them deadlier.

As we neared the mists, I was seized by a head-ache like an iron vise screwing tight on my cranium. The closer we got to the mists, the worse the pain gripped me. My field of vision disintegrated into wavy lines.

Next I was swamped by feelings of fear, despair, and horror. I must have cried out because Theo called my name. None of us deviated, but a quick glance at the faces around me verified that my comrades were feeling the same physical and emotional pain.

We were a 100 meters away, then 70, then 60. There was no change in the mists. When we got to within fifty meters, Nwokocha signaled for us to change course, but Susie burst through the pack and kept racing toward the mists. I swore and drew up in a classic racer's posture and went after her. So did the others, all of us screaming Susie's name. She charged ahead with no sign of turning back.

Ten meters from the mists, when the sweat of fear slicked over my face and every instinct in my being was screaming that I'd be killed—chewed up in the mists' maw and excreted as yellow sand—just as I was preparing to jerk hard on my horse's reins to stop him, the mists condensed and rose. What had been an ominous embankment wafted up and collapsed in on itself, morphing into a cloud. The cloud lifted as gently as a white petal floating on a breeze.

It was shocking, and the land felt suddenly empty. It wasn't, though; it was full of trees and rocks and grass, and a few piles of yellow sand where the mists had ingested animals.

"They go!" Theo called. His face was drawn and damp; he'd been weeping.

"Whew! That was close," Nwokocha said, then leaned off the side of his horse and vomited.

"Too close, but we sent them away," Donny rumbled.

"Look! People!" Susie called. She kicked her horse and galloped toward a covered wagon drawn by two pairs of oxen, and the rest of us hurried to follow her.

At first glance, the wagon was empty. When we drew up around it, we saw people on the seats, unconscious.

Susie and Nwokocha reached them first. They dismounted and ran to help the unconscious people. The sleeping ones were a young couple, swarthy and Mediterranean or Middle Eastern looking. When their eyes fluttered open, they struggled to sit upright. They wore terrified expressions, with open mouths and glazed-over eyes.

The woman spoke first, pulling her scarf tight around her head. "I . . . we thought we were dead," she said. Her face was contorted with fear, and her voice trembled. "That mist has been circling around us for the last twenty kilometers."

The rest of us pulled up in front of them, our horses nickering at the oxen.

"I give you water," Theo said. He jumped down from his horse and took his canteen over to the woman.

"We didn't know there were people in the mists," Nwokocha said. "What do you mean, they were circling you?"

The man shook himself awake. He had a short beard that he scratched vigorously, as if it suddenly itched, and dark circles ringed his eyes. "It was strange. A small bank of mists came on us and wrapped around us like a lasso. Then it moved, slowly, driving us forward. The last few hours, it seemed to be tightening around us, till there was less and less space around the wagon. It was . . . herding us."

"It was terrible," the woman cried. "I wanted to die!"

A small boy crept out of the covered part of the wagon and settled himself on the man's lap. He waved solemnly. "I am Amir," he announced, his lips trembling.

The woman wrapped her arms around him and pulled him into her lap.

Amir buried his face in her chest and shook with silent sobs.

I wondered what horrors the mists had introduced into little Amir's mind, and how he would integrate them into his daily life, from that point forward. I wondered how many years he would remember it all in his nightmares. And when I wondered these things, my heart broke for the child, for all the children of the crumbling world.

"Greetings Amir," Nwokocha said gently. He then looked at the boy's father. "Sir, the mist bank didn't start out that size?"

"Please call me Hakim," the man answered, then shook his head. "It was much smaller, when we first saw it. Then it grew when other mists floated over and joined it."

"We've never seen the mists act that way before," the woman said. She closed her eyes and shuddered, squeezing little Amir tightly.

"Were you the only ones who were caught?" Donny asked.

"Yes," Hakim replied. "The sound of your horses sent the mists away, so we are only alive because of you. Thank you." He took a long drink from Theo's canteen, then passed it back to Theo with a grateful nod. "Much obliged."

"Where are you going now?" Nwokocha asked.

Hakim and his wife gazed at each other. "I-I don't quite remember," Hakim said, his dark eyes large and round.

"We came from . . . uh . . . where did we come from, Hakim?" the woman asked, confusion growing on her face.

There were a few moments of silence.

"We have food if you need it," Nwokocha offered.

Amir peeked out from under his mother's arm and blurted, "Fatima."

"Who is Fatima?" Nwokocha asked with an air of great interest.

"Yes! Fatima!" Hakim's dark eyes widened. "She is my wife's cousin. She is alive and has a home in Havre. That's where we are heading. She invited us to join her."

The woman's face softened. "Yes! That's right! We're going to see my cousin Fatima, who is like a sister to me. We will live with her in Havre."

"Havre has been hit, but the survivors are working hard to make it safe and livable again," Donny said.

"That's what we heard," Hakim acknowledged. "We are very grateful that you have helped us. Is there any way we can repay you?"

"It would be helpful if you could answer a few more questions," I said.

"Anything," Hakim said.

"Where did you come from?" I asked.

"Minneapolis originally," the woman said. She lightened as her confusion lessened. "We've been on the move since the Day."

"Minneapolis was destroyed," Hakim said. He pressed little Amir into his chest.

"I'm sorry," I said, "but by any chance, have you recently heard anything about the raiders camped at Scotts Bluff? There was a big contingent of men, women and children led by a charismatic Russian known as the One."

The woman shuddered. "A couple of nights ago, we met a large group of settlers who were headed to the Safe Zone in Edmonton. They reported a skirmish with raiders who tried to steal some women and children. They got their people back, but one of the young women was killed."

"Friendly fire," Hakim added. "They think she was killed by one of their own arrows. Very sad."

"A terrible loss, truly. But it sounds like the work of the raiders I'm talking about," I said.

"Couldn't be." The woman shook her head, and some unruly locks of her dark hair escaped the scarf. "These raiders had made camp in Yellowstone."

"Yellowstone?" Nwokocha asked. "Are you certain?"

"Yes. The group we met questioned one of the wounded raiders, and he admitted to being a scout from a large army," Hakim said. He stretched and sat straighter, then took the reins in his hands. "I'm feeling better. We can go on. Thank you for your help. If you're ever in Havre, please look us up."

"Just one more question," I said.

"Of course."

"Did the wounded raider say anything about their leader?" I pressed. "Anything at all?"

Hakim shook his head. "If he did, no one told us about it."

"Wait, Hakim. They did say that Yellowstone was a new camp," the woman said, laying her slim hand on her husband's arm.

Hakim gazed at me steadily. "Yes, that's right. Sorry. My mind is still a bit shadowed by the mists. We didn't hear where they came from, but the wounded raider said his army had just moved to Yellowstone."

5 AGAIN, WE WERE FACED WITH A DILEMMA, a choice: We could continue south and east to Scotts Bluff, or head south to Yellowstone. We couldn't be certain the raider Hakim mentioned was one of Alexei's loyal followers, as there were many raiders in the After; for all we knew, there could be an unrelated group camped out in Yellowstone. If Alexei's raiders were in Yellowstone, though, it had been a recent move, perhaps an advance party or a small contingent. We had no way of knowing whether or not Arthur was still in Scotts Bluff with the main body of raiders.

We debated the issue over dinner, which consisted of a whitetail deer and a brace of pheasants, all spit-roasted to perfection. We sat at a picnic table by a clear, placid lake, enjoying the mellow evening as the sun painted red streaks across the vast horizon and on the surface of the water. Never one for sitting when there were things to be done and people to be rescued, I paced restlessly.

I was tormented by doubt. If we went to Scotts Bluff and discovered that the entire camp had been moved, it would mean we'd wasted precious time, hours that Arthur couldn't spare. If we went to Yellowstone and engaged the wrong group of raiders or a small contingent that wasn't the main army, we could sustain losses. It wasn't simply a matter of time in that case; we would likely be caught and captured or killed. If that happened, we'd never rescue Arthur.

Theo set the partridges on the table and split them into sixths with his big hunting knife. I let the others choose pieces, and then I took the remaining one to go and wandered down to the edge of the lake. I didn't feel like sitting, so I just kept walking, following the curve of the lake edge and nibbling the meat off the bird's thigh. I sucked every last succulent bit of meat and tendon, then threw the bone far into the lake.

Eventually, I came upon another wooden picnic table, and I sat down. I hunched into myself, even though the evening was cool but not at all cold. As always, when I stilled myself, I saw the faces of my children and my husband. I ached with love for them. Again I wondered, *How could I have left them behind?*

Will Haywood really stand by his ultimatum?

How could he force such a choice on me? Didn't he realize I had no choice at all? Of course, he was simply being himself, my husband, and I couldn't really fault the man for feeling that he had exclusive rights to me. He felt justified in demanding my presence and ensuring my safety. I understood his position. Still, after what I'd been through with Jeannie and Arthur and the others, I couldn't possibly abandon them in their time of need, even if it meant leaving Beth and Mandy behind.

My love for my family was rubbing painfully against my love for Arthur.

I drummed my fingers on the table. *What is Arthur doing now?* I couldn't help but wonder. *Is he suffering? Is Alexei brutalizing him? Will he survive until we reach him?*

Memories from my time in France with Arthur flooded my consciousness, like millions of butterflies released from a dark cage. We'd shared his tent, and so much more by the light of that small, flickering candle. So many conversations. Arguments. Sweet communion in each other's arms.

I loved Haywood, but I had never imagined it could feel with a man the way I felt with Arthur.

Arthur, astonishingly, had felt the same way. He d spent an entire evening picking lice out of my hair so I wouldn't have to cut it; he loved my long blond hair. "I'd do a lot more for you than comb out your hair, Emma," he had said. Arthur loved me.

I loved him.

In all the craziness of a world gone mad with mists and ultimatums, that was one clear truth I had to hang on to.

My fingers stopped tapping, and the water darkened with thunderclouds. In the center of the lake glimmered a light, and within the light appeared a form. The form stepped out of the light and strode to me.

Was it Arthur? My heartbeat quickened like a new infant's.

"Emma, I am Alexei," boomed the man, standing at the water's edge.

"I'm dreaming. I'm asleep again," I said.

"This is how we talk, until you come to me."

"Alexei, you must free Arthur," I said in a flat, serious voice.

"Freedom will do him no good now, for he is not fit anymore," Alexei said slyly. "My men are very angry that he made the mists. They roughed him up."

"He made the mists, and he can get rid of them. That's why you have to let him go. The world needs him. He's our only chance of dispersing the mists for good, so we can rebuild."

"France is good for Mikhail. What do I care about the world?"

"If the mists aren't eradicated, they will grow. They're evolving, even encroaching into the Safe Zones. They'll return to France and endanger Mikhail, along with everyone else. You must let Arthur go."

"You know what the price is for that!" Alexei laughed, the same rich, harsh, guttural, self-ironic chuckle I had often heard from his men. Russian humor was still as elusive as it was accessible. As if he had heard my thoughts, which I was sure he had, Alexei smirked. "I have joke for you. Man say, 'Nurse, where are we going?' Nurse says, 'To morgue.' Man say, 'But I haven't died yet!' Nurse says, 'We haven't arrived yet.'" He laughed and fixed his blue eyes on me, waiting for me to get it.

"No jokes. I'm serious." I was irritated, but even in a dream meeting, I didn't want to anger Alexei. He was unhinged, and there was no predicting what he would do. I struggled to stay calm. I wanted to scream at him, but I knew I couldn't allow myself to.

He shrugged. "So am I, Emma. Your hair looks like shit."

"So I'll schedule a trip to the salon."

Alexei raised his shaggy brows mirthfully. "You are a funny woman. Why don't you like my joke?"

"You must release Arthur," I said firmly.

"We are in contest, Emma, and Arthur is the prize."

Yes, Arthur was the prize. Arthur, whom I loved. Arthur who alone could free the world from the lethal mists he had invented. "I don't want a contest, Alexei."

"That's because I always win," he said, his gaze triumphant.

"You do. So stop sending me nightmares."

He shrugged. "As you wish. But if there is no contest, there is still a price to pay. I am a businessman, and I set the price."

I swallowed. "Where do I find you?"

"Yellowstone. I moved my camp. We are in old Army fort, never hit by mists, close to hot springs. You will like when you come to me to pay the price."

I was about to answer him, about to agree to his terms, but voices clamored in my ear: "Emma, Emma!"

I sat up and looked around groggily. Susie and Theo stood behind me, their hands gripping my shoulders. I stuttered, "Wh-what?"

"We've been trying to wake you for five minutes," Susie said, her young face full of concern. "Are you okay?"

I nodded and wiped my face, which was damp with drool or tears or perhaps both.

"Gaff come back," Theo said, then squeezed my arm.

"He has news about the raiders," Susie said.

"They're in Yellowstone," I said quietly, "in an old Army fort."

"How do you know?" Susie asked.

I shook my head. I didn't want to say. I rose wearily. I had slept poorly for as many days as I could remember, and it was finally catching up to me now. At least I knew sleep would no longer elude me, would no longer be interrupted by the man who held Arthur prisoner. I'd struck a bargain, but I wasn't yet ready to tell my friends about it.

• • •

IT WAS 600 kilometers south to Yellowstone, along that verdant, patchwork-quilted land where the Rockies met the prairie and forests erupted. There were high mountain peaks, grassy meadows, pine trees, lakes, streams, and rivers, all of it teeming with wildlife and blanketed by an impossibly, relentlessly huge sky.

We crossed the Missouri River at an old landing with a sign emblazoned "Judith Point." We piled our bags into the kayaks tied at the landing, and Susie and I paddled them across to the other side. The others waded out into the river with the horses. Luckily, it was a warm day, and neither beast nor man seemed to mind the short swim.

We reached Harlowton and found a welcome sign but no people. Streets and store fronts were intact but the town was deserted; there weren't even any packs of the wild dogs that often roamed ghost towns. We agreed that the mists must have come through, even though there was no visible sign of an incursion, no piles of yellow powder.

We found an untouched store called Remedies Pharmacy

and Hardware and decided to help ourselves to a little discount shopping. The doors were locked, and the windows were barred, so Theo broke open the lock on a back door. Inside were aisles of goods that had once been ordinary and plentiful but were now miraculous. Nwokocha and Theo went directly to the hardware shelves and filled their saddlebags with everything from knives to hammers to tape. Laurette and I went to the pharmacy section and took every tube of every cream we could find. Antibiotic and hydrocortisone ointment were godsends, given the scrapes, rashes, burns, and cuts we all routinely endured on the road.

Laurette used a precious bullet from our dwindling supply to shoot off the lock on a big cabinet behind the pharmacy counter. Inside it, we discovered the mother lode: pills of every kind, from painkillers to contraceptives to antibiotics to anti-nausea formulations. We took knapsacks and satchels from the floor and stuffed them with the precious medications; somehow we'd find a way to tie the extra packs on our poor horses. We didn't read expiration dates because we didn't care. Even old medicine was better than what we had, which was no medicine at all.

Gaff and Susie bickered continuously but mended fences long enough to scour the candy aisle. They were devouring their sixth bag of M&M's when they found a gun locker filled with ammunition. Their joyous whooping brought the rest of us running.

"This will help us get Arthur away from the One," Susie crowed as she tested a shotgun for its weight in her hands. Smiling demonically, she positioned the gun against her shoulder and aimed into the distance. "Bull's-eye!"

The others laughed and slapped high-fives; we were all a little high from the sugar in the candy, and bullets were the most prized commodity we could have hoped to find. Increasingly scarce, the precious lumps of metal could be the deciding factor in a confrontation.

I gobbled another Three Musketeers but didn't join in the celebration. Deep down, I had a feeling bullets wouldn't be necessary for Arthur's release. I just wasn't ready to admit that out loud to my celebrating companions.

• • •

WE DIDN'T SEE Kangee or anyone else during the journey. When we finally reached the ruins of Big Sky Resort community, we found a lone elderly gentleman holed up in the lobby of what had once been a luxury lodge. "Them raiders came through here and took everybody under seventy, willing or not," he grumbled. "They only left me 'cause I'm a stringy old coot, of no use to them."

"It was their loss, sir," Laurette told him in her starchy but sweet way.

He shrugged. "The leader was a big guy with one arm. Fella had an accent and didn't speak English too good, but he was totally in command of everyone." He hobbled around on his cane to fetch us water. "He shot me right here in the calf when I tried to protect my grandson. Almost pissed myself twice while I tried to remove the bullet. Hurt like the dickens, it did! I kept passin' out, and once I got the darn thing outta my leg, I was laid up for a week. I'm lucky I can walk at all now. I had an old bottle of colloidal silver, so I didn't get an infection."

Nwokocha gripped the man's frail shoulder gently. "I'm sorry for your suffering. To be clear, was this one-armed leader a blond man?"

"Yep, that'd be him," the grandfather said. "I have a few cans of beans I'd be happy to share with y'all. Could use some comp'ny for dinner if you'll just gimme a minute to heat 'em over a fire."

"I am afraid we must be on our way, but we appreciate

your gracious hospitality," Laurette cooed and stroked his arm, making him beam with delight.

In the end we left our elderly informant with a box of Hershey's milk chocolate bars, a tube of antibiotic cream, a bottle of ibuprofen, and an elk Theo shot with an arrow. Grandfather was more than grateful and warned us to beware of Gardiner, because the town had been taken over by raiders.

· · ·

WE CIRCLED AROUND Gardiner through the Gallatins and set up camp on a rolling peak overlooking Gardiner, which was perched high on a plateau. We didn't make a fire so as not to attract attention. We sat in a grove of spruce trees, ate protein bars, and drank blue Gatorade we'd pilfered from Remedies.

"It has been forever and a day since I ate anything this particular shade of blue, which does not occur in nature," Laurette said. She held up her Gatorade bottle and shook it a little. "Even blueberries are purple, not fluorescent teal."

"I know what you mean. I used to eat this stuff all the time, but now it just tastes . . . strange," Gaff commented. "Good, you know. But different, so synthetic. I'm used to fish and game now and the fresh fruits and veggies we find along the way. Dried berries and apples and jerky. Norm's delicious breads. Outpost ale."

Susie laughed shortly. "I've got a stomach cramp from all the candy I ate! I couldn't stop eating it because it's been so long. I never thought I could regret a Reese's cup, but now I do."

"Chocolate magnesium and sugar, like laxative. Big poop tomorrow," Theo warned her, with a gravitas that provoked our laughter. His face took on a serious mien. "No funny, true. Be careful, Sus. Too much poop next day."

"We should not digress to discussing our culinary and excretory situation; that's mere procrastination," Nwokocha said. He squinted grimly, then looked at each of us in turn: me, Susie, Gaff, Theo, Laurette, Donny. "It's time to face the question we've all been avoiding since we set out from Outpost City."

"How we free Arthur?" Laurette clarified.

"Yes, I've given quite a bit of thought to it," Nwokocha said. "I don't have any brilliant or original ideas, but our opening gambit is guerrilla warfare. We stalk them on their perimeter, take out a few men at a time with bullets, arrows, spears, and traps. We appropriate their weapons and gather intel. If we whittle down their numbers, we can create an opportunity to sneak in or even try a frontal approach."

"Intel backed up with bullets? I like it," Gaff said.

"From what the old geezer said, some of them are just hostages, not raiders at all," Susie noted, her pretty face taking on a thoughtful disposition. "I can tell you from experience that they're biding their time, just looking for a way out. They'll be eager to kill their captors. We can enlist them. If we get enough who aren't too scared to be on our side, we can swing the balance in our favor."

"Maybe we can find a way to arm them so they can fight the raiders alongside us when we attack, like a mutiny," Gaff suggested. "We should start with a diversion, like when we were in the camp at Scotts Bluff, and Kangee brought in her poison, and Emma put it in the food. All of a sudden, men started dying, and that threw the camp into chaos. That was how Emma escaped with Beth and her husband and how I got out with Marco."

"And how Arthur got taken," I said softly.

"We need Kangee and more of her potion," Susie said, turning to Donny. "Where is your wife, anyway? We haven't seen her since we left Outpost City."

"She'll be along when the time is right, as always," Donny

said. He gave me a pointed look, then jerked with his chin, indicating that I should say something.

I shook my head.

Donny kicked my foot with his.

I shook my head again.

Donny pursed his mouth and laid his head to one side, scrutinizing me fiercely.

"What is it?" Laurette demanded.

"Emma has a plan," Donny said.

"Donny, this mind-reading thing of yours is obnoxious," I muttered, "not to mention invasive. What I think in the privacy of my own mind is my business."

"It's not mind-reading," he said, grinning a little.

"Whatever you call it," I said, casting him a baleful look. I finished off my protein bar, a chocolate chip brownie confection that satisfied my sweet tooth while delivering thirty grams of protein and a full complement of the RDA of essential vitamins and minerals. I shook my head and laughed briefly at the wrapper in my hand; I hadn't had all of my recommended daily allowance of anything since the Day. I counted myself fortunate when there was anything at all to eat, regardless of its nutritional value. How much the apocalypse had taken from us!

"We're waiting, Emma," Gaff said in a brisk, authoritative voice. Some balls that kid had. He was getting downright bossy, of late.

I shook my head again though, as I had no intention of discussing my plans until I'd had a chance to thoroughly think them through. I had to figure out how to present them appropriately. What I had to do was required, but it would not be palatable to my comrades.

"Emma, if you have something to share, please speak up," Laurette said crisply. "I'd hate to be forced to put something in your evening tea to loosen your tongue."

Susie picked up her blonde head and gave me a quizzical

glance. "Emma doesn't need your tea anymore. She hasn't had any nightmares since Beaver Creek. Haven't you all noticed? She sleeps snug as a bug in a rug. Something has changed, Emma. What was it?"

Everyone turned to look at me.

I looked down and let my gaze follow the dirt runnels filled with clumps of pine needles. Then I glanced up into the azure sky and watched a bald eagle rising with a ground squirrel clutched in its talons.

"Emmy have plan," Theo said. "Emmy, talk."

I sighed and set the unnaturally blue Gatorade on the ground. "This isn't completely worked out in my head yet. Maybe it doesn't need to be."

"We'll decide that. Go on," Nwokocha said.

"I'll trade myself for Arthur."

A chorus of, "No!" erupted around the circle.

I held up my hands. "Actually, I think the deal has been made. In fact, I'm almost certain."

"What does that mean?" Nwokocha asked, as hotly as I'd ever heard him.

"The nightmares . . . Alexei was sending himself to me in them, haunting me and depriving me of sleep. Remember Kangee saying what a powerful mind he has?" I shuddered. "I told him he must free Arthur. He said I knew the price for that. I'm willing to pay the price, to do anything to free Arthur, and he knows it."

"The price is . . . you?" Laurette whispered, unbelieving.

I nodded. "Alexei wants vengeance. Arthur created the mists, and the mists killed Alexei's wife. So Alexei has tortured Arthur, and now he wants to take me from Arthur so Arthur will feel the same heartbreak he has. That will satisfy him, and he'll let Arthur go, let him live."

"That man is despicable," Nwokocha spat. "He will not honor his end of any bargain. He will take you into captivity and kill Arthur!"

I shook my head. "I don't think so."

"Really, Emma, you are naïve." Laurette sniffed. "Alexei is a most powerful and attractive man, but——"

"Hey!" Nwokocha exclaimed.

She reached over and squeezed his hand. "Nothing like you, my love, but in his own brutal way, he has a charm. However, he is also insane, an absolute sociopath who can reason his way to whatever he wants. He followed us to America, risking his life to do so. Why? Any sane person would have stayed in Europe with his son."

"I'm not being naïve," I retorted. "Alexei followed Arthur here for the same reason he's kept Arthur alive until now. He'll keep his word with me because he craves vengeance. It'd be far more devastating for Arthur to live knowing Alexei has me."

"You'd do that to Arthur, put him through that suffering?" Gaff asked, his narrow face more solemn than I'd ever seen it. "I don't know Arthur as well as the rest of you do, but even I know how he feels about you, Emma. He'd die to protect you. He'll never stop trying to free you from Alexei as long as he's alive. If you trade yourself for Arthur, Arthur will go back to free you, or die trying."

I closed my eyes, took a deep breath, and steeled myself. It was time to vocalize my suspicions. "Alexei has crippled Arthur. I can feel it in my body. Arthur is badly injured. He's been tortured. Maimed."

The others murmured, distressed.

"I'm sure of it." I felt faint and willed myself to go on. "There is no other way. I think Arthur's only chance to be whole again is for me to heal him."

"How can you do that if you are Alexei's captive?" Laurette asked sharply. "Do you think Alexei will let you heal Arthur before he releases him, if he complies with the deal at all?"

"No, I don't think he'll let me heal Arthur before he lets

him go, but I'll still try. I'll have to escape after trading myself, after Arthur has been released."

"Easier said than done." Laurette frowned.

"There might be a way." I looked at Donny, putting him on the spot.

"I will influence Alexei," Donny said in a matter-of-fact tone.

"I thought you said you aren't good at that," Gaff said.

Donny shrugged and adjusted his legs to a cross-legged position. "I'm not, and I'll have only one shot at it. One. I won't be able to use my mind power at all until the very last moment. Alexei can't know I have such a gift."

"I don't understand how all of this is supposed to go down," Susie said, confused and looking back and forth from Donny to me.

"I think I understand Emma's plan," Donny started.

"Understand it, or plucked it out of my brain?" I asked wryly.

Donny grinned and shook his head. "She'll make the trade. Alexei will send Arthur out of the raiders' camp to be picked up by us. A few hours later, I'll shadow his mind." Donny shrugged. "I'll do my best to delude him so Emma can leave camp, hopefully under the cover of darkness."

"I couldn't have explained it better myself," I said, blithely. "I'm starting to see the advantages in this mind-reading thing, Donny."

"It's not mind-reading," he argued again. "It's more like mind-sharing, and it's tenuous at best," he grumbled. "In fact, it may have no effect on Alexei. Maybe I won't be able to influence his mind. Even if I am, there's no guarantee that it will be enough to provide you with an escape. You'll be taking a huge risk, Emma, and if my powers don't work, we don't have a play. Even Kangee's afraid to go into Alexei's camp. We can't send her in to retrieve you."

"No, but you'll have Arthur, and he'll be alive," I said. "Even if he's crippled, as long as he's alive, he can control the mists."

"If Alexei have you," Theo said, chewing his lower lip, "Arthur not forgive us. He won't care about mist."

"This is a shitty plan if I ever heard one," Nwokocha said, disgusted and glowering at me.

"Come on! We specialize in pulling off shitty plans," I joked. "Where's our old camp spirit?"

"Lying broken and crippled in Yellowstone Park, if you are correct," Laurette snapped.

"Yeah, Emma. It really is a shitty plan," Susie said.

"If you've got a better one, I'm all ears," I said, "but I'm sure if I don't show up to make the trade and we engage in this guerilla warfare of yours, Alexei will execute Arthur."

"How could he execute the one person who can stop the mists?" Susie challenged.

"Yeah. Arthur is his one bargaining chip," Gaff added.

"Alexei believes his son is safe because France is a Safe Zone now. He's so bent on revenge that he doesn't care about the mists roaming the rest of the world. I think killing Arthur is and always has been Alexei's end game. It's payback for the death of his wife. That's the only reason he wants me. This way, if I trade myself, even if I can't escape later, Arthur's got a chance."

"He does not want a chance without you," Laurette said. She ran her fingers restlessly through her short, chic bob. Her pixie face was thoughtful and arresting, and I wondered how she always managed to look so good, even in the wilderness, after days without a shower.

"If he's been tortured that badly, he won't have a chance without your healing ability. You said so yourself," Gaff observed. "Arthur's an athlete, a proud man. He won't want to live if he's crippled and can't walk and take care of himself. That's not his idea of living."

"He has to live because he's got a bigger purpose than walking or me," I said. "Arthur has to face the mists because he's the only one who can. He can do it without being able to walk, if necessary. But we humans can never start over and rebuild as long as the mists are hunting us. Until we deal with them, we're just barely surviving, just hanging on. If we can get Alexei to release Arthur, you must make sure he lives, no matter what happens to me."

"So it's not just about Arthur. It's bigger than that," Susie commented. She gave me a long, troubled look.

Nwokocha steepled his hands in front of his chest. "If Donny's powers don't work, we will need a Plan B."

"So we go with our usual," I said.

"And what's that?" Gaff asked.

"Make it up as we go along," Laurette and I said, at the same time.

"Or guerrilla warfare, I suppose," Donny said, "the original idea."

Susie leaned across the circle and put her arms around me in a rare, sweet squeeze. None of us had ever known her to hug anyone voluntarily, so we were all surprised, me most especially. Susie leaned back in her seat after the impromptu and unexpected embrace and said, "Emma, it's so brave of you, to give yourself up to the raiders' camp. I thought you were doing it because you love Arthur, and I'm sure that's part of it, but there's so much more to it than that."

"Do not idealize Emma. She is a pain in the ass, always getting herself in trouble and needing to be rescued," Laurette warned. "Alexei's camp in France, the gallows at Outpost City . . . she has a talent for mishap."

"Lucky for her you are here to save her," Susie said, in such perfect mimicry of Laurette's French-accented intonations that we all laughed, except for Susie herself, who continued to gaze at me somberly.

I lowered my eyes; I couldn't bear such admiration. I knew

my motives weren't as noble as they seemed. The truth was that I was deeply in love with Arthur and bound to him. I would have sacrificed myself for him whether or not he could rid the world of mists.

· · ·

I ADVOCATED EXECUTING the trade immediately. I had felt the pain of Arthur's torture in my own body and couldn't bear the thought of him enduring another moment of it.

The others refused, demanding a night's sleep. Interaction with Alexei was bound to be complex, unpredictable, and possibly even fatal, and we were all exhausted from traveling fast and hard. None of us were at our best to face him and the challenges he was sure to present.

So, it was decided that we would ride through Yellowstone to the Army fort the next morning. Susie, Donny, Laurette, and Gaff would hang far back, five kilometers from the fort. Nwokocha and Theo would accompany me in moving much closer to the fort but remain hidden when I entered.

"You have to be where you can see Arthur brought out or at least where I can signal you to retrieve Arthur," I said.

"We find place." Theo squeezed my shoulder. "No worry, Emmy. We get Arthur. And then we get you out too."

"I hope so," I said. "If this doesn't work, it'll be twice as hard to get him out from now on, because Alexei will be on top of us, expecting anything and everything."

"I thought you said this will work, that Alexei will keep his end of the deal, as long as you willingly exchange yourself for Arthur," Gaff said, narrowing his eyes at me.

"Well, there's always Murphy's law," I said.

"Murphy? Who's he? One of the raiders?" Gaff asked, clueless.

"No," I said, then laughed. "Whatever can go wrong usually does." I sighed.

"With those inspirational words ringing in our ears, let's make camp for the night," Nwokocha said. "Gaff and Theo, you take first watch. Wake Laurette and me around midnight. Donny, you and Susie will come on just before dawn."

"What about me?" I asked from my horse, where I was getting my blanket.

"You have the toughest role to play tomorrow," Nwokocha answered. "You get a full night's sleep. You'll need your rest."

6 I STOOD IN THE SHADOW OF PINE TREES on the snowy side of a rolling mountain, looking far down at the red-roofed buildings in the village in the northern section of Yellowstone Park. It was there that tourists had, until a few years ago, entered the park. My eyes went to sandstone double-barracks that had once housed Army troops, then served the park, and now served an army once again, albeit a far more sinister one. Somehow I knew that Arthur was in that building. So was Alexei.

Theo touched my arm, and Nwokocha nodded. Nwokocha's large, dark eyes were luminous, and Theo's face was wrung tight with anxiety, but neither spoke. They wished me well, hoped I would succeed, worried, and cared; their feelings were palpable, familiar, deeply valued.

I smiled a little, an expression of a hope I didn't feel. Talking the plan over with my friends had made it seem plausible. But now that I stood there in the moment, preparing to hand myself over to a sociopath, I realized how thin and brittle the strategy really was. *What will Alexei do to me once he has me?* He'd always observed certain proprieties around me, but I wondered how long he would continue to do so. *Will I really be able to escape?*

Theo and Nwokocha melted back into the woods, disappearing into the waist- and shoulder-high shag of young lodgepole pines from which we'd just emerged. The trees swayed and squeaked and absorbed my friends, and the red squirrels chattered as if attending a tea party.

My heart thumped and raced and stumbled and cart-wheeled. Before I could step forward, a drumbeat sounded from far to the south. Then other drums joined in, until the plateau below me swelled with percussion. The mists were coming: That was the only reason for pervasive, rhythmic sound.

I squatted and waited. It was about twenty minutes before I spied the first white tendrils creeping along the ground toward the village at Fort Yellowstone. The drumbeat picked up its cadence, and its volume also increased.

The mists must have caught a group of people too far away for me to see, because distant screaming erupted. The forest came alive with animals rushing, flying, thrashing, leaping, and escaping. Deer and gray wolves and even a bighorn sheep, coyotes, fox, and elk, raced past me in a panic, not even both-ering to cast a glance my way. A ground squirrel ran over my foot. Ravens and magpies shrieked. And still, the drumbeat intensified.

All at once, the mists froze. Then they curled into them-selves, compacting into a tight white ball. The ball rose above the fort and hovered. It rose higher and kept rising until it was nearly as far above the Earth as the artificial satellites that had once navigated the planet's atmosphere.

The drumming slowed and lost volume, until it spiraled down into rich, saturated silence.

I looked up and could still faintly see a tiny white flash. The mists had only been temporarily displaced. They would return.

Sparrows and finches sang, and the park returned to nor-mal almost immediately. A swathe of pavement had been eliminated, and only brown scars of earth and yellow sand were left behind.

The time had come for me to surrender myself. I took a

deep breath and carefully trekked down the sloping mountain toward the fort. Alexei would know I was coming; he would feel me, and he would leave word with his men. I would pass through the guards unmolested until I was in his presence.

One minute I was maneuvering my way down to the fort, trying not to lose my footing, and in the next, I was walking into an underground tunnel. It was shocking, and I froze, wondering where I was. I looked around quickly and anxiously and saw a painted white line in the middle of a road. I identified a mountain underpass, the kind blasted through solid rock. The air on my skin was cool and damp.

What am I doing here? How did I get here? Have I somehow lost track of time?

I took a deep breath and eyed my surroundings carefully. I was standing in the center of a manmade rock cavern, disoriented and with no idea which direction I should take to get to the fort, since bright sunlight gleamed at both ends of the tunnel. Finally I just let instinct direct my feet and walked along the white line. I arrived at the lip of the tunnel and was about to step out when laughter erupted behind me.

"You like games, Emma?" asked Alexei.

I whirled to face him. "I played a mean Pictionary in the Before."

"Me too. I like games." Alexei winked and motioned for me to approach him.

I stalled. "What game?"

"Hide-n-seek," he sang in a mocking, joyous tone. "I hide, and if you find me, you will stay and your lover can go."

"I'm supposed to believe you'll keep your word?"

"Emma, I swear to you on life of my only son Mikhail that if you find me, I shall set your lover free!" Alexei threw up his one arm and vanished.

I changed course and walked all the way back through the tunnel, emerged, and looked around. There was more roadway with strips of field alongside it, flanked by trees, rocks, and underbrush. Birds called, and squirrels chattered, but none gave away Alexei's location. I took a few steps off the road into the dirt and looked around. No Alexei.

I turned and walked back into the tunnel. I was in the center when a voice boomed, "Getting warmer!"

The voice was so loud, right at my left shoulder, that I jumped and exclaimed. I spun around, but he wasn't there. I looked up: No Alexei. I walked through to the other side. The other side looked exactly the same as the first, so much so, in fact, that I was convinced I'd gotten confused and retraced my own steps. I walked to the edge of the road and knelt down, peering at the ground, to see if my tracks were there. Faint and barely discernible, I spied the outlines of my hiking boots.

I turned around and reentered the tunnel, resolving not to stop for any reason whatsoever. Alexei's laughter followed me as I marched in a direct line toward the other opening.

But when I exited, it was the same vista as before. I returned to the edge of the road and once again spied my own tracks. I turned and ran back through the tunnel, as fast as I could, without stopping, only to emerge in the same exact spot.

I stood still, panting to catch my breath. A game, Alexei had called it, but it was only for his amusement. The only way to end the game was not to play it, so I walked off the road and crossed the grassy field to the woods and found a boulder. I climbed up and sat on it, waiting. I slowed my breathing and tried to relax, though I felt tense and anxious in every cell of my body.

About twenty minutes, a petulant voice sounded. "You are not playing, Emma. You are boring."

"I don't want to play. I want to get on with it."

"You are no fun." Alexei strode out of the tunnel. He came

over, hoisted himself onto the rock with his one arm, and sat beside me. His hip and arm, warm and hard, brushed against me.

"Alexei, where are we?" I asked.

He smiled faintly. "Do you know what pain is, Emma? I never asked you. Do you know?"

"I know pain very well."

"No, real pain," he admonished, "not the pain of this frail thing." He touched my arm with his remaining hand, then gestured, indicating my entire body.

"I know real pain," I snapped, losing patience. "Real pain is loss and worrying about your loved ones! I know it damn well, much of it thanks to you."

"Loss, yes." He nodded in satisfaction. "Every day I have real pain but not for world. World is bad, but I survive, and Mikhail lives. World gets what it deserves. But Mikhail's mother was good, and every day she is in my heart. Every day I remember her face as mists eat her. I shot her to stop her suffering. I shot my beautiful, good wife. That is pain." A gun appeared in his hand, and he pressed it to my temple.

I held very still. *Is Alexei going to kill me?* "Yes, that is real pain," I breathed.

As quickly as it had appeared, the gun vanished. "All other pain is secondary, less real. Pain of burning eyeball or testicle with red hot stick or cutting flesh off body in strips or smashing bones is all secondary pain."

"It hurts too," I said cautiously, as I didn't know if his gun would reappear or if he was planning to do to me the awful things that he'd mentioned.

"Not like real pain. Not like pain if you lose daughter, beautiful sweet Beth or funny Mandy. If you lose them, that would be real pain."

"A pain I could never recover from," I admitted, still feeling wary.

Alexei leaned toward me. "I like your daughters. They

are very good girls. You do good job with them, you and Haywood."

"Thank you," I whispered, awash in terror. *Is he threatening my daughters?*

"I do not threaten your sweet girls." He eyed me in puzzlement. "Why do you think such things? Maybe Mikhail marry one of them and make beautiful babies. You and I could share grandchildren. It is my dream."

I didn't speak because I didn't know what to say.

"Do you have a dream, Emma?" he asked.

I gathered my courage. "Yes. I dream of Arthur being free and safe."

"Arthur? Pssh," Alexei spat. "Why do you want him? Haywood is good man, willing to die for you and daughters. He is brave, gallant. I like him. He does not bring mists to world. No one dies because of Haywood. Why do you not stay content with Haywood, father of your sweet girls?"

I found it strange that he asked me the same unanswerable question I asked myself every day. "The heart wants what it wants," I said dully, my chest throbbing. I wrapped my arms around my knees and squeezed. "I didn't mean to love Arthur. I never intended for that to happen. When I met him in France, I was just trying to take care of my daughter and a group of orphans. Arthur had a camp, a safe camp, and safety was the most important thing for us after a winter of running from the mists. It just happened."

"Lame," Alexei uttered, like an epithet. "Very lame."

I shrugged. "Sometimes the truth is lame."

"Like Arthur. He is lame now, since his Achilles tendon is cut." Alexei said, and now it was his turn to shrug nonchalantly. "After everything, I think I would feel good to hurt him, but I still have pain. Arthur suffers very much, but I still see my wife's face just before I shot her. My pain is not less, even if Arthur's pain in body is great."

"Maybe you weren't supposed to make him suffer.

Vengeance is mine, saith the Lord!" I cried. "Maybe you were supposed to leave him to his destiny!"

Alexei picked up his head and tilted it, his blue eyes huge and vacant, like the sky. "Vengeance and the Lord? Hmm. Maybe you are not boring, Emma, even if you do not play." He vanished from the rock.

For a split second, I was alone on the boulder. Then there was a kind of implosive percussion, and I was blinking my eyes. I lay in a crumpled heap on the side of the mountain, where I had been before. There was blood on my mouth and chin, leaking down from my nose. Weak and trembling, I stood. I wiped myself off and continued down the mountain.

A group of eight men met me and positioned themselves around me in tight formation. They kept me in the center as we descended.

• • •

AT THE ENTRANCE to the village, a bulky, scarred man stepped out of the crowd of raiders who had gathered to watch my ingress. The man gave me a serious look and smiled, the ropy scar on his face contorting his mouth.

"Dmitri!" I exclaimed when I recognized the medical doctor from Alexei's old camp in France, someone I hadn't expected to ever see again.

"Emma," he said. He laid a big hand on my shoulder and looked at me with great compassion.

"I had no idea you were here. I didn't see you in the other camp, the one at Scotts Bluff."

"I saw you," he said in a low voice so only I could hear. He scowled. "I saw you in the pen with the crazy ones, your beautiful blonde hair dyed and cut." He ruffled my hair affectionately. "I knew you right away." He took my arm and drew me away from the other men.

"Then why didn't you didn't say anything?" I asked, sotto voce.

Dmitri glanced around from under hooded eyes. He leaned his head close to my ear. "None of my business if you wanted to hide yourself. We are friends. You helped me and my patients in the old camp, and I will never forget that." Then, scowling a warning at me, he picked up his pace and escorted me through the visitor center village to a building marked "Park Administration."

We entered the front door of a three-story building through a big door on the left, and I saw Alexei first, a one-armed colossus, his blond head and broad shoulders filling the hallway, sucking all the life out of everything else. There was no electricity, just some hurricane lamps that spread gray light through the hall; when his mad eyes caught the light, they tripled it back.

"Welcome, Emma, to your new home!" Alexei said, waving his hand.

But I stopped paying attention to him when I caught sight of a body lying on a desk. The body was curled up in fetal position on its side. It was covered in blood. Black hair marked strips of scalp that had flopped down around its neck.

A sudden, horrified knowing dizzied me, from my knees up to the crown of my head. I knew that it was Arthur, but when I ran to his side, I froze.

Arthur was horribly hurt. His clothes were in scarlet and brown tatters and he stank of vomit and putrefying flesh.

Fighting nausea, I leaned closer.

Half of Arthur's face was black and charred; the eye on that side of his face was a pool of bloody gel. Strips of skin had been cut away, like a peel sliced off an apple, leaving fascia and muscle and the rainbow slick of periosteum exposed. He must have felt my gaze in his semi-conscious state because he writhed slightly and moved an arm that ended in a crusted, blackened stump just below the elbow.

Seeing him hurt and maimed like that evoked contrasting images of him whole and perfect, entwined in my arms. I was shocked by the forcefulness of those images: his gray eyes alight with passion or anger or pleasure; the perfect symmetry of his features; his smile when I moved beneath him.

My hands trembled as they reached for him. I did not know how he could still be alive in such a condition, and I wasn't sure my healing gift would be of any use to him, as far gone as he was. Everything in me ached for him. I had never felt so sorrowful.

"No, dear Emma, no," Alexei said. He clasped my hands together tightly in his big one. "Your sweet, healing touch that saved my son Mikhail is not for Arthur."

"Alexei, please! Even you cannot be so cruel," I whispered.

"Is it cruel to visit retribution upon the man who brought the apocalypse?"

"I told you, retribution belongs to God, however you conceive of God."

"I don't. God took His leave of people and gave Arthur freedom to do as he would. If not for Arthur, the world would be as it was three years ago. Billions of people would still live. My wife would be alive. Mikhail's mother would hold him still."

Tears fell down my cheeks. "Alexei, Arthur may be the only man alive who can eradicate the mists. He may have created them, but he did it with good intentions, to save the world from war."

"Intentions? Pssh," Alexei snorted. "You Americans have funny saying about intention and road to hell, have you not?"

"Please let me help him," I begged. "I don't know if I can, but I have to try."

Alexei shook his head. Still gripping my wrists, he pulled me aside. He lifted his chin to a cluster of men standing behind us, and they bustled forward, carrying a makeshift stretcher. "Take Arthur up the mountain," Alexei said. "Two men hide there, waiting for him. I remember them from my time in Arthur's camp: Charles Nwokocha and Theo. You will give him to them."

The men grunted and set to work, rolling Arthur off the desk and onto the stretcher and not being at all gentle about it. Arthur was so bad off that he couldn't even moan. I could do nothing except weep.

"You see, dear Emma? I am generous. You did not win our game, yet I keep my word anyway. I set your lover free." Alexei released my wrists and swept me to his side with his one arm. "It is good, Emma. You will come to see that."

"Alexei, Arthur has no chance of survival without my healing gift," I said, sobbing silently. "Please let me work on him before he goes. Please."

"Arthur will take his chance with God's healing gift," Alexei said in a tone of satisfied finality. "Come, I will show you to your new room. Then we eat lunch. I make good food for you."

• • •

IT WAS EVENING, and the sky was purple, the stars shaking themselves out from beneath the blanket of daylight. We sat on wooden chairs by a big campfire in a field outside the village, just on the other side of the parking lot.

As in his other camps, Alexei had organized his personnel according to a hierarchy that made sense to him, if to no one else. The upper echelon of raiders and a few women sat near me on office chairs that had been dragged out of the park administration building. Other raiders and women spilled over the ground and settled around several other fires. At each, food was being cooked: deer, antelope, and elk, as well as grouse. Big pots bubbled with stewed plants and mushrooms. It smelled good, the roasting meat and the mushrooms, but I couldn't think of eating. My fingers twisted themselves together over and over again in front of my chest.

"You must eat, Emma," Dmitri said softly, pressing a plate of food into my hands. "Maintain your strength. You know how the world is. You cannot turn down food when it's available."

"I do know how the world is," I said numbly. I had been hungry many times since the Day the mists had torn through the streets of Paris and through every other city in the world, devastating everything in their path. Nevertheless, I placed the plate on my lap and refused to touch the venison. All I could think about was Arthur, my Arthur, whole and perfect in my arms. Then I thought of Arthur as he was now, almost unrecognizable after Alexei's torture, and any appetite I might have had was quickly lost.

Alexei didn't sit. Rather he walked around, bantering with his men and flirting with women. He was jovial and expansive. He meandered back to our fire and traded jokes with Dmitri. I wasn't really paying attention, as I was lost in a fugue of mourning for Arthur, but then I heard Alexei calling my name.

"Emma, why you not eat delicious food? Is feast prepared in your honor!" He touched my cheek with his hand, then took hold of my chin and tilted up my face to meet his eyes. "You must eat. You have not eaten all day."

"I'm not hungry, Alexei."

"This will not do," he frowned. "You must eat. One day you will see your girls again, and you must be strong for them. Come now. Eat. I command you."

Reluctantly, I put a bit of meat in my mouth.

Alexei beamed. "Good! You please me." He stroked my cheek again and went off.

There must have been a contingent of Russians besides Dmitri, because the sound of Russian folk-singing, accompanied by some kind of hearty flute or clarinet, rose up from a nearby campfire.

I choked down a few bites of meat before Alexei returned.

"You are done?" he asked.

I nodded.

"Come." He held out his hand.

I rose and set the plate on my chair.

Alexei took my hand and led me away from the fire, back toward the buildings in the little village. "You and I have shared much, Emma. Remember when we go with Mandy to my camp in Le Havre?"

"Not really. I wasn't sane for most of that."

"You saved my life and Mandy's by becoming mad," Alexei said solemnly. "I saved yours in battle with cannibal army. You save mine at Allier River. You sacrifice yourself to save me."

"And Mandy," I said dully.

"And Mandy," he echoed, then pointed to the duplex sandstone building in front of us, roofed with red clay tile. "This was Captain quarters, now is mine . . . and yours." He led me up concrete steps on the north side and opened the door.

"I want my own quarters."

"I will not force you into my arm, Emma," Alexei said, his lips quirking. "My one good arm is very good arm, good enough to hold you. Too bad only one. You will come to me when you are ready, but for now, you will share my bed."

"I most certainly will not."

"You and I have danced around each other for so long. It is time for us to come together." Alexei struck a match and lit a candle which he used to light others. He led me through a kitchen and living room to a bedroom with a double-bed. He set his candle down on a dresser.

I walked past the bed to a bathroom. In my backpack was my toothbrush and a tube of toothpaste. Brushing my teeth was a ritual to which I had adhered since the Day. It grounded me and steadied me somehow. If nothing else held true in the world, no matter what and no matter where, regardless of the apocalypse, I would attend to my teeth. I collected tubes of toothpaste wherever I went, and I had not gone a day without brushing. I had often brushed dry and spat foamy spittle on the ground.

Arthur had even teased me about my fixation on dental hygiene when we lived at his camp in the south of France. *Arthur, whole and perfect.*

"Take candle, or pee in dark," Alexei said. "Water works."

I took the candle from the dresser, carried it into the bathroom, and brushed my teeth by its flickering yellow light. The faucet actually did work, and I rinsed my mouth carefully, washed my face, and drank several handfuls of water. I went back out and replaced the candle on the dresser.

Alexei was sitting on the side of the bed. "You hope for rescue, but there is none this time, Emma. Now you are with me."

I couldn't speak. Numbly, I went around to the other side of the bed. I took off my hiking boots and coat and settled my backpack on the floor. I lay down on my side and curled up into a tight ball, reminding myself that I had slept in worse places, albeit not with worse people.

Alexei pulled the cover up over me. He lay down and curled up around me, spooning me. "Be peaceful. Your friends have Arthur. I have you, and you have me."

"We are not for each other," I said softly but stubbornly.

"You must let him go, Emma. He is damaged goods. Is not man anymore. You would not want him how he is." Alexei's tone was dismissive.

The candle was still burning, shedding pearlescent radiance over the quiet room. Far away in Carstairs, my husband and daughters were sleeping, missing me. I had given them up for a man I'd never intended to love, a man whose inventions had visited horrific destruction on the world. A man who lay in agony a few miles from me. And now I knew that I loved him no matter what, even if he was damaged goods, even if he wasn't a man anymore. I just loved him.

• • •

SOMETHING WOKE ME just before dawn, like a breeze fluttering over my face. I sat up, shrugging off Alexei's arm.

Alexei continued to sleep, snoring softly.

In my head and in the room, I felt rather than heard a single word: "*Go.*" Something about that word had the flavor of Donny, or at least I thought so. I desperately hoped so.

I rose quickly, slipped my feet into my boots, shrugged on my coat, and scooped up my backpack. I did not glance back at Alexei as I soundlessly left the room through the door we'd entered last night.

The sky was deep indigo and spattered with stars. A faint, pale, milky scrim was just beginning to paint the horizon lavender and gray. I walked through the somnolent village and saw no one moving. I knew, however, that there would be patrols, and my mind raced, wondering how I'd slip past them. I pulled a wool cap from my pocket and tucked my hair up inside it; I didn't want it to be obvious who I was, as anyone who recognized me as Alexei's special guest would return me to him promptly.

Sure enough, at the edge of the parking lot, a two-man patrol stopped me. They were raiders, young guys garbed in heavy coats and armed with machine guns and ammo belts. Each also wore a bow and quiver of arrows slung over his back. One carried a torch, and the dancing orange flames threw distorted shadows onto his face and the ground below.

"What are you doing?" demanded the raider with the torch. "Why are you out of your bunk?"

"I, uh . . . have to go to the bathroom," I lied.

"The latrines are that way," the other raider said, pointing.

He'd cut the fabric of his glove so his index finger would poke through.

"I have a strong sense of smell, and I prefer the woods," I said with a wink, as if that would explain everything.

Mr. Pointy cocked his head. "Don't I know you?"

"I don't think so, but if you wait until I'm finished doing my business, maybe we could get to know each other better," I said suggestively.

He smiled. "I think we can work something out."

Mr. Torch grimaced. "Look, woman, go back to your bunk. It's dangerous out there, with all the animals, crazies, and mists. Use the latrines, like everyone else."

"Come on, boys. There's plenty of me to go around. We could have some fun." I stepped close to him and laid my hands on his chest, then seductively dropped one hand to cup his crotch. "Gimme ten minutes, and then you boys come see what I'm doing. If you've got one, bring a blanket."

Wavering, Mr. Torch chewed his lip. "We're not supposed to allow women out of the village."

"No one will know," Mr. Pointy said with a hungry look. "Let's do it!"

"You'd just be doing your job," I coaxed. "If I slipped past you and you heard a noise, surely you'd come to check it out. Dutiful scouts that you are, you'd have no trouble finding me." I paused and rubbed my hand up and down the guy's pelvis. "A little while later, you bring me back. No one will know anything except that you're patrolling. Doing a good job." I dropped my hand away from the growing bulge and stepped back.

"Hell yes!" Mr. Pointy said eagerly. "We can spread my coat out on the ground. It's not that cold out tonight. It's not cold at all."

"Ten minutes," Mr. Torch growled. "And I go first!"

Mr. Pointy objected, and I skedaddled while they bickered. I had ten minutes. I had to make them count.

I ran up the trail I'd come down so many hours earlier, then cut out into the underbrush at the first opportunity, then turned to go back up the mountain. I proceeded that way in zigzag fashion, ducking low and moving as fast as I could in the dark, making my way toward where I'd left Nwokocha and Theo.

My laces weren't tied, and even with my eyes adapted to the dark, I was struggling. I tripped and fell and banged my head on something that tore a deep, bleeding gash into my forehead. I kept going. My internal sense of time counted five minutes gone. Some big animal crashed nearby, perhaps scenting me, but I kept going. *Seven minutes gone.* I knew the two guys would come looking for me soon, or maybe Alexei would wake and rouse the whole camp to look for me. The dark was lightening into murk, and I could feel my heart pounding as I desperately tried to get as far away as possible. *Ten minutes.*

They were calling out cautiously, "Where'd you go?"

"Where are you? Hey, woman? Ain't we gonna have some fun?"

I tried to move more stealthily while also moving faster. I was working my way uphill, dodging trees and bushes and rocks; it was like swimming through molasses.

Sixteen minutes. It had been about nineteen since I'd slipped out of Alexei's room, and I wondered how much longer before he stirred and didn't find me lying next to him. I pressed on desperately, barely able to see. Low-hanging branches whipped back into my face.

A *crash* sounded behind me, not an animal this time; one of the men was hot on my trail. Not Mr. Torch, because no light flickered nearby. I leapt forward, caught my foot on something, and sprawled out, facedown.

"There you are!" Mr. Pointy laughed. "Led me on a pretty chase." He grabbed me by my ankles and pulled me toward him.

I kicked, and my shoes came off in his hands. I lunged up like a runner on a block and sprinted forward.

He took a flying leap and tackled me. "This works just fine," he panted, his hot breath grazing my ear. "I wanted you to myself anyway." He thrust his knee down on my back, slamming me down as I scrabbled to get away. His pants dropped, his metal belt buckle thumping on my back. He grabbed my hips and dragged me backward, then reached inside my coat for the belt of my pants.

I fought him, rearing up and twisting around to scratch at his face and eyes.

He smacked me hard, with the flat of his hand, causing my head to bounce backward like a basketball being dribbled. Then he jerked off my cap and grabbed a fistful of my hair, yanking so hard that I cried out. "Be still, bitch," he growled.

There was a *hiss* and a *swish* of air next to my head. A curtain of wet splattered all over me. The raider gurgled, then fell silent. A second later, his hands unfurled, and he crumpled to the ground, with an arrow extending from his throat.

I would have cried out in surprise and delight if someone hadn't whispered a "Shh." I leapt to my feet, whirling around. In the gloom, I spied Susie, standing tall and straight, not two meters in front of me.

She had shrugged off her hood and set her blonde hair free, and that faint yellow glimmer around her head drew my attention. Her lips were pursed to hush me, and her hands held an arrow nocked into her bow. Near us, down the slope of the mountain, a ball of orange light bounced through the trees.

"Hey! Where'd you two go?" called Mr. Torch. "I'm supposed to go first!"

"Here," I called softly.

Susie smiled.

"That's more like it!" Mr. Torch stepped into the clearing where I stood.

Susie released her arrow.

The raider's mouth opened in surprised at the arrow protruding from the center of his chest. He pitched forward.

I scrambled out of his way, then took up his torch. The ground was damp from melting snow, but there was plenty of kindling, and the torch could conceivably ignite a fire, which would alert Alexei and the others to my whereabouts. I exchanged a glance with Susie, then put out the torch by plunging and rubbing it into the earth. When it was dowsed, I located my boots, pulled them on, and tied them tightly.

Susie was stripping the dead raiders of their weapons and ammunition. "We have to hurry. We don't have long. Donny said he can only keep Alexei asleep for about a half-hour, and even that would be a stretch."

"It's been almost that," I said.

Susie touched my forehead. "This is bad."

"I know."

"Can you go fast?"

"Yes. Thanks. Good shots, so . . . timely."

"Such fun, right?" she chortled softly. "It's a good night, two for two." She clasped my arm in a moment of good spirits. Susie liked killing raiders.

"Theo and Nwokocha take Arthur?" I asked.

Susie nodded and didn't say anything. The two of us set out at a lope up the mountain. Sure-footed like a goat, she expertly picked the path for me.

7

THEO AND NWOKOCHA HAD TRANS-ported Arthur five kilometers, to the others' location. "I only saw him for a moment," Susie said, "and then Nwokocha sent me back here to help you. But that was enough. I've never seen anyone in such bad shape. He didn't even look human. Do you really think Arthur can be saved?"

It was the same question I asked myself when I joined the others, in a little stand of aspens. Arthur lay on the stretcher on the ground, bleating occasionally. I ran past the others, murmured, and knelt beside him. Tears ran down my face.

"You can't work on him now," Nwokocha said, his voice tight. "Donny says Alexei is awake and is raising hell down there."

"We must get away, as far and as fast as possible," Laurette added as she grabbed my shoulder and pulled me upright. She eyed me carefully, put her cool hand to the gash on my forehead, then dabbed at it with a piece of cloth from her pocket. "Let me clean and dress this before we go."

"No," Nwokocha said. "Our time will be better spent putting distance between us and Alexei, immediately, not playing nursemaid. Emma is strong, and she will be fine."

Laurette shrugged. "Emma, you must at least take a dose of the antibiotics we took from that store in Harlowtown and something for pain, if necessary."

"How are we going to move Arthur?" Susie asked, standing at the foot of Arthur's stretcher with a horrified expression on her young face. She stroked her long, blonde hair over her shoulder, caressing the tresses like she would a kitten.

"We will lash him to a horse. I realize it sounds crude," Nwokocha said, glancing at me, "but we have no choice."

Theo and Gaff emerged from behind a copse of fir trees. Between them, they supported Donny, each with an arm under one of hiss burly shoulders. Donny's head was lolling down onto his chest, bouncing as they walked.

"Donny!" I called.

"I . . . we must . . . we've gotta go," Donny stuttered. He pushed away from Theo and Gaff and leaned against a tree, trembling. "Alexei is awake and mad as a hornet. I can feel his mind, his fury. He's determined to find us, to get you back, to kill Arthur. We have to get as far away as possible."

"Are you okay?" I asked.

"Took everything in me to use my mind that way, to hold Alexei's mind in sleep. I've never done anything like it before. It was like using muscles I didn't even know I had. I feel nauseous." Donny picked up his head and smiled a little, in spite of the pastiness and green hue in his dark skin. His eyes met mine. "But at least I look better than you do."

"Emma look bad," Theo said. He crossed over to me and laid a warm hand on each side of my face, peering at the gash on my forehead.

"It's not all my blood. Susie shot a raider who was right beside me," I said. "I can ride."

"You sure, Emma?" Gaff asked. He looked worried for the very first time since I'd met him. "Did Alexei, uh . . . hurt you?"

Laurette sniffed and continued to wipe my face. "If Emma is talking, she is fine. We only have to worry when she is screaming or cannot talk."

"I'm fine. And no, he didn't hurt me," I said somberly. "We should tie Arthur on in the front of my horse. Maybe I can use the healing gift to stabilize him while we ride."

"You think Arthur wants to be stabilized?" Gaff asked as he stared down at Arthur, shuddering. "You think Arthur would want to live like this?"

"If he did not want to live, he would not still be alive," Laurette said, her harsh tone softened. "He has a powerful life force."

The rest of us looked at each other but didn't answer. We had Arthur back, and that was enough for now. What to do with him would come later.

Theo, Nwokocha, and Gaff maneuvered Arthur up onto my horse and secured him as best they could.

Gaff vomited twice, because oozy red chunks of Arthur's skin came off in his hands. "Man, what did they do to him?" Gaff asked, scrubbing at this mouth with his hands.

"I just hope he can hang on a while longer," I said, breathing through my mouth so I wouldn't have to smell the salty, metallic stench of his blood or the caustic aroma of burnt flesh and pus, vomit, urine, and defecation. Arthur had been left to rot in his own body fluids.

Nwokocha and Gaff were helping Donny mount when a cheery voice rang out.

"Greetings!" said Kangee. She stood directly in our midst, wearing her pink Juicy Couture tracksuit topped with an unzipped parka.

"Kangee!" we all cried in unison.

"Miss me?" she asked. She then walked over and poked Arthur's calf, which was largely peeled of its skin, revealing blue and red veins running over the ball of his calf muscle. "You have your work cut out for you, Emma."

"Can I do anything for him?" I wondered.

Kangee smiled. "I'll be you."

Nwokocha finished fixing Donny's foot in the stirrup. "What do you mean?"

"I will be Emma, or at least Donny will start thinking I'm Emma, while I ride with you. Emma will leave us when we get a little north of here. She'll take Arthur with her. We'll divert Alexei and his gang and lead them away from Arthur and the real Emma."

"That'd be a great plan if I wasn't sick," Donny called, struggling to hold himself properly on his horse.

"You'll be okay," Kangee said. "You have to be. All you have to do is look at me and think of Emma. That will be enough to fool Alexei when he looks into your mind."

"It's a good plan, to misdirect Alexei and allow Emma to escape with Arthur—a very good plan, if we can pull it off." Nwokocha tilted his head, thinking it through.

"I want to do it. The thing is, I'm real sick," Donny rumbled. "I don't have the focus I'd need to pull it off."

"You were real sick in the Royal Alberta hospital," Kangee said, "but Emma saved your life then by putting her hands on you. Now we must help her and give her a chance to help Arthur."

"This plan will leave the rest of you vulnerable," I noted, troubled. "If Alexei catches up to you, it won't go well. You'll have a battle on your hands."

"We'll ride fast," Kangee said. "Donny will know if they get close to us. He'll warn us."

"We have a shitload of bullets," Gaff said cheerfully. "Their supplies have to be running low, but we stocked up in Harlowtown."

"We have plenty of arrows too," Susie added. "You saw how good I am with a bow. I'm an expert archer."

"Still, Donny is weak," I said. "It all depends on him. If I take Arthur and Alexei realizes we've split up, we'll be vulnerable."

"I'll get myself together." Donny took a deep breath and exchanged a fond smile with Kangee. "Kangee's right. I have to do this. I'll find a way to make it work. I'll start right now, seeing Emma when I look at my wife."

"I've always wondered what it would be like to be blonde," said Kangee. "Now I'll know." She saddled one of the packhorses.

"We will all look at Kangee and think of Emma. That will support Donny," Laurette said. She reined in her horse, who started to prance, as if he sensed the inevitable pursuit.

Donny nodded. "It will help. Call her that by name too. It will strengthen me."

"Where will I go?" I asked.

The others stared at me, and for a few beats, no one answered.

"You'll go far away, where Alexei won't be able to find you," Kangee said finally, wearing her usual inscrutable smile.

• • •

WE LOOPED EAST and joined the Beartooth Highway, which we took for hours. It was often exposed, but when it wasn't, we trotted along a series of steep zigzags and switchbacks; I didn't dare look down. Nwokocha felt that the good, paved roadway, which allowed the horses to go hard and fast, more than compensated for the danger.

I kept my eyes on Arthur, who was little more than a lump of flesh on the saddle in front of me. I couldn't believe he was still alive, but periodically he would groan or hiss, indicating that he was. I tried to will the healing energy into him, but it didn't work that way. I would have to put my hands on him to complete the circuit, and my hands were busy with the reins. I could do little more than pray that he'd stay alive long enough for me to help him.

As we rode through open land from the west toward

Beartooth Pass, Nwokocha drew up his horse. "Here," he said.

We all reined in our horses. Donny drew away from the rest of us, keeping his back to me. He hadn't looked at me or spoken to me once since we'd set out. It wasn't rude or malicious; he had expunged the real me from his thoughts so he could see me when he looked at Kangee.

I was in awe of his self-discipline. And grateful.

"I've been thinking about this, let's give Emma some food," Gaff said, dismounting.

"I can't take care of another horse," I objected.

"I'll just tie on a few saddlebags behind you," Gaff said, throwing a crooked grin over his shoulder as he marched to the packhorses. "You're gonna need food and water and you won't be able to hunt and gather while you're caring for Arthur. You've only got two hands."

"Gaff's right," Susie decided. She slid down her horse and stretched, arching her back and shoulders. "I know where the protein bars are." She went to one of the packhorses and unbuckled a bag, which she tossed to Gaff.

Gaff had thrown two packs over his shoulders. He trotted over with them and the one from Susie. He stepped around to the left of my horse and patted my calf. Then his nimble fingers worked to clip on the packs.

"Gaff, look at you! Mr. Pickpocket Information Broker, thinking ahead and looking out for someone else's wellbeing," I said playfully but solemnly. "When did you grow up?"

"When I had to." He craned around so I could see his skinny face with its shock of blond hair poking out of the tattered leather cap. "Probably when I was standing on the execution platform with a noose around my neck, next to you." He stepped back. "I can just about fit one more if I do it right."

"Medicine," Laurette suggested.

"Extra gun and ammo," Nwokocha corrected.

Laurette and I looked at each other, and I swallowed hard. *Will I ever see her, or the others, again?*

She shrugged, and her gamine face tightened with worry. "Gun and ammo."

So Gaff made another trip to the packhorses, checked through the packs, and grabbed one, then ran back and buckled it on behind me. "Good luck, Emma. Ride safe," he said before he clambered back up onto his horse.

"Godspeed, Emmy," Theo said softly.

"Good luck," Susie said. "Be careful, because I won't be there to shoot any raiders who've tackled you."

"I will not say goodbye, because we always reunite somehow," Laurette said lightly. "I will say, à bientôt, see you soon. Try not to do anything stupid and get yourself into any mishaps until we are around to rescue you."

"We're going east and eventually south," Nwokocha said. "We'll stay on the move."

"When and where will we meet?" I asked plaintively.

"Six months from now, in Outpost City," Nwokocha said. He shifted both reins into one hand and saluted me with the other. "Bring Arthur with you, eh? Whole and sound. I'll buy the two of you some Outhouse Ale."

"Uh, don't you mean Outpost?"

"Not particularly," he said with a smile. With that, he kicked his heels into his horse and led the others off the Beartooth Road to the east.

I watched for a few minutes as their horses' hooves kicked up dust, and then I lifted the reins and guided my own toward Beartooth Pass. A keen ache settled into my bones. I had never felt so lonely. The huddled near-corpse in front of me groaned, but I couldn't soothe Arthur yet. I had to get him to safety before I could even try to heal him.

• • •

WE RODE NORTH, then north-west. I didn't stop other than to pee and to let the horse drink water. He was a tallish bay quarter-horse with a dyspeptic disposition. While he slaked his thirst, I dribbled water into what was left of Arthur's mouth, then gulped down a few mouthfuls of fluid myself.

At sunset, I dismounted and let the horse graze. I left Arthur tied on the horse because I wasn't sure I'd be able to heave him back up once I let him down.

Arthur showed a little more movement after taking a drink, so I gave him regular sips, every twenty minutes or so. His face was a mushy, blackened rag of what it had once been, and he was still oozing fluids.

How can I heal him, even with the healing gift? What is the best outcome I can even hope for? Look at him, for God's sake! My heart despaired. *This is what I gave up my husband and children for, this doomed shell of a person?* Unanswerable, irresolvable questions writhed inside me.

We rode through the night and into the next day. The horse wheezed and slowed, and he got cranky and stopped to graze at random intervals. I would have liked to let him feed, but I didn't dare stop. I didn't know if Alexei and his men were close or if the others had successfully led him away from us.

We skirted the town of Ennis. I didn't see anyone, which was a relief. I knew if the town had survived the mists' incursion, it might harbor raiders loyal to Alexei. Even regular folks might mention seeing us if Alexei sent scouts this way. Arthur and I had to disappear, to stay out of sight and out of mind of everyone.

North of Ennis, we reached a lake and the horse got very stubborn. I had taken to calling him Edgar, which seemed like a fitting name for a cantankerous old man. I had to keep kicking Edgar and cursing at him to press him forward. I smiled to think how Arthur would have responded to my inept horsemanship, had he been conscious. Arthur had once been an Olympic equestrian. His grace on the back of a horse was legendary.

We came to a cluster of deserted lake houses, cabins with their own docks that looked out over the lake. Edgar dug in his heels and refused to go any farther. Stiff and sore, I dismounted and led the unwilling Edgar along a gravel driveway, toward one of the structures. It had stained pine siding, a two-car garage, second-story windows inset into dormers, and views over the lake to the Madison Mountain Range. I tied the horse on a long lead to a tree outside and took off his packs, then parked them on the porch. The nasty creature immediately fell to grazing, heedless of Arthur's dead weight on his back.

"I'll be back," I said to Arthur, though I knew he didn't understand a word of it. I walked to the front door, which was open. Inside were sculpted moldings and carefully painted earth tones, with matching furniture turned over on its side. Lamps, CDs and DVDs, books, pictures, dishes, cutlery, vases, and assorted detritus were scattered everywhere. The living room, family room, dining room, kitchen, and office downstairs were a disaster. I walked up a grand staircase to three bedrooms that were equally chaotic; clothing, linen, and various personal items, the appurtenances of a vanished life, were strewn everywhere in utter disarray. Still, the place would do for the night, and we could get back on the road the next day.

I went downstairs to the living room and struggled to right the couch. I cleared a space on the floor, then dragged a mattress off a twin bunk upstairs, pushed it down the steps, and laid it in the cleared area.

Untying Arthur and lugging him down off the horse proved to be a nauseating task. I didn't want him to fall, so I cushioned his drop off the horse with my body. He couldn't walk and was mostly unconscious, so I hooked my arms under his armpits and dragged him inside. I caught a full view of what the front of his body had endured, the burnings and beatings and breakings and cuttings. It sickened me.

Inside, I laid him on the mattress on the floor, since I didn't have the strength to hoist him up onto the couch. Once he was situated, I dropped my backpack on the floor and lay down on the couch. I didn't have the energy to eat or drink or even take off my boots. I just slept.

• • •

I AWOKE WITH a start. The room was pitch black, and Arthur was making snuffling noises. I sat up, disoriented, and waited for my eyes to adapt. When I could see faint, darker outlines in the night, I got off the couch and stumbled through the room to the front door. I went outside, where the stars shed a milky light by which I could navigate. I went to the saddlebags and found the one with Gatorade and protein bars. In another bag was a flashlight whose batteries worked: score!

Inside, by the white beam of the flashlight, I took my canteen out of my backpack and drizzled water into Arthur's mouth. Then I drank, only to realize the canteen was almost empty and that I'd have to fill it tomorrow. I gave a couple capfuls of grass-green Gatorade to Arthur, then drank some myself. I tore off a bite of protein bar, masticated it well, then took it out of my mouth and put it in Arthur's. I thought I saw his throat move, so I stuck my finger back in his mouth and felt around among his swollen gums and few remaining teeth. No food; he'd swallowed. I chewed a few more bites for him, then finished the bar. I lay back down on the couch, and fell instantly into a deep sleep.

• • •

IT WAS A brilliant morning when I woke, probably ten o'clock. Arthur seemed to be sleeping; his eye was closed. I went to the bathroom and flushed out of ancient habit, before even thinking about it. When the toilet worked, I turned on

the faucet. Cold water streamed out. I turned it off and ran
for my canteen. I rinsed and filled the Gatorade bottle too.
Then I sought out the biggest pan available, a giant chrome
turkey roaster that was lying in the family room, and filled it
with water for the horse.

Outside, Edgar slurped every drop of liquid in the pan.
His head swiveled up, and he looked at me as if asking for
more, so I gave him a refill.

I checked on Arthur, who was making harsh, breathy
noises. I gave him water and chewed bites of a protein bar. I
ate two bars myself, a chocolate chip protein bar and a chewy
cherry granola bar, then put my hands on Arthur.

The healing energy refused to flow. I waited, but my
hands didn't fill with tingles like a current of running water.
In fact, nothing whatsoever happened. My hands felt normal,
like regular human hands, capable of work and love and play
and killing and perhaps prayer one day. *Has the healing gift
deserted me?*

I tried for a while longer, then decided to pack and go, in
case Alexei and his men were tracking us. I picked through
the house quickly, in the most cursory way. There were no
guns or ammunition, as one might have found in a private
residence in Montana.

One of the former inhabitants had been a teenage boy
about my size. I changed out of my blood-spattered clothes
into a pair of his jeans. I threw a t-shirt and sweater over
it, then shrugged on an Army surplus-style coat. I also took
some women's underwear and snagged a few pieces of clothing for Arthur, since the former man of the home had been
tall like him. Of course I couldn't even attempt to change
Arthur until he was healed. There was no point before then.
Arthur would just lose skin and blood in the process, and he'd
soil fresh garments with waste and pus.

The stream of water was running thin from the faucet; it
was definitely time to leave. I found an unopened bottle of

scotch on the shelf and took it. *Never know when that might come in handy.*

I brushed Edgar quickly, picked out his feet, then saddled him. I tried to arrange the saddlebags so they would be tolerable for him. Then I took Arthur under his armpits and dragged him outdoors. By dint of pushing, pulling, and swearing vociferously, I convinced Edgar to kneel on his front knees and managed to flop Arthur over his withers. Then I mounted and pulled and heaved to get Arthur upright. It wasn't easy or quick, but we finally set out.

We rode for several days, usually from early in the morning until late at night. The scenery, though arduous, was spectacular: forested ridges, snow-capped mountains, and high plateaus of granite and limestone. Cairns of stones stood in meadows or between boulders, as if they'd grown there themselves, like weeds that had grown in cement cracks in the vanished cities of Earth.

Somehow, with water, antibiotic capsules opened up into Gatorade, and willpower, I kept Arthur alive. The healing gift wouldn't flow through me, but I gave him what drugs I had and kept him hydrated and nourished him with chewed bites of protein bars. We spent our nights in abandoned buildings, usually homes, but once we stayed in a gas station and once in a very large, very empty, very creepy church.

The church had a basement, one corner of which was stocked with cartons of vanilla meal replacement shakes, the kind drank by the elderly or those on a diet. In the Before, such specialty drinks were found in health food stores; after the Day, they had been hoarded by a vanished congregation. I wondered where the would-be drinkers had gone, whether they had been lost to the mists or to the raiders, had become raiders themselves, or had died some other way, as was so easy to do in the After.

The expiration dates stamped on the cans were a few years in the future, so I created a saddle pack out of a drawstring canvas bag I found at the church and filled it with plenty of shakes. I also stuffed some into every backpack and saddlebag already tied on. Edgar nickered with complaint at the extra weight, but Arthur now had a meal source that I wouldn't have to masticate for him, and that was a relief.

We stayed three days at Lost Creek State Park, a narrow, boulder-strewn valley situated between sheer pink and white cliffs. I'd developed saddle sores on my rump that demanded care. They began as little abrasions, then morphed into a heated, stinging rash. After that, they abscessed rather painfully. I had to tend them for a few days or risk serious infection.

Abandoned RV's were scattered through the park, so I chose a big one at the foot of the Lost Creek Falls. The date escaped me, but it was spring running into summer for sure, and the weather was warm, sunny, and dry. Trees fuzzed over with bright green leaves, a few flowers poked their bright heads out of thawing soil, and animals were frisky. I saw mountain goats gamboling and bighorn sheep butting heads. I killed a deer with an arrow and skinned and roasted it for myself, laughing because Theo and Robert would have poked fun at my appalling lack of skill. But it didn't matter. The fresh meat, even hacked grotesquely, was delicious.

It was a quiet interlude to spend washing my throbbing, burning bottom with eighteen-year-old alcohol from Scotland before applying ointment to it. "Surely the Laphroag Distillery would approve of the medicinal usage of their single-malt," I mused, trying to laugh but finding it impossible in the midst of such pain.

After three days, my derriere was healed enough that I could consider riding again. I repacked everything and saddled Edgar, who brayed like a donkey, registering his disapproval. It took an hour, but I managed to hoist Arthur up onto the horse. I mounted behind Arthur, and we rode out of the valley, Edgar picking his way carefully through the scree.

I didn't sense Alexei following us, nor could I feel him in my dreams. I wondered if that meant anything, if it was good news, if my comrades had managed to draw him off my trail. *Are they safe, or have they been captured?* I couldn't answer those questions, nor any of the ones I asked myself about Arthur and the absence of the healing ability on which I'd come to depend. All I could do was ride on.

8 SOMEWHERE IN THE FOREST NORTH OF Coeur d'Alene, we rode past a bear, the biggest one I'd ever seen. When he rose up on his hind legs, Edgar fled up a nearby mountain. He galloped high up and didn't stop until we came to an uninhabited cabin alongside a creek. The cabin exterior was sumptuous log and stone, and it was expertly landscaped, designed to blend in seamlessly with the mountain and trees. I almost didn't see it until we were right up on it, even though it was a sizeable two-story building, a structural masterpiece that some architect had spent loving and inspired thought on and some builder had constructed with meticulous attention to detail.

The front door was locked, but I found a window around back to pry open. I crawled into the kitchen and sat on a granite countertop and beheld a custom electric Viking stove and matching subzero refrigerator. When I noticed a light glowing blue on the ice-making gizmo, I hopped down and skipped over the travertine floor to flick a light switch. The lights came on: The place was equipped with a working generator.

Then and there, I decided to call the well-appointed mansion home for a while. I walked into the next room. The entire place was covered in a thick suede of dust but was completely untouched by the apocalypse. Every room had working electricity. In the basement was a billiard room, and next to it was a laundry room with a washer, dryer, and spacious freezer, still filled with frozen foods. It would have been luxurious in the Before, but in the After, it was undreamt of.

Still, it wasn't the luxury that persuaded me to stay; I'd learned to live without creature comforts. It was our haggard condition. We must have ridden 800 kilometers since Beartooth Pass at Yellowstone. Arthur was still a battered, shredded wreck of a human being, missing skin and a limb and half his face, oozing blood and pus, and ready to die at any moment. It was a miracle he had lasted so long on the road, a miracle I could only attribute to his own indomitable will to live, since I hadn't been able to heal him.

Also, my saddle sores had flared up again, and I desperately needed rest. So did the crotchety horse that had caused them. Most urgently, I needed to regain my healing abilities, Arthur's only hope. Willpower or not, even he couldn't live forever in such a dilapidated condition.

We couldn't stay on the road forever, so we would stay in the mansion for a while, perhaps until it was time to make our way to Outpost City and rejoin the others. We would be as safe there as we could be from the mists, random raiders and crazies, and Alexei and his men. Uneasily I thought of the bear, but I remembered that bears were usually more afraid of people than people were of them.

An elegant guest bedroom on the ground floor served as Arthur's abode. I heaved him into a bed outfitted with Pratesi linens, certain that it was the most posh bed he'd slept in since the Day. I hoped the silky sheets would give him ease, though it seemed a shame to stain them with his blood and pus and feces, drool, and urine.

I set myself up in the master suite upstairs. The first night in our new home, after seeing to Arthur and Edgar, I ran a steaming-hot bath in a giant brass claw-foot tub. I poured in lily-of-the-valley foaming bath gel, then slithered into the water and soaked myself until it cooled to tepid. I sat on the rim of the tub and did something I hadn't done in forever: I shaved my legs.

I then wrapped myself in a fluffy blue Turkish cotton bathrobe and brushed out my hair. Most of Laurette's brown dye from a few months ago had worn off, and the shaggy blonde layers fell past my collarbone. I found scissors in a drawer and carefully trimmed my hair to make it even. I ended up with a long bob that wouldn't have passed at a salon but looked spiffy after my time in the wild.

The former mistress of the home had been dark-haired but had seldom used the hairbrush that now lay beside the sink; I could tell that from the paucity of long, dark strands tangled into the bristles. She was also taller and broader than me, as attested to by the upscale wardrobe in her walk-in closet. Some of the clothes I could wear as they were anyway, some could be rolled or belted to fit, and others could be tailored. I'd become as adept with a needle and thread in the After as I was with a gun. I chose a pink silk peignoir to sleep in and sent a silent thanks to her, wherever she was, alive or dead.

I stood by the bed and ran my callused, tanned hands and their ragged nails over the plush bedclothes, marveling at their softness. Then I put my gun beside the pillow and crawled in.

• • •

I TRIED REPEATEDLY to run the healing energy into Arthur, to no avail. The healing tingles simply wouldn't flow through me. I calmed myself with my breath and let myself sink into a peaceful, meditative state, I opened to allow the healing current, but it still didn't respond. I even reached for it, with all the yearning of my spirit. No go.

I had always known the healing current wasn't mine, in the sense that it didn't originate within me. At the same time, I always thought I'd be able to tap into it at will. But now, when I needed it most, it eluded me. I felt broken. Worse, I was failing Arthur, whose one eye opened less and less frequently as he dwindled away, making a slow journey toward death. I spent hours next to his bed, but it was useless. I couldn't help him other than to give him water and nourishment.

When I wasn't nursing Arthur, I explored the property. I discovered that it had belonged to a couple who had made a fortune off an Internet company, one of the dot.coms that didn't fall prey to the economic collapse. The house was a cornucopia of delights. It had been built to be self-sufficient and entirely off the grid, with a solar-powered generator, solar panels fixed on the south side of the roof and mounted on arrays, and virtually soundless wind turbines. I discovered the turbines attached to thirty-foot towers back of an apple orchard planted into a plateau near the house. The grounds boasted a toolshed, a small, bean-shaped swimming pool cunningly sunken into a side yard, a separate apartment over the garage, and a terraced garden for growing vegetables. I found seeds and gardening implements in the shed.

Edgar was ensconced in the garage at night. During the day, when I wasn't grooming him, he grazed placidly near the house, occasionally lifting his stubborn head sideways to glance at me with condescension. He was thin and could have used a farrier's services but seemed otherwise to be in good condition.

It took a few days to gather my courage before I inventoried the contents of the freezer in the basement. I thawed a small batch of foodstuffs to test it. That big Viking range, with its six electric burners, cooked like a dream. Standing beside it, waiting for a whole chicken to bake and for frozen peas to simmer, I collapsed into a fit of giggles. After three years of cooking over fires and eating only whatever could be shot, dried, picked, or salvaged, except when I was in Edmonton, Outpost City, or Carstairs, it was surreal to be able to use such a high-performance appliance. I couldn't stop laughing and finally surrendered to it, stretching out on the travertine floor as rich gales of laughter rolled up out of me. The bottle of nebbiolo I'd prized out of the wine cellar probably had something to do with my hysteria.

Plenty of the food in the pantry had to be thrown out, but a surprising number of items remained edible. The honey, salt, sugar, pasta, white rice, powdered milk, dried fruits, dried beans, baking soda, bouillon, and whole spices were all fine. A large bag of flour had been kept in a vacuum-sealed container, and there were no mealy bugs to be seen. Three boxes of couscous looked and smelled good, and all the canned goods were more than acceptable. Pristine instant cocoa and coffee in various gourmet flavors was a luscious find.

The food supply was impressive, but I knew it wouldn't last forever. I would still have to hunt animals and butcher them myself, as horribly inept as it as I was, despite my luck with the deer in Lost Creek Park. It was undreamt-of beneficence that I could freeze the meat after butchering it.

I daydreamt about acquiring livestock. Some chickens or a cow would have been a godsend, worth their weight in gold or stocks, bonds, and the old instruments of value in the old, now valueless world. I remembered reading that during the German occupation, the Parisians of World War II had raised rabbits for food, and I wondered if I could trap some rabbits outside, on the mountain.

I discussed the situation with Arthur as he lay there silently, oozing bodily fluids and disintegrating. I sat on a stool beside his bed, desperately trying to access the healing gift that had, always before, been readily available. When my hands remained empty, I started talking. Arthur's good eye was closed, and he didn't answer; he was long past speaking. I just hoped he was also past feeling pain.

"Must have been white rabbits those Parisians bred on their balconies and in their basements," I told him. "At least that's the way I've always imagined it. White rabbits, like Alice's in Wonderland. Did you know I once illustrated that book and won awards for it? It was a different world then, but I still remember. Do you, Arthur?"

He didn't answer, not even with a moan or a blink of his eye. He was dying, and I couldn't save him because the healing gift, *my* healing gift, had abandoned me when I needed it most, when *he* needed me most.

I had no idea how much time Arthur had left. *A week, a day, an hour?* Ten minutes was my guess, and that hurt. I hadn't been able to save him. He wasn't going to save the world from the mists.

Disconsolate, I stared out the window. It was an exceptionally fine day, warm and bright, with butterflies gliding on the breeze. I was struck with a notion: *I'll take Arthur outside for fresh air.* He hadn't been outside since we arrived at the mountain house. I couldn't expose him to sunlight because of the burns and exposed fascia, but I could take him to the back porch, which was covered. There, if he managed to turn his head and open his remaining eye, he could at least see the sky. *Yeah, Arthur would like that . . . even if it's the last thing he sees.*

The house of wonders had an air mattress in the linen closet upstairs. I inflated it out on the porch, then went back in and engaged in the usual strenuous, disgusting rigmarole of moving Arthur.

At last, he lay outdoors. I couldn't be sure, but I thought he was breathing easier. As of late, he breathed ever more shallowly, and now not even into his throat. He was on his last hard-won breaths. At least they could be taken outdoors, in spring air fragrant with fir trees and running streams. It seemed the only thing I could do for him.

I left the porch to examine some shrubs; their dense, arching stems reminded me of blackberry bushes. I examined the leaves and concluded that there was a high probability that they were and that there would be fruit to enjoy in the summer. If they had been ripe already, I could have mashed them for Arthur; the sweet softness would have felt good on his tongue. It was also probable that the plants would attract deer, to be dispatched at my leisure. I would easily fill that splendid freezer.

I wandered around the perimeter of the house, looking at plants, identifying some and wondering what was edible and what was just for show. Around front was a sweet-smelling white lilac bush with a smattering of open buds. Lavender crocuses stood up out of the sugary loam. I was always discovering something enchanting in or around the house, and each time I did, I sent the absent owners a blessing. They had lavished their prosperity on their home, and Arthur and I were now reaping the benefits.

It was silence that caught my attention. All the ambient noises of the woods and mountain, sounds I hadn't consciously noticed, hushed at once, their sudden absence making them conspicuous. Then Edgar brayed, a horse's high-pitched scream of fear.

I raced around to the back porch. I came to a flying halt. Standing more than seven feet tall at the porch with its paws on the railing, leaning over to look down into the porch at helpless Arthur, was a giant brownish-black bear, the same beast who had frightened Edgar up the mountain.

"HEY, YOU!" I screamed. It was instinctive, and not at all planned.

The bear dropped to its four feet, turned to face me, and growled. It had giant shoulders and a prominent ridge across its forehead. It had to weigh three hundred kilos. How big was it in the fall, after eating all summer?

Drawn by the coppery smell of Arthur's blood, thinking him a carcass, was it scoping him as a potential meal? I was horrified at the thought of Arthur's body being scavenged. The horror and fear that the bear would attack me jarred me out of the apathy that had settled into my bones, an insidious numbness I hadn't even been aware of, until that moment, facing the bear.

"Go away!" I yelled, waving my arms. "Get away from him!"

The bear growled again, a long, deep, powerful noise that elicited primitive terror.

I grabbed for my gun, but it wasn't in my waistband. I'd left it on the dresser in Arthur's room when I'd dragged him outdoors. *How could I be so careless, so stupid?* In such treacherous times, I knew better than to stray far from my weapon.

I thought hard, my mind racing back to what I'd read about bear encounters, long ago, before the girls were born, when Haywood and I had gone camping. The books warned against running away from a bear in close proximity, so I stayed rooted in my tracks, but I spoke in a loud, fierce tone. "You leave right now, buster, or I'm gonna get my gun and shoot you in that big ole face of yours, right between your eyes!"

The bear stared directly into my eyes. Its ears flattened back against its head, like a feral dog's. Its jaw chomped, as if its teeth were working over an old piece of leather.

Some unknown sense buried in my oldest ancestral DNA alerted me: I had only a few seconds before it charged. I had never faced a bear before, but everything in me woke up at once. Not only was the hidden apathy gone, but I shifted into a preternaturally alert, ready state. I was going to die, but in those few seconds before I died, I was more alive than I had ever been.

The bear exploded into a run. It barreled at me like a million-ton truck equipped with sharp teeth and giant claws.

Stark terror eclipsed everything else. I couldn't possibly outrun the animal, and I didn't have my gun. *This is it,* I thought. For a split second, I felt bitter regret that I would not be able to help Arthur. He also would die, likely as the bear was eating his innards, if the creature had room in its gut after it devoured me.

My hands tingled. *Now?* They rose of their own accord out before me, as if to command the bear to halt. A stream of

energy erupted from my hands. The energy wasn't really visible, except as a very faint but palpable laser beam. It felt like
lightning pouring down through my arms and out my hands.
It hit the bear in its head and shoulders, and the bear flipped
over backward.

I stood as immobile as a sculpture, my mouth agape, my
hands outstretched. *Where did that come from?* I had never felt
nor suspected such an ability in myself.

The giant bear grunted and snuffled. It twisted around to
right itself, then stood up on its hind legs, sniffed the air, and
eyed me.

I didn't move.

Not dissuaded, the bear dropped to all fours again. Again
it charged.

Again, the lightning from my hands zapped it.

Again, I was astonished. *Has this power resided in my hands
all the time? Was it given to me by the mists and somehow called forth
by the extreme danger posed by the bear? Is this the same power as the
healing current, or is it a new phenomena, an evolution of the mist-
given healing gift?* My mind jumped from question to question,
never waiting around long enough for an answer. *What are the
uses of this powerful energy stream, besides as a bear repellant?*

This time, the bear was slower to rise. It growled and
groaned unhappily.

"I'd go away if I were you," I told it in a shaky voice. "I
don't know why or how, but if you keep coming at me like
that, you're gonna get hurt."

A third time, the bear charged.

A third time, the beam of energy shot from my hands and
slammed into the animal.

Several minutes passed before it could sway and stumble
upright, so the bear sat back on its haunches and stared at me
with glassy, unrepentant eyes. It tilted its snout upward and
sniffed.

"Go!" I demanded, my voice stronger. "I don't want to hurt you anymore. Just leave."

Long, slow minutes passed before the bear got to all fours again. This time, it crawled backward a few feet, then turned and ambled off into the forest.

I was palpitating in every muscle and bone, and all I could think about was Arthur. I vaulted up onto the porch and laid my hands on him. Beneath my palm, I felt the brittle rasp of a charred ear stub, feverishly hot. I closed my eyes and breathed deeply, filling myself from pelvis to chin, from toes to brow, with air. I forced myself to soften and relax, even though I was hyper-adrenalized from my encounter with the bear.

My hands still thrummed from the lightning beam. I wanted to know what it could do, if it could be harnessed for healing, which Arthur desperately needed. I focused on my hands and on my intent to heal the man, my lover, my Arthur, for whom I had sacrificed so much and who had sacrificed so much for me. Somehow, we were inextricably bound together. My heart softened, opened, and luminesced.

A tremendous force poured through me. It felt like the lightning but had its own distinct flavor: rich, fertile, fluid, and bursting. It rose from the Earth through me, like molten lava. It drained out of my hands into the battered, maimed, destroyed body beneath them.

Suddenly, with a *twang* like a guitar string plucked, my mind was catapulted inside Arthur's. My awareness went deep inside him, deeper than I'd imagined possible, deeper than his identity or his cells, all the way into a blueprint that was the foundational pattern for his healthy body. I'd somehow reached the psychic structure underlying his body and all bodies; the ideal template from which all human bodies formed, including his. To my mind's eye, it looked like a stick figure with a grid superimposed on it.

The grid pulsed and breathed and changed colors in

patches. It had a sound too—a rich, deep tenor note that uni-
fied it. I had never imagined such a thing. Now that my consciousness brimmed with it, I was astonished at its power. It,
not I, would heal Arthur. I didn't have to do anything other
than complete the circuit. I relaxed, and the blueprint flowed
out through my hands and into his burnt and flayed head. It
slurped into him with a juicy, salty force, like ocean surf.

I lost all sense of time. I was simply a vibrating conduit for
the healing flow and for its foundational image of an unscathed
body. The scorched half of Arthur's face filled out and pinked
up; his eye reformed itself out of the red jelly in his socket;
his black eyelashes grew back on the pale, veiny lid. Skin
hanging off in flaps fit back into place like pieces of a jigsaw
puzzle, their edges smoothing over and vanishing, leaving an
unblemished surface. Where the skin was gone, it regenerated, thickening on the exposed fascia and muscle like a high-
speed film of scum forming on the surface of a pond. Arthur's
ear, like a butterfly unfurling itself, stood up against his head.
The seared, peeled skin of his neck and shoulder plumped up
with moisture and the rich mineral stew of healthy cells.

I was fascinated and could not tear my eyes away from the
process. All the healing I had ever done before seemed crude
in comparison.

His amputated hand was the last challenge. It had to be
regenerated from the stump. I was unsure of how to proceed,
but luckily, the pattern was smarter than me. It pushed my
brain aside and directed the healing current. It told me what
to do, and I obeyed. Swallowing revulsion, I laid one hand
directly on the bloody stump.

With a detached part of my awareness, I felt the gooey
slick of meat, tendon, vein, and charred skin peeling in curls
from the bones like tulip petals from a stamen. Alexei's men
had not been neat about their work.

Pulses with the acrid taste of electricity surged through

my hands. After some span of time, the current evened out, and Arthur's arm grew back, centimeter by centimeter.

When Arthur's long fingers lay, newly curled, in my gore-spattered hand, I released him. The flow through me dissipated. Like waking from a dream, I grew aware of myself. I was sore, exhausted, and lightheaded. I smelled of curdled bodily fluids: blood, sweat, and ooze. I was trembling and limp and soaked in perspiration that felt uncomfortably cool.

But Arthur lay whole and perfect on the floor in front of me. His clothes were in rags, but he was completely healed. Even his old scars had vanished.

"Arthur? Arthur!" I shook his shoulder. "Can you hear me? Wake up!"

His eyes fluttered, and he sat up.

"Arthur!" I hugged him, squeezing tightly.

He didn't answer.

"Arthur?" I asked. I leaned back on my haunches to stare into his face. That's when I noticed that his clear gray eyes were empty, and that his symmetrical, sculpted face hung slack.

Arthur's body was finally whole again, but his mind was gone.

9 ARTHUR ATE CONTINUOUSLY. HE FOL-
lowed me around like a lamb, unable to understand anything but the simplest commands: "Sit
here. Stay there. Eat this." He didn't speak. He
just pointed to his mouth when he was hungry, which was all
the time.

In the first hour after his healing, I made him an entire
box of macaroni with tomato sauce from a jar. He ate every
bite with his hands, smearing the sauce on his face. Then he
pointed at his mouth, wanting more.

I cooked a box of couscous and stirred in cans of mushrooms, succotash, and Vienna sausages. Arthur ate all of that,
too, and again he pointed at his mouth.

"No. You're going to wait a few hours for more," I said,
wiping his face with a towel. "I don't know how much your
stomach can handle."

His shoulders slumped, and he sat at the center island bar
with vacant eyes and a blank expression on his face.

• • •

WE WENT THROUGH provisions so fast that I was forced
to go hunting. I considered taking Arthur with me, but I
was worried he would wander off, distract me at the wrong
moment, or make noise and frighten our prey, so I decided
to leave him at the house. I had already stripped his bed and

bundled up the soiled linens, which were beyond salvage and would have to be burned. The mattress was stained but serviceable, so I placed a blanket over it and directed Arthur to sit on his bed.

Arthur got up to follow me every time I left the room. It took me a dozen tries to make him understand that he had to stay seated. Finally, he slumped over and stayed put.

I killed two deer with arrows that day, one of which I was pretty sure was a nursing doe. I felt bad about that and hoped her fawn would survive. I left the carcasses out back by the orchard, in case the bear was nearby. I felt I owed the bear something in exchange for awakening something within me, the powerful new healing ability, and at just the right moment, as Arthur lay dying. It was almost enough to make me think divine providence still had a hand in human affairs on Earth. *Maybe we aren't all meant to die, after all. Maybe there is hope. Maybe rebirth will follow the apocalypse.*

In his bedroom, Arthur was exactly as I had left him, slouched on his bed. He looked up at me, and his expression didn't change. He still didn't utter a word, but he followed me out and watched me dress the deer.

I had watched Theo and Robert many times after hunting, so I knew the basics. First, I had to open the animal and remove the entrails inside the chest cavity, then use a saw to cut open the tailbone, remove all entrails, clean the body cavity with water, and pack it with ice if available. Then I had to hang the carcass from a tree nearby and remove the feet. Then I began at the neck, skinning the animal by cutting through the filmy connective tissue between the skin and muscle. That was supposed to release the hide. Halfway down the carcass, I had to pull the hide. I tried to instruct Arthur to help with this chore, but he didn't understand. He just stood and stared. He didn't react to the mess I made either, incompetent as I was.

After the deer was skinned, it had to be quartered, with

the front quarters first, followed by the hind. Then we had to remove the backstrap, the tender strip of meat along the spine. Theo and Robert always enjoyed that particular cut of meat. Theo liked to sear it fast over a very hot fire, and Robert and he had once had a lengthy discussion about slicing the backstrap into medallions and frying them in oil with salt, pepper, and Worcestershire sauce. At the time, Arthur had commented that the recipe sounded delicious. I figured I would try it in his honor, since all the ingredients were available and the Viking stove made cooking easy. After cooking on a campfire, the stove practically did the work for me.

Arthur stood at my shoulder while I fried the backstrap. I led him to the stool at the center island bar and settled him there, but when I went back to the stove, he hopped out of his seat and returned to his place at my elbow.

"Arthur, this will not do," I scolded, pointing the spatula at him. "Sit down and stay there! You'll get splattered with grease if you stand here."

Arthur looked at me with his void, infantile expression. He didn't move.

I led him back to the stool and pressed his shoulders down firmly. "Stay!"

Arthur waited a beat, and then, when my back was turned, came right back over.

When three succulent medallions were cooked, I piled them on a plate and set them at his place at the bar.

Arthur clumsily grabbed a piece of meat with both hands, then dropped it in surprise. He stared at the reddened tips of his fingers.

"It's hot," I said, then fetched the knife and cut it into bites for him. I gave him a fork but he had no idea how to use it and preferred his hands, when the venison had cooled.

• • •

ARTHUR NEVER SPOKE. I talked. I talked to hear a voice
speaking sentences. I talked about nothing and everything. I
talked all the time. I talked while cooking meals and brushing
his teeth and bathing him. I talked while dressing him in clean
t-shirts and sweatpants from the closet of the former owner.
I talked while changing his underwear and wiping him, since
he wasn't potty-trained anymore. There was a drawer full of
tightie-whities, but they fit too snugly on Arthur; he didn't
like them and pulled them off whenever I wasn't looking.
Then he crapped on the floor.

I got sick of cleaning the giant, stinking pile of turd made
by a man who stood nearly 190 centimeters tall, so I led him
outside to watch Edgar crap on the lawn.

Arthur observed Edgar without any sign of comprehen-
sion, but thereafter, he went outside and squatted on the lawn
to do his business.

I talked for companionship, for I was even lonelier with
Arthur's perfect but empty body than I had been when he
was maimed. At least then, I still had hope that he would be
healed and we would be reunited. Now Arthur—the Arthur
I'd known—showed no sign of coming back from his debili-
tating second infancy. I often looked at him and felt despair.

To comfort myself, I recounted stories from my childhood.
From the time I was six years old, I had known I wanted to
be an artist. I'd spent hours outside drawing trees and flowers and garbage cans and mailboxes. I'd had taken drawing,
painting, sculpting, and pottery classes in elementary and
high school. I reminisced about museums in different cities
and countries. After a flash of inspiration, I set myself the
mental task of remembering every piece of art I'd ever seen in
every museum I'd ever visited. If those works of art and those
institutions had not survived the mists, at least they would
live on in my memory, forever beautiful, forever treasured.

I was pleasantly surprised to discover that my mind was
plastic and liked to oblige. Once it got the hang of the game,

it coughed up paintings and other *objets d'art* I had forgotten about. I started with the Metropolitan Museum of Art when I was eight, and by the time I got to the Uffizi in my twenties, after graduating art school, the paintings were preternaturally, viscerally vivid, almost like stepping inside the building.

"The room with the Botticellis is extraordinary," I told Arthur as I led him to the bathroom. I put the seat down on the toilet, then pushed him to sit. I ran water on a washcloth. "It's a big hall with many paintings." I paused to recall as I dampened Arthur's face. "Twenty five maybe. The *Primavera* and the *Birth of Venus* would take your breath away, but there are many gorgeous paintings in that room, even a stunning triptych by a Flemish painter."

I sprayed shaving cream in my hand and applied it gently to his stubbly cheeks and chin. "The *Portinari Triptych!* Yes, that's it, by Hugo Van der Goes. *Adoration of the Shepherds.*" I wet the razor and carefully stroked with the grain of the stubble on Arthur's beautiful blank face. I didn't know how to care for a beard, so I didn't want to let him grow one. I shaved him every other day. I got good at it. The secret was in the wrist.

"The central panel has shepherds falling to their knees, worshipping the Christ child. The infant Jesus isn't in a crib. He's lying on the ground, swaddled in golden light, radiating it. Very lovely representation. Unusual." I finished his left check, rinsed the razor, and started on his right.

• • •

ONE EVENING, THE lights dimmed and flickered, and then half the lights in the living room went out. It was a lovely late-spring evening, so I knew the power flicker wasn't the result of a storm. I checked the wind turbines, and they were happily spinning on their poles out behind the orchard. I poked around the basement and finally found a crawlspace with batteries and wires and boxes and what had to be a generator or something for adapting the energy collected by the solar panels and turbines. There was a red light on it, but I had no idea what that meant or how to fix it.

I looked around the house for manuals for the novel electrical system, to no avail. I didn't know what else to do, so I turned off extraneous lights and unplugged appliances I had carelessly left on. We didn't use all the rooms anyway; mostly we stayed in the kitchen and our bedrooms. Those rooms and the basement seemed unaffected, and the freezer kept humming, so I hoped it was a localized issue.

Arthur raided the pantry when I wasn't watching. He ate all the pretzels remaining in an old, unopened bag. He devoured a box of raw pasta and drank a precious, irreplaceable bottle of chartreuse olive oil. He gulped down a bottle of maple syrup. He got into the honey and ate the entire jar, scooping it out with his fingers and smearing his face until it was sticky with gold. He left handprints and splatters on every surface of the kitchen.

When I yelled at him, it startled him, and he threw the honey jar through the window. Shards of glass flew everywhere, and I spent the next hour sweeping the floor. I found plywood in the toolshed and duct-taped it over the hole, only to discover I'd cut my palm and had leaked blood all over the cabinets and floor without realizing it.

Arthur let out a ruckus in the back yard. He'd encountered a skunk who didn't want to play with him and wasn't amused when he picked it up by the tail.

I ran outside with a towel clutched around my sliced hand and tried to calm Arthur, who was running in circles and flailing his arms in horror at the stink that had enveloped him. He let out baritone roars of indignation. Not at all pacified by my pleading, he barreled into shrubs and trees. He was going to hurt himself.

Edgar trotted over to investigate, and I could have sworn, that damn horse stood there guffawing at us.

It was more than I could tolerate. I flopped down on the lawn and cried. I kicked my heels and pounded my fists, wailing at the top of my lungs. I thrashed and screamed and cursed at God.

Arthur and Edgar fell silent.

I let out a last, long howl and sat upright. I pushed the hair out of my face.

Arthur stood in front of me, reeking of skunk, holding a shining yellow daffodil. Slowly, he extended the flower toward me.

I burst into tears. "Arthur, where did you get this?"

He glanced at the tree line, at a bright and riotous patch of flowers weaving around the leathery boles of the trees. I hadn't even noticed them before, but they were almost done blooming.

So I wiped my face with my arm, scrambled to my feet, and hugged him. It was our most complex interaction since before he was captured by Alexei. It could have even be called communication.

• • •

ONE DAY, WHEN summer was in full bore, a lone man walked up the driveway.

I sat out on the back porch, cleaning my gun and calculating how much ammunition was left, knowing it was imperative to conserve bullets. It was also time to make arrows. The freezer was crammed full of venison, so there was no urgency in terms of hunting for food, but arrows would be necessary for self-defense. I was no arrowsmith, but I began retrieving nice, straight fir and pine boughs whenever I explored the woods. The toolshed was well-stocked as well, so I was sure I could fashion something that would leave the bow quickly enough to deeply penetrate an oncoming animal. Or raider.

Heavy footsteps crunching on gravel startled me. That

wasn't Arthur walking on the driveway. I'd put him in his room so he wouldn't mess with the weapon while I was cleaning it. Besides, he had a light tread. Even with his mind gone, he walked softly for a man his size.

I loaded the gun, ran down the steps, and trotted around to the front, keeping out of sight until the last moment. Then I sprang around the corner of the house with the gun held out in front of me.

"Do not shoot!" Alexei called in his thick Russian accent. He raised his arms, the whole one and the one that was only a twisted red stump. "I come alone and in peace."

"Go away!" I fired a shot a meter in front of his feet.

Alexei jumped. "I need to speak with you. Emma. Please. I have never hurt you."

"I'm not playing games, Alexei," I said fiercely. "Go away right now!" I fired another shot at his feet, closer this time.

"Please, Emma," he begged.

Not wanting to hear it, I fired a shot so close to his foot that chunks of asphalt flew up and lodged themselves into his ankle and shin. His pants grew dark with blood where the shrapnel had hit.

Alexei fled.

I hoped he would bleed and hurt. I hoped the wounds would get infected and that his legs would rot and fall off. Most of all, I hoped he was gone and would stay gone.

But it was Alexei, and I knew how relentless he was. I was certain he'd be back. I climbed to the roof of the house and perched there with binoculars, watching as he made camp halfway down the mountain, by a crook in the stream. He used his one arm to great effect, building a shelter of tree limbs and leaves. He seemed to be settling in for a long stay.

I checked on him every hour. At dinner he built a fire and roasted something over it. I went inside and locked all the windows and doors before feeding Arthur, then clambered to the roof one last time at midnight. No movement at Alexei's campsite. By the moonlight, I just made out a pair of feet extending from the shelter.

Whatever he wanted, whatever his reason for appearing, Alexei clearly planned to stick around. I wondered if I'd get my opportunity to kill him, and I wondered if I'd actually take it. I wondered if I had been right when I'd told Alexei that vengeance belonged to God.

• • •

THE NEXT MORNING, Edgar started screaming, that shrill whinny of terror that meant the bear was nearby. I locked Arthur in his bedroom, grabbed my gun, and raced outside, but I didn't see the bear.

Then I heard Alexei hollering.

I ran headlong down the mountain to Alexei's camp. He wasn't there. The yelling sounded again, downstream this time. I raced along the curves of the stream and came on Alexei and the bear.

Alexei was standing in the waist-deep stream, completely naked. He looked more vulnerable than I'd ever seen him before.

On the opposite shore from me, the bear reared up on his hind feet. It sniffed and looked at me, but when I held up my hands, it dropped to all fours and hunched into itself. It sniffed some more, then turned and waddled off.

"Shoot it!" Alexei called. "You have a gun. Shoot it, Emma!"

"No," I said. I wouldn't shoot the bear yet, if at all, unless I had to. I felt I owed it something for the powerful stream of energy it had galvanized within me. That stream of energy had saved Arthur. But I didn't explain any of that to Alexei. Nor did I put the gun away. I pointed it at Alexei. "You have to go. Leave my mountain."

"But Emma . . ." he chided.

I gestured with my gun, and he raised his arm and his stump. "Where's your horse?"

"Broke leg. I walk last four days."

I didn't need to ask how he'd found me; obviously he'd used his powerful psychic senses. "And your weapons?"

"Pile of clothes behind you."

I stepped backward, gingerly, knelt on the ground, and groped his clothing with my free hand. I found a Beretta in a black nylon shoulder strap inside a coat. Inside one belt loop of a pair of pants was a Glock. Beside his socks lay the little Walther PK 380 that Alexei kept at his ankle. "Is this everything?

He shrugged, philosophically. He kept his arm and the stump up and arched one eyebrow, then stepped forward.

"Stay back! Don't you dare come out of that water. Tell me, Alexei, where's your knife?"

He made a face but froze. "My knife is at the campsite where you need a blade most."

"I should shoot you where you stand for what you did to Arthur!"

"But you will not. Emma, you cannot shoot unarmed, naked man asking for peace—especially one-armed, unarmed man." His lips quirked in a grin. "Even if that man is me."

I thought of what he had done to Arthur and my hand trembled with a deep yearning, wanting, of its own accord, to squeeze the trigger. I was holding a SigSauer 9mm, a neat and trusty shooter with minimal muzzle flip, and it longed to unleash its power on Alexei's chest. *Or maybe I could just open a big, gaping hole in his forehead. He deserves that, doesn't he? After all the evil he's wrought?*

"Vengeance is mine, say the Lord," Alexei said.

Is he mocking me?

Slowly he walked to the water's edge, unconcerned about being naked and looking me straight in the eye. He stopped a few inches in front of the muzzle of my gun, which was leveled at the center of his chest. "That is what you told me. You are right."

My hand, torn between desire and judgment, shook uncontrollably. Some sound, maybe a yelp or snarl, exploded out of me. I lowered my weapon.

"Good choice," Alexei approved. He looked up the mountain to the house. "Nice place you find. Please, let me come in. I could use a real bath, not in river with hungry bears."

I barked with incredulous laughter. "You think I'm gonna let you into my home?"

"You have my weapons."

"I don't think so, Alexei."

"You want to hear what I have to say," he said slyly.

"Arthur is here."

"I will not hurt him. I am done with that. I promise, on life of my only son Mikhail."

I shook my head. "No."

"Emma, please. I have always kept my word with you. I came to find you. I ride alone, then walk all this way. Please talk to me, for all the times we have shared. I bring you to Le Havre to meet Haywood. I take care of Mandy when you were mad. Please, Emma. I was gentle with both your daughters, gentle with you. I could have waited until dark and broke into your home before you know it, but no. I approached openly. I let you see me. I have something to discuss with you. Please hear me."

I waited and thought. What he said was true, at least in part. There were several ways he could have taken me unaware. He could have broken in after dark or hidden and pounced on me, but he hadn't. Instead he'd marched right up to the driveway and made himself known. Finally I said, "If you promise to leave when I ask you to, I'll give you an hour. One hour, Alexei. One. Sixty minutes and you're gone, one way or another." I turned on my heel and marched back the way I'd come. I took his weapons with me.

His cheery voice rang after me. "You have vodka?"

Refusing to answer, I rolled my eyes and remembered to stop and grab his knife from his campsite.

• • •

ALEXEI FOUND A bottle of Stolichnaya in the liquor cabinet in the kitchen, and he brandished it triumphantly and kissed the label. "I am happy first time since mists destroy world."

I pointed my gun at Alexei's chest. I still desperately wanted to shoot him. "It's the small things in life that make it worthwhile."

Alexei took two crystal highball glasses from another cabinet and set them on the center island bar. He lifted one side of his mouth in a sardonic grin. "You are funny woman. I think you are pretty, but I forget you are funny, too. Too bad glasses are not cold. That is proper way to drink vodka."

"It's ten o'clock in the morning," I said.

"Never too early or too late for vodka," Alexei said. From the fridge he took a plastic container filled with cooked backstrap medallions. "You have food and refrigerator that work," he said in a reverent voice. He rummaged through drawers and shelves. "Pickles are good."

"Those are at least three years old." I imagined a bull's-eye on his back, centered around the middle of his chest.

"Pickles live for century." He set the jar and the container of venison on the center island bar.

Then, suddenly, as if he'd been summoned by the aroma of pickles and venison, Arthur appeared at the kitchen door.

Alexei heard the noise and swiveled around to look. He took one glance at Arthur's slack expression and vacant eyes and burst into roaring laughter. He leaned against the fridge, shaking and booming, tears forming at the corner of one eye. "Arthur's body is whole, but he is mad! I win."

"Alexei, stop!" I hopped down and handed Arthur a cold medallion, then led him to his room. Once he was settled on his bed, cross-legged, chewing the venison medallion, and staring blankly out the window, I smoothed down his hair. I'd need to trim it soon. It had grown past his shoulders, into a long pageboy. *Poor Arthur. If he was himself, he'd be trying to kill Alexei right now.* His disinterest in Alexei showed, more than anything else, just how far gone Arthur's mind really was.

When I returned to the kitchen, Alexei had set out a feast. He'd found a package of multigrain Wasa crispbread in the freezer and had arranged it on a plate with sliced pickles and bite-sized pieces of backstrap. He had poured the two high-ball glasses full to their brims with vodka.

"I can't drink that much," I demurred.

"I show you Russian trick to drink a lot." He gestured at the stool.

"If I drink a lot, I may not be able to restrain myself from killing you." I seated myself. "Why are you here, Alexei? What do you want? Your hour is waning."

"To drink vodka with you."

I snorted.

"Emma," he chided, "what do we toast? Only problem-drinkers do not toast before drinking. Come now. What toast do we make?"

"To Arthur's good health," I said sarcastically, raising my glass.

"*Budem zdorovy!*" He lifted the highball glass, clinked it against mine, and threw down its contents without stopping for air or spilling a drop. It was an impressive performance.

I put the glass down. I didn't want to drink with Alexei. I wanted him to leave.

"No, Emma, please. That is not the way." He clucked his tongue and refilled his own glass. "Let me show you." He lifted my glass to my mouth.

I couldn't protest because when I opened my lips to do so,

Alexei poured in most of the vodka. I choked and coughed but gulped it down; it was pretty clean except for the charcoal kicker.

"Your vodka technique needs much work." He handed me a crispbread with a bit of backstrap and a slice of green pickle on it.

I devoured the snack but never took my glare off of him.

Alexei refilled my glass. "To love!" He wagged his brows at me and downed his glass.

I didn't take a sip because I was already feeling a head rush from the spirits, a buzz that caused me to sway in my seat. I grabbed a bigger piece of the crispbread and more venison. "Alexei, how long did it take you to find me?"

"Almost did not. Your friends lead me on wild turkey chase. They think that other girl is Emma, Emma, Emma. But when I find them, no real Emma."

I took a deep breath, steeling myself for the worst. "What did you do to my friends?"

"Nothing. I let them go. I feed them first," he said with an indignant edge in his voice. He leaned toward me and gazed deep into my eyes. "I tell you, I learn lessons. You teach me two. First, vengeance belongs to God. Second, Emma does not like to be captured."

"Does anyone?"

Alexei smiled and held up my glass again.

I shook my head but he urged me with a motion of his shoulder. *What the hell?* I thought. After all, it was helping me deal with him without making a mess of my kitchen by splattering his brains all over the place. I wrapped my hand around his on the glass and allowed him to pour the liquor down my throat. I gargled charcoal. We both took more Wasa bread and trimmings.

"Third toast for fallen comrades." Alexei refilled our glasses.

"Third toast, and I'll *be* a fallen comrade," I warned, "but

I'll take you down first." I gestured with the gun still in my hand.

Alexei glanced at the gun, then ignored it. "Third toast, and I'll say why I come."

I looked at him askance, but he nodded solemnly. There was no help for it. I lifted my glass. "To fallen friends."

Alexei said something in Russian, and we both drained our glasses.

"Speak," I said. I wasn't feeling as groggy as I should, by all rights. I bit off a big chunk of uncut backstrap, noticing how delicious it was, peppery and savory with Worcester-shire sauce. I hoped the food would cut the intoxication and cushion my stomach from the next drink.

"I come to warn you. Mists are coming."

"The mists are always coming," I responded, uneasily. "That's not news."

"Mists are coming *here*."

"You mean to this house, where we are?"

"Yes. Mists come soon. They cut a path direct. Now they eat trees too. At will. New trick. I ride around them to this mountain. They will be here in ten days, maybe two weeks. Be ready."

"I will."

"I can help you get ready, since I am here."

"I don't need your help. I need you to leave."

"I will go when you ask, as I promised." He paused and seemed to resolve himself. "I also come to seek favor."

"Of course!" I laughed, a shrill sound that would have been harsher except for the emollient effect of alcohol.

He laid his one hand on my arm, then brought over his stump and leaned forward until the scarred tip of it touched my cheek. "Please, Emma. Give me my hand back. Heal me. I come to ask you this, with all my heart."

"Alexei . . ." I pushed away his stump with both my hands.

"Your heart is a cold, dead thing." But despite myself, and cursing inside, I was moved by his plea.

"Death of my wife kill my heart," he said softly. "She was my heart." His head drooped and he wore an expression of pure vulnerability.

The alcohol and uninvited, unexpected pity choked me for a moment. I laid the gun on the stool beside me. "Alexei, I don't know if I can."

"You healed Arthur."

"I love Arthur."

"Love me, if not forever, for now. Long enough to heal arm." Whimsy passed over his angular face. "Do this for me, and I will leave you alone forever. Love for solitude is good deal, no?"

I sat up straight in my seat. "You'll leave me alone? And Arthur too? Forever?"

"Vengeance is mine, say the Lord." Alexei tilted his head. "You heal my arm. That is ransom for you and Arthur. Bah, I have hurt Arthur already. Now he is gone. His body you healed, but his mind is no more. I do not need to punish him anymore. But I do need my arm."

I leaned away from him and chewed Wasa bread. My mind felt supernaturally sharp, not drunk at all. I felt a keen sense of hope that Arthur could live without being pursued by Alexei. But could I really trust Alexei? "Did you really let my friends go when you found them?"

"On my word as Mikhail's father," he said quietly. It was the most solemn oath in his repertoire; it was likely to be true. Alexei deeply loved his son. He poured another glass of vodka. "They ride east. I tell men not to follow."

"That was decent of you."

"I am better man than you think." He gave me an appraising look. "Next toast is that we do not toast each other with third toast next year."

"Will this bottle never be empty?" I picked it up and stared at the label.

"We can drink to seal our deal," Alexei said. "You give back my hand, I no longer hunt you and Arthur, and there will be peace between us."

Peace with Alexei was a powerful incentive. I took a deep breath. "I can't promise. For weeks I couldn't access the healing gift. It wouldn't come to me."

"But then it did."

"At the very last moment. Arthur was dying, almost at his last breath."

"I am not dying," Alexei said in a soft tone I had seldom heard him use. "I am living and learning." He smacked the countertop with the flat of his hand, making our glasses rattle and dance. "Ha! I am forgiving. That is hard for Russian. We do not forgive so fast."

"I can only *try* to heal you, Alexei. I can't promise. As I said, the healing gift eluded me for a long time. I can't promise I will succeed. I can only promise I will try."

Alexei scrutinized my eyes with his blue ones. He seemed to be looking inside me. He probably was, using his psychic gift. After several minutes, he nodded. "Emma's *try* is better than most people *do*. I accept your offer." He stretched his good hand toward me.

I shook it, something I thought I'd never do.

Alexei's face lit up, and he brought my fingers to his lips in a quick, dramatic kiss. Then he threw my hand into the air. "Now we drink! To our deal . . . and that we do not toast each other next year!"

10

I ROLLED OUT OF BED WITH A SPLIT-ting headache and an uneasy tummy and made my way down to the kitchen.

Alexei set a steaming mug of tea on the center island bar.

"Argh," I grunted gratefully. It was Earl Grey, very hot and sweet, and it slurped luxuriantly down my gullet, cozening my stomach into compliance. "Good. Thank you."

"We have to work on your drinking, Emma. You have no tolerance."

"Do I need one in the After?" It was meant to be withering but came out pitiful.

"Frozen fries not bad." Alexei set down a plate of roasted French fries; the bag had been in the freezer downstairs. "Good stove you have. It will be shame to move."

"I'm not moving," I said over a delicious mouthful of potato.

"Mists are coming." He leaned against the center island and glanced out the window. Something he saw made him smile broadly.

I stretched up in my seat to see. Arthur was out in the backyard taking his morning dump. I focused on the fries.

"I fed him this morning. He is . . . how do you say? Pungent."

"Skunks. He finds them fascinating. I don't know why. What did you feed him?" I asked suspiciously.

"Rice and venison, what do you think?" Alexei shook his head at me. "I like him this way. Empty and innocent like child. First time I ever like Arthur."

"You didn't like him when you met him?"

"I disliked him at first look. He asked me to find nuclear bomb to destroy laboratory outside London, where he make mists. I knew he was trouble. I want to kill him, shoot him in head and dump body in ocean. My wife, she like him. She tell me to help him. I am good husband and did as wife say." Alexei laughed in his throat and shook his head. "Emma, once I have meeting with colleagues, businessmen like me, successful and rich. I ask them, 'Are you afraid of your wife?' Every man say, 'Of course!' How do you like that? Men are pitiful lot." He shook his head again.

"I won't argue the point."

He shrugged. "I find Arthur a bomb. Iranians sell me one for money to make more, but it is too late. Mists already escaped from laboratory. No point. Arthur paid me for bomb but never used it."

"I didn't know all of that, just bits." I guzzled the tea. "Where did he get the money for a nuclear bomb that he planned to detonate outside London?"

"Arthur is resourceful. What does it matter now? World is gone." Alexei chucked me under the chin. "Ready to give me hand back?"

"When the hangover passes, I'll be ready to try."

"No sauna, so no perfect cure, but we have pickles in juice. Good for hangovers." Alexei's rugged face was wreathed in smiles. He fetched the pickle jar from the fridge and poured some brine off into a teacup. "Good cure, so you can drink more later, to celebrate new hand."

• • •

AFTER LUNCH AND a pair of fried rabbits that Alexei shot not far from the house, I situated Arthur in his room. I led Alexei outside to the porch, where Arthur's healing had taken place. I seated him in a rocking chair and opened a folding lawn chair for myself. I dragged it around to Alexei's side, close enough that his stump could rest in my two hands.

"What do I do?" Alexei asked, looking curious. "You never healed me before."

"Just relax." I took a deep breath. I'd never tried to heal someone I disliked and distrusted to the degree I did Alexei. But we had a bargain, and Alexei had, until now, kept his word with me. It was one positive trait I could cling to as I settled into the healing space. It was there immediately: a warm, tingly rush like a current of water running through my arms and out my hands.

"Your hands feel good, Emma," Alexei whispered. "You can heal my heart, too, make me a better man?"

"I didn't know you wanted to be one."

"I tell you, I'm learning."

"It's up to you to be a better man. I'm not a good enough healer for that or to heal your heart." I was breathing slow and deep into my diaphragm, filling all of my lungs, from the low floating ribs all the way up the front of my torso to my throat and up my back to the occiput of my skull. The slow, even, full respiration altered my state, and the healing energy flowed more strongly.

It was ironic to me that I had tried so hard and so long to access the energy on Arthur's behalf, but it had eluded me. Now, for Alexei, it sprang to the ready.

But Alexei's stump would need more than energy. If he was going to regenerate his hand, the deeper pattern was necessary. It was that deeper, foundational pattern that had healed Arthur, and it, not I, would heal Alexei.

I had barely thought of the pattern when I sank into it; it was that easily evoked.

Alexei exclaimed.

I slit open my eyes to see why.

His red stump had burst open like a bud bursting into bloom. Flaps of red skin waved in the air like anemone fronds in the water. Alexei's blue eyes were huge and awestruck.

I concentrated once again on the healing pattern that streamed like liquid lightning out of my palms and into Alexei's stump.

Slowly but with great precision, the stump reformed into an arm. This time, the arm seemed to generate itself by growing in a spiral direction, not in a straight linear vector. I wasn't sure if the spiral motion had been present in Arthur's healing or not, but it was remarkably effective.

In little swathes, bone and muscle and veins and ligaments and tendons and fascia and skin regenerated. It wasn't quick, but I submerged myself in the process, and the passing of time fell away.

Alexei was fascinated, but at a certain point he dozed. His craggy features smoothed out, as if their outlines were being smudged by a cosmic thumb. He looked young and peaceful. He looked innocent. If I hadn't known him to be a conscienceless sociopath, I would have been moved to tenderness toward him. As it was, even knowing well the cruelty which Alexei practiced as a matter of course, I couldn't help softening toward him. The energetic current passing through my body demanded that my heart be open.

His arm finished regenerating. It was whole and perfect, his hand without one single scar. Even his new nails were distinctly healthier and better kempt than those on his other hand.

I laid his hand in his lap, stood, stretched, and yawned.

A gust of rank air alerted me: Arthur was nearby.

I turned and caught him watching, his face blank as always. I really had to do something about the way he smelled. I bathed him regularly, using the lavish array of bath scents in the master bath, and his odor was less offensive after that, but it was still noticeable.

Arthur was waiting for me to lead him back indoors.

"I don't have any tomato juice. That's what you really need," I told him. "But how about more of that lily-of-the-valley gel?"

. . .

ALEXEI WAS JUBILANT. He slept until evening, then waltzed into the kitchen where I was cooking. He grabbed me by the waist and threw me into the air. "I have hand, A beautiful new hand! You heal me, Emma! You beautiful woman!"

"Put me down, you big Russian oaf," I sputtered. "Now you can leave. I'll give you back your weapons, and you go."

Alexei laughed and squeezed me in the biggest hug I'd ever survived. "Beautiful, good, kind Emma! I love you! You give me beautiful, good, new hand!" He kissed my cheeks and neck repeatedly.

"Stop it right now and put me down! I'm glad it worked, but it's time for you to leave!" I squirmed and writhed and smacked him with a wooden spoon, but it wasn't until a particular odor assailed us that Alexei settled me gently on my feet.

We turned as one to find Arthur standing close, staring wide-eyed.

"Arthur, I have new hand!" Alexei waved his hand, demonstrating. Then he clapped Arthur on the shoulder. It was nearly a blow and would have dropped a smaller man to his knees. "You are forgiven, Arthur. Now go shit on lawn like good idiot."

"Alexei, please." I took Arthur's arm and led him to the barstool at which he usually sat.

Arthur pointed to his mouth.

"It's coming," I said. A venison leg roast was cooking in the range and would be finished soon.

"He smell like whorehouse. Flower soap not helping skunk smell," Alexei observed, his lip curling.

"You would know whorehouses." I went back to the stove to stir the pasta.

"Yes. I own some before mists. Very good business, if run properly." Alexei hugged me from behind one more time. "We will drink to celebrate my hand! If only we had good champagne from my whorehouses, we would have party!"

"No more parties for me. I drank enough last night to last me until the next apocalypse," I muttered. "No more drink for you either, Alexei. It's time for you to go."

"Not yet! Please, Emma. We must celebrate my new hand. We are almost out of vodka. I will get wine from cellar. But first I help you, Emma. Lights in other room are dim, and some not work. Show me electrical panel."

"We're not playing house," I said crisply. "We had a deal. I expect you to keep your word. You have your hand back, so you have to go and leave Arthur and me alone forever."

"Emma, sweet Emma, let me fix your problems in house first," Alexei wheedled. "You don't have to do everything yourself. I can help. I am good at fix-it. I am, how do you say? Handyman!" He flexed his new hand joyously.

"I don't need your help."

"You are strong, tough woman, but everyone needs some-one. Electrical work is mechanical. Maybe you don't know it. I study it in university. I am good at it. Come, Emma. Let me repay you with kindness. It will make me happy. Then we drink. We have dinner. It's late. I leave in the morning." His blue eyes were earnest, his voice soft and coaxing.

I had misgivings, but I figured a few more hours wouldn't hurt. It was late, and I did want the house to be in perfect order, in case the owners returned someday. I wanted to leave it for them in the same perfect state I'd found it. So I turned down the roast, covered the pasta, and stuck Arthur back in his room so he wouldn't mess with the food on the stove and burn himself. Then I showed Alexei the generator I had found.

First he explained that it was not a generator but a power inverter. He pointed to other gizmos and called some of them charge controllers and others storage batteries. He asked about tools, and I pointed out the toolshed, and then I left him to his puttering.

Alexei made a trip outside and came back carrying a yellow toolbox, singing at the top of his lungs. He went back to the crawlspace and sang while working for the next hour. Then he ran upstairs and performed some Russian dance squat kicks, still singing, and announced that he had repaired the electrical system. He flicked the lights on and off a dozen times to demonstrate. He even asked about other repairs.

I made a plate for Arthur and left him to eat, and then I showed Alexei the kitchen window I'd tried to repair.

"You do a good job on window," he said when we examined the honey jar's trajectory. He prodded the plywood panel that covered the broken pane. "Nice work. You are pretty woman and a good carpenter."

I giggled at the incongruity. "I'm a piss-poor carpenter! I just didn't want the rain to get in."

"Or snow in winter."

"I won't be here next winter," I murmured, thinking of my friends in Outpost City. *Had Alexei really released them?*

"True, you will be far from here." Alexei studied me for a moment through lowered lids, then shrugged. "Put that big, smelly child to bed, and I will get wine."

· · ·

IT WAS ALMOST midnight, and still we hadn't eaten. Alexei was too excited to sit and kept gamboling around the house;

as undignified as it was, that was really the only word for it. He danced and pranced and sang in Russian and waved his hand around like a new toy. He fixed things and straightened things and moved things around. He tried on shirts that had belonged to the former owner of the house. Then he took off his shirt and stood in the kitchen half-naked, juggling forks, spoons, and knives.

"You're like a little kid," I grumbled. "Mind those knives. They're sharp!"

He reached for me, letting the silverware clatter on the floor.

"Quiet! You'll wake Arthur, and it took forever to get him settled in tonight." I threatened to smack him with a spatula. "I'm hungry, Alexei. It's time to eat."

"You set table in dining room. Very nice furniture there. I get wine from cellar, red and white and pink—whatever they have." Alexei held up his regenerated hand and snapped his fingers gleefully. Then he twirled me around and dipped me while singing lustily. Finally, he flittered down the stairs.

I hadn't yet eaten in the dining room. Arthur and I always sat at the center island in the kitchen. But the formal dining room was furnished with an eight-seater carved cherry table and a matching demilune sideboard. In the sideboard I found a linen tablecloth, elegant woven placemats, real silver place settings, and crystal barware. It was a pleasure to set the table. I even lit tall wax candles that had stood like silent sentinels in their Baccarat candelabra since before the world had ended.

"That is beautiful, Emma!" Alexei boomed. "Now you are understanding!" He had a bottle of wine in each hand and two more tucked in the crook of his new arm.

"You open the wine, and I'll bring out the food."

Finally we sat down together. Alexei poured ruby-red wine. I served the pasta, stewed field greens, and roast.

"I thawed the frozen raspberries for dessert and made a warm cocoa sauce."

"Delicious!" he exclaimed, lifting his wine glass. "To Emma, most beautiful healer, excellent cook, and clever handy girl."

"You're leaving tomorrow," I reminded him. "Don't try to butter me up."

"You don't need butter. You are tender as you are," he joked.

I laughed, shook my head, and clinked my glass against his. It was red wine full of sun, more delicious because someone was sitting across from me for real two-way conversation. It felt so good to not be alone. I couldn't help smiling at Alexei, who was beaming at me. But I had to wonder if it was such a good thing for that particular man to be so pleased with me, and, even more so, for me to be happy in his company. I set down my glass and sighed. "I hope the raspberries are still good."

"Subzero refrigerator, everything frozen very good," Alexei said.

"Or we'll be sick tomorrow."

"Alcohol kills germs. Let us drink much wine." He refilled my glass.

I laughed again. "Nothing could make you sick tonight. I could serve you spoiled meat, and it wouldn't affect you. You're too happy."

"True, Emma. I am very happy with my new hand. I am very happy with you," Alexei leaned toward me and gazed into my eyes. "How do you do it, Emma? So hard for one woman, all you do. Hunt food, heal Arthur. Before Arthur heal, you take care of him. Drag him all the way here, 1000 kilometers, on lazy horse."

I blushed. "You figured out Edgar's lazy? You haven't even tried to ride him!"

"Pain in the ass, that horse. If you had other horse, I would shoot him for you. Horse meat not very good, but since you have no beef, maybe you make tasty stew."

I wasn't grossed out because I'd been so hungry in the After, that I would have happily eaten horse. But I had to admit, grudgingly, that I'd grown fond of Edgar. "Don't shoot him. I'll need him yet."

"To get away from mists." Alexei drank more wine and refilled our glasses. "But you have not tell me, Emma. How you do so much? Since I first hear about you in France, you take care of children, take care of Arthur and his camp. Then you come to Canada with Haywood, steal Beth back from me, steal Arthur from me! You are busy woman, stronger than you look. What makes you so strong?"

It was a serious question, and I swirled the wine in my glass, wondering how to answer it. Finally I realized there was no answer. It wasn't about strength. I just met the exigency of every moment. "I do what I have to."

"You do much more than that," Alexei said. He speared a bite of venison but remained focused on me. "Who helps you? Who takes care of you?"

I wanted to say, Arthur. That had once been true, but no longer. Now Arthur couldn't take care of himself, let alone another person. Nor could I claim that Haywood took care of me. Reflectively, I took a bite of meat, chewed, and swallowed, then shook my head.

"I could take care of you," Alexei said in a soft, haunting tone.

"Alexei, you promised you would stop pursuing me and leave Arthur and me in peace if I healed your hand."

"I will keep my word. I will go. I will leave you in peace . . . unless you ask me to stay. Maybe you will do that. Maybe you are tired of taking care of infant who cannot speak. Maybe you want more than you have here or than Haywood can give you in Edmonton. Maybe you want a man who is partner and companion, a man who will talk to you, who will listen to you, help you, hold you."

I was so mesmerized by his words that I could barely breathe. It was as if he had read my innermost thoughts, everything I had ever wanted but had never spoken aloud. I couldn't tear my eyes from his piercing blue ones.

"A man who will love you," Alexei murmured. "You are a beautiful woman, Emma. You are a strong woman, but you are lonely. This is no life for you. Arthur's mind is gone. Haywood is a good man, but he is no match for you. You need a strong man." He touched my mouth with his new fingers. "I am a strong man."

"Alexei, no . . . ."

Delicately he stroked my cheek and lips. "I know I have been a bad man, a crazy man. But I am a better man now, Emma, because of you. You teach me. I am willing to learn."

I wanted to believe him. "Alexei, please. I—"

"I am still strong. Now I am a strong man with two good arms to hold you. I will take care of you. I promise." He kissed me.

I kissed him back.

In the next few minutes, we were a tangle of arms and clothes. I was not proud of it, but it was so tempting to be held by a man that I allowed myself to be swept up in the headiness of passion and wine and companionship.

I was lonely, and canny Alexei had seen that with perfect clarity. Since setting out from Carstairs over my husband's objections, I had felt alone, even in the fellowship of my comrades. The feeling was amplified into near bereavement when my friends left me with broken, damaged Arthur at Beartooth Pass. Arthur's healing had not lessened my ache but had only exacerbated it. Arthur couldn't even communicate with me as well as the damned lazy horse Edgar could.

Now, in Alexei's arms, with his desire and his warmth engulfing me, I felt the ache diminish. It receded like a tide ebbing. Finally.

We made it upstairs, trailing articles of clothing. Alexei murmured Russian endearments and kissed me soulfully. His lips pressed against my collarbone, and in the next moment, his tongue luxuriantly tasted mine. He ran his hands over my waist and cupped my bottom, then pressed against me so that I felt his erection, and it was pulsing hard and delicious. He was a man, a real man, and he wanted me.

I tingled all over, groaning with desire. My body cried out to feel his weight on top of me. We were mostly naked when we made it to my bed. Alexei kissed me deeply and he rolled on top of me, gauging me, accurately, to be soft and juicy and open. I had never been so ready to receive a man. It had been so long since I had been held and loved.

Suddenly, the door to my room swung open, startling us both.

I pressed up on one elbow, my breasts grazing Alexei's chest.

Arthur stood in the doorway.

I cried out.

Alexei rolled off me. "He is a child! Put him to bed and come back to me."

"I . . . can't."

"Then I will," Alexei said in a tone of supreme annoyance.

"Alexei, don't hurt him."

"I lock his door." Alexei rose and padded out, speaking Russian to Arthur in a threatening tone and gesturing for Arthur to descend the stairs.

I remembered myself suddenly, like waking from a dream. I was Emma, an artist in the Before and a healer in the After. I was Emma, who was in love with Arthur and married to Haywood. I took care of children and those who were hurt or sick. I loved my friends. And I never, ever slept with sociopaths, even charming seductive ones who could give voice to the deepest, most secret yearnings of my heart.

I sobbed silently as I rose and went to the dresser and found some soft gym pants and a t-shirt.

Alexei leaned against the lintel of the door and watched me slip on the pants. "Arthur is no reason to stop. He is a child. He is gone."

"But I'm not." There was a quiver in my voice that I couldn't control. "I am not a child, I'm not gone, and I can't sleep with you, Alexei. Too much has happened."

Alexei sighed, then went to my bed and stretched out on it. He held up both arms and looked at them, then clenched and unclenched his new hand, examining it back and front. He rolled over onto his side and gestured for me to come to him. "I will hold you, Emma. Come."

"I can't." I had given up everything for Arthur, even my husband and daughters and my safety in Carstairs, and he wasn't Arthur any more. I had sacrificed all for an infantile shell of a man. I was alone, really alone. I felt small and adrift.

"I will hold you, only hold you." Alexei's voice was kind, which seemed rare and even dissonant coming from him. But he kept his word and held me gently all night, first as I wept with pent-up sorrow and frustration and bitterness and loss. Then he held me as I slept.

• • •

IN THE MORNING, breakfast awaited on the kitchen table. Beside a plate of venison roast and some crispbread was a piece of heavy-ply cotton stationery on which were scrawled a few lines:

Emma, you must come to me now, I cannot chase you anymore. I will not say no to you. You have haven in my arms.

Remember, the mists come. One week, maybe two. Mists move in a line to your mountain. Please be safe.

Thank you for new hand. Love, Alexei.

Arthur was locked in his room. He saw me at his door and pointed at his mouth.

"You're hungry. I know," I said. I turned away so he wouldn't see me crying as we walked to the kitchen, for he wouldn't be able to make sense of my tears. Still, I wanted to spare whatever feelings lingered in him of the man he had once been. Perhaps the empty child contained vestiges of the old Arthur, the one I'd given up hope of ever seeing again.

11

IT WAS JUST AFTER DAWN WHEN THE MOUNtain came alive with sound. I awoke instantly, rolled out of bed, and leapt to look out the window. Ignoring each other, intent only on their escape, animals thundered across the yard from east to west. Their hooves and paws threw up twigs and leaves and dust and trampled down bushes and plants and saplings. Single birds and whole flocks of them fluttered and flew in the same direction.

Only one thing could cause such a focused eruption: The mists were approaching.

Edgar neighed and stamped in the garage.

I was prepared to flee, more or less. I had packed my backpack and the saddlebags soon after Alexei's departure so that Arthur and I could go at a moment's notice. I threw on my clothes and shrugged on a Ralph Lauren jacket I'd taken out of the closet a few nights earlier. I threw my gun into my backpack, shouldered the bag, then raced downstairs with boots in hand.

Arthur sat up on his bed, cocking his head like a puppy, listening to the clamor.

"Arthur, get up! It's time to go!" I grabbed his shoulder and felt his silk nightshirt while stepping into my boots. It was long and slinky, regrettable really, but it would have to do because we were in a hurry. I tied a t-shirt around his crotch; we had to ride hard and fast, as quickly as Edgar's four legs would allow, and there would be no time for Arthur to relieve his bladder. He stood passively as I yanked sweatpants up his legs and over the makeshift diaper. With my heart hammering in my chest, I knelt to tie my boots.

The ruckus outside grew louder as daylight brightened the horizon.

I took Arthur by the hand and hurriedly led him out to the garage. I saddled Edgar faster than I'd ever saddled a horse before, then hastily buckled and tied all the saddlebags on.

Arthur stood with his face pressed into the garage door windows, staring outside.

"Arthur, come here!" I pushed him back and rolled the garage door open by hand. I grabbed the reins in one hand and Arthur's hand in the other and led horse and man into the yard.

Hordes of animals of every variety—deer, elk, moose, caribou, squirrels, foxes, wildcats, skunks, rabbits, possums, and others—sprinted past us, ignoring us and each other. Bird droppings rained from the sky. The air boomed and roared around us from the sound of animals running and screaming and of wings flapping, louder than a jet engine and far more terrifying. It sounded and felt as if we were in the fulcrum of a living tornado, a twister made up not of wind and water but of beasts of the Earth.

It took a few minutes to make Arthur understand that he had to mount Edgar, who was stamping nervously. Finally I managed to get the uncomprehending man on the jittery horse. Arthur was so tall that he'd have to ride behind me, which meant he had to wear the backpack. I passed it up to him, but he just stared at it blankly.

A low growl sounded nearby, the kind of menacing, ominous sound that pierced even our current epic cacophony. It made the hair on my neck stand up, but I swiveled around to look.

Barely ten meters from me, the giant grizzly reared up on his hind legs, brandishing claws and teeth. He glared at me with an expression of unmitigated memory and anger.

I didn't think; I just reacted. I slapped Edgar's rump and sent him cantering down the mountain, along with all the other fleeing animals. Next, I reached for my gun. But it wasn't at my waist, where it belonged. It was then that I realized it was in the backpack in Arthur's hand. Fortunately, I still had my hands, which had served me well in our last encounter, so I raised them.

Snarling, the bear dropped to all fours.

Just then, a giant ball of white mist rose up over the crest of the mountain, bigger than the house we'd inhabited for the last few months. It was rolling straight at me and the bear. The sickly sweet scent of flowers and sulfur choked out every other smell.

Suddenly, Edgar and Arthur reappeared behind me. Arthur held the reins and galloped against the stampede, straight at the mists.

The bear launched itself at me.

The ball of mist rolled inexorably and seeped over the house, crushing and imploding it. Gritty yellow sand, the mist's excretion, filled the air like confetti during a parade. The sound of wood splintering, rebar twisting, and glass shattering surged, then finally gave way to the whooshing of sand.

Still, through a stampede of panicked animals, the bear was coming for me.

The mists rolled toward us.

Arthur and Edgar raced toward the mists.

I cried out, fearful of man and horse entering the vast mist bank, but I couldn't hear the sound of my own voice over the mists' destruction and the screaming uproar of a multitude of dying animals.

Arthur stood up in his stirrups and stretched out his hands.

In an instant, the giant ball of mist vanished as if it had never existed. A deep, eerie silence lowered on the mountain as birds and beasts adjusted to the absence of the mists.

The bear froze in its tracks.

"Emma, drop!" yelled Arthur.

I dropped, and curled into a ball.

When the bear pounced, I steeled myself, trying to prepare to feel its claws and teeth in my back.

Two shots rang out. The grizzly crumpled over onto its side just in time for me to crawl out of reach of its massive claws.

With gun in hand and his face carved into grave lines, Arthur stood before me.

I gasped. "Arthur! You're . . . all right?"

He stepped up to the still-moving bear and pumped two more bullets into its brain through its thick coat of brown fur. "Evidently."

I threw my arms around his neck. "Arthur, you're all right! I-I didn't think you'd ever come back. I thought you'd be an idiot forever. You wouldn't believe how hard it was, how hopeless and alone I felt," I babbled.

Arthur pushed me away, none too gently. "You put a diaper on me." He reached inside his sweatpants and pulled out the wadded-up shirt, then threw it on the ground with an expression of contempt.

"Huh?"

"A diaper, for God's sake! And what is this smell?" He lifted his arm to his nose and sniffed, then curled his lip. "I smell like a skunk in a brothel," he said, casting me an accusatory raised eyebrow. "Care to explain that?"

I took a deep breath. I watched as birds sang and ascended up into the sky, then flew off in all directions. Deer scurried off, and ground squirrels melted back into the woods, through which ran a broad swathe of emptiness, marking the mists' passage. I wondered how far the swathe extended, whether it was 100 kilometers or 1,000. I wondered how many buildings had been destroyed, how many people, precious survivors, had perished.

The one thing I did know for sure was that we would never be truly free to rebuild until the mists were gone. Still, there were other thoughts on my mind. *Isn't it odd that the mists headed here so directly, to Arthur's location, when he's the one man on the planet who can dissolve them at will?* It was clear that the mists were evolving, as they'd never before consumed trees. *But are they now, in fact, hunting Arthur specifically? Maybe trying to make a preemptive strike?*

"A goddamn diaper, Emma." Arthur's sharp tone pierced my reverie.

"I didn't have tomato juice."

"Tomato juice?"

"You don't remember? You got friendly with a skunk. Multiple skunks actually. You had a thing for skunks, and they didn't reciprocate. I did the best I could to clean you up." I faced him. "Do you remember anything at all, Arthur?"

His gray eyes turned to follow the path of the mists' destruction. "I remember Alexei's camp. They tortured me. Then there are long periods of nothingness, except for disjointed images, isolated pictures in my head. They don't connect into a narrative. They just . . . don't make sense."

"You were hurt badly," I said quietly.

"That I know," he replied grimly. He spread out his hands in the air before him, holding my gun loosely on the thumb of the hand that had regenerated. "They cut off my hand so I'd know what Alexei felt. Then Alexei cauterized the wound with a torch so I wouldn't bleed out. So he could keep me alive to torture me some more." He inhaled deeply and raggedly, and his face paled. "Tell me the rest."

"We're supposed to meet the others in Outpost City," I said. "We have a long journey ahead of us and plenty of time to talk. But first tell me, how did you come back to yourself?

I didn't think you ever would."

"The mists woke me. They were engineered to affect the human brain, mostly through the pineal gland."

"Pineal gland?"

He nodded. "It's a receiver, the physical seat of the bio-mind. The mists got close enough to tweak my pineal gland. My head started to ring, and the suppressed, sane part of me began to emerge. That part knew I needed even greater proximity to the mists, so I drove the horse toward the mists. That massive formation set up a huge resonance in my head."

"But the mists usually cause madness, not cure it," I said, curious.

"The mists operate via a resonance that affects the human biomind. That resonance acted as wave interference for the pattern of madness that was afflicting me. I knew I needed to be closer, and I remembered that I could disperse the mists. When I got close enough to do so, the mists' resonance restored me to myself," Arthur said, then tilted his head. Various expressions chased over his beautiful, perfectly symmetrical face: curiosity, uncertainty, chagrin, shock, reserve, sorrow, and anger.

Why anger? I wondered, but I could tell he didn't want to explain himself—at least not yet. That was something he'd have to do in his own time.

I looked at the yellow sand that now blanketed the land where the beautiful house had stood only minutes before. I spared a moment to mourn the house, which had sheltered us so graciously in our time of need. In the After, such respite was rare.

"Let's get Edgar. We'll need provisions for the journey to Outpost City, and we can't get them here," I said.

Edgar was grazing nearby, and Arthur snapped up his reins with the confidence of a master. Edgar's ears sprang to attention; damn horse knew right away that he couldn't misbehave anymore, that his laziness wouldn't be tolerated.

Arthur checked the saddle and exhaled in disgust. He tightened the girth and adjusted the reins, shaking his head.

"We were in a hurry," I said, feeling defensive. It wasn't my finest saddling effort, but it had done the job.

"I'm not criticizing."

"Good . . . because you shouldn't!"

"I wasn't. I'm just surprised that you're still so sloppy with the girth."

"Sloppy with the girth!? I've managed to keep us alive for the last three months. I kept *you* alive when you were a disintegrating wreck of a person, and we had to ride hard and fast for 1,000 kilometers. *I* healed your ghastly injuries. *I* found us a place to rest and recharge while you were busy being an imbecile. *I* hunted animals, butchered them, and cooked them. It was *me* who fed us, clothed us, and kept us safe. So, if you ask me, you have no right to say anything about how sloppy my girth is!"

Arthur gave me an impenetrable look. "Did I say I wasn't grateful, Emma?"

"You didn't say anything at all except 'sloppy with a girth' and 'god-damned diaper'!"

"Well, hell, woman, what do you expect? I'm a grown man!"

"You weren't potty-trained. You were crapping on the lawn," I said, trying to keep the disgust from my voice; though truthfully, I didn't try that hard. I was pissed with Arthur. *How dare he be so ungrateful and standoffish?*

Arthur's lips tightened, as did the skin on the bridge of his nose. "I remember something about that."

"Good. Then you tell me, what was I supposed to do? I didn't want you to wet yourself while we were riding Edgar. I didn't want you to pee on me. I got terrible saddle sores while we were riding out here, and it took a month for them to heal. I never want to go through that again." I shuddered.

Arthur wouldn't look at me. He just held the stirrup in a

white-knuckled death grip. "Get on. We'll ride together until we find another horse."

I climbed up.

"Take the reins," Arthur said as he mounted behind me. "How far do you think we are from Outpost City?"

"We're just about due north of Coeur d'Alene. You're better at directions than I am. You estimate."

"I'd say 700, maybe 680 kilometers north and east, as the crow flies," Arthur said. He put his arms around me stiffly and took the reins in his big hands, which were soft and smooth after his months of idleness. "Glad to hear you still need me, even if it's only to estimate directions."

"I need you, Arthur," I said quietly.

"Yeah," he muttered. "Sure you do, Emma."

• • •

ARTHUR REMAINED ALOOF as we rode.

I recounted the last few months, including his healing, purposely omitting Alexei's visit and the healing of Alexei's arm.

We passed three cairns en route to Sandpoint, one almost ten meters high; I pointed them out and commented that I'd seen them with increasing frequency along our journeys.

He nodded but didn't answer.

Finally, when we reached Farragut State Park, he halted Edgar and dismounted.

"What are you doing?" I asked, confused.

"There's a community nearby," he answered, his voice taut. "See? There are signs of human habitation everywhere," he said, pointing here and there at the so-called "signs" I couldn't really discern. "I don't want anyone to see me like this. Do you have any other clothes for me besides these ugly pants and this swell nightie?"

I rummaged through the saddlebags until I found the

garments from the lake house in Ennis, Montana, a pair of canvas painter's pants and a long-sleeve, red and gray-checkered flannel shirt. "This is the best I can do," I said, handing them to him.

Arthur grunted, but it almost sounded like approval. "I need a knife."

In the backpack, I found the hunting knife, and I passed it over in correct fashion, handle first.

Avoiding my eyes, Arthur took the knife and the clothes and marched around behind a tree. The silk nightshirt he was wearing fluttered out onto the ground, followed by the sweatpants.

"You're embarrassed to undress in front of me?" I called. "Since when are you so modest?"

"Since you've been wiping my ass." When he walked out from behind the tree, he was holding the flannel shirt loosely in one hand. His chest seemed curiously white and flat, like a prepubescent boy's, devoid of its usual rolling pecs, defined abs, and ragged scars. He noticed me looking, and he flushed. He sliced the sleeves off the shirt before he shrugged it on and buttoned it. Then he held out a handful of his black hair and chopped away at it with the knife.

"What the holy hell are you doing?"

"You think I'm gonna let anyone see me looking like little lord Fauntleroy?" Arthur asked, tossing me a look of consummate disgust.

"At least let me help you," I said, then stepped toward him.

Arthur took a step away. "No. I can do this myself," he said, in a steely voice. "Thank you very much." He hacked at his hair until it was a short, ragged mess.

What is wrong with him? Is he still insane? I wondered but didn't dare say aloud. I watched as he felt his head for any remaining longish strands.

"Good," he said when he finished. He looked at the blade and wiped it carefully. "Do you have a holster for this?"

"No."

"Fine. Let's go. We need to find some Sandpointers and another horse," he said sternly, motioning for me to mount the horse.

"It wasn't bad, you know," I said once we were both atop Edgar.

"What? Wiping my ass?"

"No," I said over my shoulder, almost cracking a smile. "Your hair. It was just a bit long."

"I looked like a little girl. It's bad enough that I smell like one. I don't have to look like one too."

• • •

A LIVELY COMMUNITY had grown up around Lake Pend Oreille. The area was largely unscathed by mists, and the shores of the lake and of west-flowing Pend Oreille River were built up with crude shantytowns, as well as structures from the before. We hugged the lake and soon ran into a group of six fishermen coming in off the docks.

The fishermen welcomed us to the area, assuring us that we were safe and congratulating us on being alive. They directed us to the refugee center at the Athol Public library, where we could obtain food, water, and information.

"About nine kilometers west along Smylie Boulevard," said a young guy who sauntered over to stand next to me. He smiled pleasantly and offered me dried fish rolled up in tree leaves.

"Hmm. I've never had that before." I smiled back and broke off a chunk to taste. It was savory, with a rosemary tang. "Not bad."

"Pretty good, once you get used to it. One of the Japanese families showed us how to make it." He was dark-haired and stocky, with an angular, strongly boned face. He was only average height, but he boasted thick triceps and thoughtful, quick-moving eyes that took in everything.

"People pull together now, in the After—or at least sane people do."

"That they do," he said. "Teamwork is our best chance for surviving the mists. Even the crazies can pitch in. Another piece?"

"That's very kind of you, but no thanks," I said with a smile.

He smiled back. "I'm Jeremy."

"Good to meet you, Jeremy." I shook his hand. "Emma."

"I'm Arthur," Arthur said coolly. He turned to speak to an older, Asian-looking gentleman who was dressed in a collared gas station attendant's shirt with a name embroidered on the pocket. "Are you Ravi?"

"I am," affirmed the man, shaking Arthur's hand and pointing proudly to his name on his shirt. "I used to work at a Citgo, in the Before." He dipped his head, acknowledging me.

I waved back.

"Ravi, we don't want to trouble anyone. We won't be staying in town." Arthur glanced pointedly at Jeremy, then returned to Ravi. "We just need another horse and a few provisions, and then we'll be on our way."

"Do you have anything to trade?" Jeremy asked. "Everyone will pitch in to get you settled in if you're homesteading here and to take care of you if you're hurt, but horses aren't free."

"We can find something," Arthur said, giving me a questioning look.

I nodded. In one of Edgar's saddlebags, I'd packed the fancy silver cutlery from the mountain house. It was ornate Reed and Barton sterling, heavily laden with fruit and flower clusters, and there were twelve place settings. I was sure it would be enough to buy us a horse, maybe two, along with tack and feed. "We can trade."

"My uncle stables some good horses," Jeremy said. "I can take you there."

"How convenient," Arthur muttered.

I elbowed him in the ribs.

Jeremy grinned. "He lives just north of here, off Bayview. You can look at his stock and see if there's a horse that will serve your needs."

"We need a well-broken one in good enough shape to travel about 700 kilometers," I told him, "preferably one that isn't lazy."

Jeremy raised his eyebrows. "You're going to Outpost City?"

"Good guess," Arthur said, his tone glacial.

"All right. Well, let me just get my horse and lead you to Uncle Jake's." With that, Jeremy scurried off at a fast clip, disappeared down a trail through some trees.

"Uncle Jake's stock any good?" Arthur asked Ravi, once Jeremy was out of sight.

"Yeah. Uncle Jake's got the best stock around. That's his business," Ravi answered.

"Any other game in town?" Arthur asked.

"Uh . . . a woman north of Sandpoint who keeps a big ranch, a guy on the other side of the lake who specializes in quarter-horses, a couple west of Athol with an Arabian farm, and two places near Schweitzer," Ravi said, counting off the five horse-dealers on his fingers.

"Good to know," Arthur murmured.

The quick clip-clopping of horse hooves caused the group to turn toward the path, and we saw Jeremy trotted toward us on a sweet-looking Morgan horse. He rode to me and looked down with an inviting demeanor. "Emma, you want to ride with me and give your friend a break?"

"I don't need a break," Arthur snarled. "Emma rides with me."

I rolled my eyes, having forgotten just how overbearing

Arthur could be. I made a mental note to discuss with him later, in private, the respect he owed the person who'd saved his life, healed his wounds, and kept him safe until his mind returned to him—not to mention wiped his ass.

• • •

UNCLE JAKE OWNED a sprawling ranch that covered the side of a respectable hill that overlooked the lake. He was a quiet, compact man; it was clear where his nephew got his looks. He came out to greet us when we rode up close to his house, which was perched high on the hill, with sweeping views of the surrounding area. Even from a distance, he would have seen us riding toward his grounds. "Jeremy, my boy! Looks like you brought some friends," Uncle Jake called.

"This is Emma and Arthur," Jeremy said, dismounting. "They're looking for a horse." He embraced his uncle loosely but affectionately.

"Might be able to help 'em out." Uncle Jake tied Edgar to a nearby fencepost, then shook Arthur's hand, looking him right in the eye.

Arthur brightened and stood a little straighter; it was clear that he liked the man right from the get-go. "I hear you've got the best stock around."

"Entirely true," Uncle Jake said proudly. He shook my hand and looked me over thoroughly, but it was congenial and inoffensive, the way he might have appraised a mare with good conformation. "You folks look good, like you've been restin' and eatin' okay. Those mists south of here didn't bother you? We heard they were ferocious. Cut a path as wide as a city block over a 200 kilometer stretch of land. Just gobbled up the damn trees. Folks around here been real nervous, fearing the mists were coming our way."

"We've got a speaker system," Jeremy interjected. "It broadcasts the sound of horses galloping and sends the mists away. We expanded that in a hurry."

"The mists dissipated near us," Arthur said, a half-truth. He unbuckled the girth and hung Edgar's saddle and packs over the fence.

"Lucky," Uncle Jake said. "Would you like to come in for dinner?"

"Maybe after we look at your available horses," Arthur said.

Uncle Jake gestured for Arthur to follow him, and they walked around the house to a big barn down the hill.

"I don't see a ring on your finger," Jeremy said, touching my left hand gently. "You aren't married to him."

I sighed. "It's kind of hard to explain. I'm *with* Arthur, but I'm married to someone else. It's . . . complicated."

We approached the big red barn, which was topped with a mansard roof.

Jeremy paused and, as if he couldn't resist touching me, he laid one uninvited hand on my shoulder. He was warm and grounded and emanated a feeling-sense of kindness and respect. "Life in the After is complicated for everyone, Emma."

"Mine is downright messy," I said, though I wasn't about to broach the subject of being followed by a Russian sociopath from Europe, one who wanted to wreak revenge on Arthur and to obtain me. Strangely, Alexei had kept his word and had left us alone. He'd even been kind to me that last night, had held me without asking anything in return. It didn't compute. I didn't believe Alexei had changed—or even that he could. I still couldn't fathom that I'd almost slept with him. *What was I thinking?*

A moment later, I realized Jeremy was still talking. "Everyone's got a messy story these days. We all know that, and we've learned to be tolerant. The old rules from the Before don't apply and don't matter."

"That's a good way to look at it."

"We can talk about it more on our way to Outpost City."

"Wait . . . *our* way?"

"Uh-uh. I received word that my brother's there," Jeremy said, grimly. He grasped my elbow gently and ushered me forward. "We haven't seen him since the Day. I've been meaning to ride over and find him so I can bring him back here, but I didn't want to ride alone and risk running into raiders or wild animals without anybody to help me. I'm going with you and Arthur."

"Emma!" Arthur's stern voice issued from inside the barn. "Would you come look at this thoroughbred and see if you think you can ride him?"

As Jeremy and I headed inside the barn, I grabbed his arm. "Let *me* tell Arthur your plans," I whispered. "He's a touch cranky."

"Well, I'm easy to get along with," Jeremy whispered back. "Even-tempered. You'll like that."

The black thoroughbred was young and finely boned, but at not quite fifteen hands tall, he wouldn't be able to carry a lot of packs. Still, the animal had an air of frisky intelligence that Arthur seemed to appreciate.

"I don't know," I said uneasily. "I'm okay with Edgar, but this guy is too small for you, and he's got a lot of spirit for me to handle."

"Edgar needs a firm hand and an experienced rider. He's been getting away with murder." Arthur ran his hands over the young thoroughbred's withers. "This guy will grow with you."

"He's not stubborn, just young," Uncle Jake added.

"If the lady wants a more tractable animal, how about the bay mare, Mona Lisa?" Jeremy suggested. "She's older, but she's got a few good years left in her, and she'll be easier to handle. Maybe that's what Emma needs."

"Great name too," I commented, exchanging a smile with Jeremy.

"I think *I* know what Emma needs and what she can handle," Arthur said in a bone-chilling tone.

"Maybe *Emma* knows what she needs and can handle," I snapped, throwing Arthur a defiant stare. "I'd like to see the mare."

Arthur's eyes narrowed, then dropped. He took a breath, then met my gaze. "Fine. Let's see her."

From a nearby stall, Uncle Jake brought out a sedate bay who came with him amiably. Her spine and withers showed more prominently than I'd expected. "She's seventeen but in good condition," Jake said. "She's got some solid years in her yet." He tied her down the aisle from the thoroughbred so I could examine her.

Arthur lifted her lip to examine her teeth. "Her teeth show wear and a few points, but they're not bad." He knelt and lifted her front foot. "How's her digestion? Does she have habitual pain, arthritis, or joint disease?"

"As you can see, she's not too thin, so she's digesting properly," Jake answered. "She's a slow eater for sure. She doesn't show signs of pain or disease, except a little stiffness sometimes. She needs to be exercised regularly. Her feet are good."

I stroked her neck and forelock as she drooped her head. "She seems quiet."

"That she is," Uncle Jake said with a smile. "She's a good girl." He patted the horse affectionately.

"Is quiet right for you now?" Jeremy wondered.

"Good question," Arthur said. "Emma, you're a better rider than when we met in France, far more experienced and confident. You can handle a horse with some spirit. You can think about horsemanship and about developing a relationship based on trust and good communication. A sensitive horse that hasn't been hardened by rough handling will be a better mount for you in the long run, and you'll probably be with this one for a while. You can ride and live with the animal in harmony."

He had a point, though it annoyed me to admit it. I returned to the thoroughbred and stroked his neck, considering my options. After dealing with temperamental Edgar, I wanted an easier horse, but I knew Arthur had made a good point: I needed a horse who would grow with me. I finally nodded, looking at Arthur from lowered lids.

Arthur smiled his old sardonic half-smile. "We'll take him."

"Let's see what you've got to trade," Uncle Jake said.

As it turned out, the Reed and Barton pattern was a big hit with Jake's wife Eleanor, a shapely brunette with a melodic voice. She laid it out on her kitchen table and cooed. "Why, it's absolutely beautiful! I haven't seen such fine tableware since the Before!"

Uncle Jake scrunched up his face, as if he didn't understand her excitement. He and Arthur fell into a lively discussion about the value of the silver, what we would get in return for all twelve settings.

I leaned back against a counter and listened to Arthur bargain. He spouted off a whole laundry list of what should come with the horse and even included a second horse as a pack animal. Uncle Jake minimized Arthur's list to include just one horse and tack essentials. Arthur listened carefully and countered by offering four place settings.

The wheeling and dealing went on that way for twenty minutes before Arthur fell silent. He shook his head, frowned, and stared off into space, as if thinking. I was sure it was a ploy; I'd forgotten what a skilled negotiator Arthur was.

"Some performance," Jeremy murmured in my ear.

I stifled a grin.

"Jake, dear, it just wouldn't be right to split up the set," Eleanor said, breaking the silence and staring admiringly at the silver pieces.

Jake gave her a reproachful look and rolled his eyes.

"There is the Arabian farm west of Athol, but your wife

loves the silver, and I'd hate to see it go to someone else," Arthur said, in a confiding tone. "I'd love to see your wife happy."

Jake harrumphed, but he and Arthur shook hands.

Eleanor grabbed Jake and kissed his mouth with a big smooch.

With his eyes gleaming, Arthur gave me a small, triumphant smile.

I tilted my head in deference, acknowledging Arthur's score.

"Hold on," Jeremy said. "There's one more thing."

"Jer, I already shook on the deal," Uncle Jake said, clearly puzzled by his nephew's interference.

Jeremy held up his hand. "I'm going with Emma and Arthur to Outpost City."

"What!? No," Arthur said, through clenched teeth. "That's not even up for discussion, and—"

"Mister, my brother is there, in Outpost City. We just found out, and we haven't heard from him since the Day. We thought he was dead," Jeremy said. "I want to bring him home."

"Jeremy can't go by himself. We could never let him take that risk," Eleanor said. She put her hand on Arthur's arm. "We all want to see James again. It would be good of you to let Jeremy ride along."

"You know how you like to see Eleanor happy," said Uncle Jake wickedly.

Arthur's eyes blazed at Jeremy, and then he clasped Eleanor's hand on his arm. "To please Eleanor, of course Jeremy may accompany us." He removed Eleanor's hand and swung back around on Jeremy. "You ride armed and fend for yourself. We ride hard and fast, and we aren't going to babysit anyone."

"That won't be a problem," Jeremy said. "I was a rodeo

rider in the Before. Couldn't be unseated. Quick on the draw too."

"We'll see about that," Arthur muttered.

"Would you folks like some dinner before you ride? You must all be hungry," Eleanor said. "I'd love to serve you on my new silver!"

12

ARTHUR SLEPT ON THE FLOOR.

First Eleanor prepared a delectable feast of beefsteak, sautéed onions and baby eggplant, boiled carrots with parsley, baked potatoes, and a side of green tomato and basil salad. The meat and vegetables were expertly cooked on a cast-iron wood stove that filled the kitchen with a mouth-watering aroma. I couldn't help but admire Eleanor's talent as a chef, and I wondered what she could have done with that gorgeous range that existed now only as yellow sand scattered on the side of a mountain.

I insisted on helping with the dishes while the men went outside to talk livestock. Eleanor chatted with me about James, the missing brother. He was sixteen months younger than Jeremy, and the two were close.

"Like all brothers, they argued all the time and were very competitive with each other," she said, "but no one else could look cross-eyed at either, or the other one would jump in with his fists at the ready."

"Jeremy must have been happy to hear that James is alive," I commented. "It's always a miracle these days when a family is reunited."

"Yes, the mists have taken so much from so many," Eleanor said grimly. She dried the dishes I washed and carefully placed them in their designated spots in the cabinet. "A big family group came up from Outpost City ahead of that last bank of mists, and they had news of James. Jeremy's been over-the-moon happy ever since. He would have set out that same day, but Jake and I asked him to wait until someone could go with him."

By the time we finished cleaning, the sun had set. Eleanor lit candles and lamps throughout the living room, kitchen, and bedrooms.

When the men wandered in, Eleanor showed Arthur and me to an attic bedroom with a full-sized bed set up under long, sloping eaves. There was a washbasin and chamber pot in one corner and a stack of towels and blankets in a dresser drawer. Eleanor apologized for the crudeness.

"We're delighted with the accommodations!" I assured her.

She smiled slightly at Arthur. "I've got a few old cans of tomato juice, if you need them. I was saving them, but it seems you've had a close encounter with a real stinker. Take the juice out back to the horse trough and lather up. Rinse yourself real well after."

"I'd be obliged, Eleanor," Arthur said. "I can't stand my own stench." With a sheepish smile on his face, he followed our thoughtful hostess out the door.

I changed into a t-shirt and leggings. On the road, I seldom got to change into sleeping clothes, but it did make for a better night's sleep. This time, I had a mattress as well. I crawled under the coverlet to the far side of the bed, leaving space for Arthur.

When he returned, smelling faintly of vegetables, he stretched out on the floor and performed several sets of push-ups. He was soon panting and sweating. He continued with sit-ups, then used the beam running between eaves for pull-ups. He was red-faced and shaking when he dragged one of the pillows onto the floor. He shut his eyes and rolled over with his back to me, a clear signal that he didn't want to talk.

I blew out the lamp and listened to the soft sibilance of

Arthur's breathing as he slept. I wondered if he understood how deep was the ache of loneliness. If he had, he would have wanted to hold me as much as I longed to hold him. But this was the After, and longings were like firefly trails against the night sky, a brief passing of passion. Nothing to hold close.

• • •

JEREMY, ARTHUR, AND I made ready to leave right after breakfast. Eleanor and Uncle Jake filled saddlebags with feed for the horses. For us, there were dried meats and fruits, hard breads, canteens full of water, and bottles full of water and tea.

"Kootenai Forest is inhabited by some real crazies," Uncle Jake said as he showed me how to properly cinch a double-girth on the new horse, whose name was Bucky.

"I'm not in love with that name," I muttered. "It doesn't bode well for me."

"Well, he's your critter now, so name him whatever you want," Uncle Jake said, grinning. "This is an Australian saddle. Arthur said you had some real bad sores before. This should help. Your bones will make contact with a surface that gives, like a hammock. It's also lighter and more comfortable for the horse, and young Bucky—or whatever you call him— needs that right now." He glanced over his shoulder at Arthur, who was already astride Edgar. "You folks be careful now. The mist crazies have organized into some kind of religious commune, or at least that's what we heard."

"We haven't heard that they're dangerous, just that they warrant watching," Eleanor noted. She tucked something in my pocket and winked at me to keep quiet about it. She hugged me briefly and smoothed a few errant strands of hair out of my eyes. "Be safe, hear? You never know how people's minds will unwind once the mist sickness sets in. Even the seemingly harmless can turn into monsters."

"I'll take care. Besides, I'm a good shot," I assured her.

"We ran into cannibals in Europe, but we haven't seen that here," Arthur said, closely watching Jake, who was saddling his own horse.

"Count!" I exclaimed as I decided on the perfect name for my new ride. I slid my finger under the girth and felt the tautness for myself. I nodded at Uncle Jake, who squeezed my shoulder, then helped me atop my young steed. I noticed immediately that the saddle naturally put me into a balanced riding position. "You're right. This is great."

"For days of riding, you can't do better," Uncle Jake declared. "These pads are called poleys, and they should run parallel to your thigh, about a centimeter away." He walked over to Jeremy, and uncle and nephew embraced. "Ride safe, Jer."

"You bet, Uncle Jake," Jeremy said. He swung himself up into his saddle, a compact Australian one like mine, sitting atop his spirited black and white palomino. "James and I will be back in no time. Don't you worry, Aunt Eleanor."

"Anything else we should be aware of, any trouble we should be on the lookout for between here and Outpost City?" Arthur asked.

"There's ongoing talk about an army of raiders led by a one-armed Russian. They capture people, mostly women and children. They've been south, by Yellowstone," Uncle Jake said. "A few days ago, we heard they're on the move again."

"They won't bother us," I said with certainty.

Everyone looked at me strangely, including Arthur, who cocked his head, suspicion on his face.

I didn't elaborate.

"Kootenai is full of all kinds of survivors," Uncle Jake said, glancing away and stroking his jaw. "Once you get close to the Safe Zone, the Mounties get touchy and take horses based on eminent domain. They'll take your weapons, too, if you aren't careful."

"They can try," Arthur said coolly. "We'll set a path between the Safe Zone and Kootenai."

"Wise," Uncle Jake said. "Lethbridge is a nice city, and you'll be able to get more supplies there. Just ride safe and send my nephews home in one piece."

"We'll do our best," Arthur promised. He leaned down and shook hands with Uncle Jake and Eleanor.

"Thanks again," I said.

Arthur steered his horse toward the north, and we followed him, with Eleanor and Uncle Jake waving farewell behind us.

Jeremy rode up alongside me as we left Uncle Jake's grounds behind. "Emma, do you know something about that Russian and his army."

"Ah. The million-dollar question," Arthur said. "What does Emma know about Alexei and his depraved band of thugs?"

"I know they won't bother us," I repeated. Then, tight-lipped, I kicked the horse and trotted ahead of the two men.

• • •

WE MADE IT to Bonner's Ferry late in the day and found a ghost town, at least the remains of one. Big swathes of the city had been devastated by an incursion of the mists and were blanketed by yellow sand. Like a crazy quilt, parts of the city stood up out of the sand, unscathed. We reined in our horses on a bridge that crossed over the Kootenai River and surveyed the devastation.

"The damage looks recent," Arthur observed.

"Yeah, it happened about two months ago. Mists came out of the Columbia River. Until then, this town was untouched. About 5,000 people had come here since the Day, and the place was growing, with survivors trickling in," Jeremy said, his voice flat and uninflected, the way we all talked about the ruin wrought by the mists. It seemed particularly fitting in the violet dusk of the summer evening, ringed by forested mountains and serenaded by humming insects and the soft swishing of the river flowing under the bridge.

"Did they have warning?" Arthur asked.

Jeremy nodded. "A couple thousand got out, and about half as many made it to Sandpoint. The rest went elsewhere, mostly to Calgary."

"No protection system?" Arthur wondered.

"They had a system like ours, speakers blasting the rhythmic cadence of horse hooves," Jeremy said. "I guess it worked, because the mists dispersed, only right into the city."

"It always seems to work out that way. Too little too late," I said softly.

Arthur gave me an inscrutable look, then turned back to Jeremy. "Any idea where we can hole up for the night?"

"There's an untouched stretch of Main Street. I'm sure we can find suitable shelter there," Jeremy said.

Sure enough, we found a women's clothing boutique, which afforded both shelter and articles of clothing for me. Few fashionable items were left from what had obviously once been a thriving enterprise, but I scored a pair of jeans in my size and two turtlenecks, a heavy, ribbed one in black wool and a sheer, mercerized cotton in eggshell blue. It was a treat to have such spiffy new clothes, and I was happy and humming in my throat as I packed them away with the ill-fitting garments I'd taken from the mountain house.

I noticed the slight bulge in my pocket, the souvenir from Eleanor, and when I drew it out, I realized it was a piece of chocolate candy. "Wow!" I exclaimed and could barely contain myself from dancing. I popped the chocolate in my mouth and groaned with delight.

"You light up a room when you smile," Jeremy said, squatting down to watch me as he unrolled his sleeping bag in a clearing in the center of the boutique.

"Wait till she laughs out loud," Arthur said from the corner, where he was doing push-ups again. "It's like a Mozart piece, ringing out and lifting everyone's spirits."

I turned in surprise at Arthur's words, but he was already walking out the door to find something to use as a pull-up bar.

• • •

WE MADE IT most of the way around Kootenai Forest, encountering only gray cairns. They were perfectly conical, exactly three meters high, as if created in a robotic factory on an automated assembly line. The cairns were also spaced at precise one-kilometer intervals.

I grew curious after a few days and rode up to one of them. I urged Count closer and closer, leaning forward in the saddle. Suddenly I was sailing through the air toward the pile of stones. I had a brief second of forethought and wrapped my arms around my head, knowing it would do me no good to crack my noggin on a death monument.

Fist-sized gray stones flew everywhere but mostly avoided my body. I lay amidst the messy heap of rocks for only a second before I quickly scrambled upright and backed away. Surprisingly after such a tumble, I was intact other than a few bruises; I was grateful I hadn't been hurt worse.

Arthur and Jeremy called my name, but their voices diminished into a distant buzzing. The scattered stones seemed to fill with life and hop around like jumping beans. I stared at a stone, and a wraith rose up out of it, like a genie arising from an uncorked bottle. Another wraith funneled up out of another stone. One by one, a wraith came from each stone, and I stood in the center of them, quaking in disbelief. The wraiths stared at me, then two joined hands, and others followed suit. As they connected, they began to slowly circle me in a great, ghostly carousel. They circled faster and faster, and the day was dimmed over, as if by an eclipse.

Count bolted, whinnying with fear.

The fallen stones rose and hovered in the air, and the wraiths spun faster.

I found myself at the center of a vortex of shades. I reached out to touch one of them, a man.

He paused out of the carousel of ghosts, and his mouth dropped open into a giant, engulfing void. My hand lost its warmth and color as he howled, the sound of regret and loss and suffering coming from the gaping hole. The others joined in. It was symphony of pain, ripping my heart open in my chest, overwhelming my senses.

I swayed on my feet.

Suddenly, with a *whoosh*, the stones reformed into a three-meter high, conical cairn, the wraiths vanished, and the day returned to its normal brightness.

"Emma, are you all right?" Arthur leapt down from Edgar and grabbed me by the upper arms, shaking me.

"I . . . my hand is cold," I murmured sleepily, as if I'd just woken up from a dream.

"It's white and freezing!" Arthur said, dismayed. He took my icy hand in both of his and rubbed it furiously. "Emma, talk to me. Your eyes are glassy. What happened inside that whirlwind?"

"Uh . . . I-I don't know. I . . . um . . . "

"Emma, tell me! Exactly what did you see?"

"I saw . . ." I felt myself slipping back inside the circle of wraiths.

"Emma!" Arthur grabbed my head on both sides and leaned close to me, his eyes urgent and black. He shook me, said my name again, and finally penetrated the reverie that had descended over me.

"I saw . . . wraiths." A second later, I cried out in pain.

"Ow!" Pins and needles flooded my hand like electric shocks. "That hurts!"

"It's just the circulation returning to your hand," Arthur said, his relief palpable.

"What did you see?" I asked, surprised that I could finally put together a complete sentence.

Arthur shook his head. "From where we were, it looked like the stones flew up and circled you. There was dust and wind."

"There was a wraith, a ghost, inside each stone." I pulled my hand back and shook it several times, flicking my fingers to get the feeling back.

"I saw faces," Jeremy said from atop his horse a few meters from us.

"Odd." Arthur grunted, then walked around the cairn, perusing it. "The stones reformed themselves into a cairn. There must be a field of psychonoetic energy holding them together."

"Psychonoetic?" I asked.

"From the Greek, meaning 'soul' and 'knowing.' It refers to the deeper facets of human consciousness," Arthur started in his professorial voice.

"You mean the human biomind that contains psychic abilities like the mists have given us?" I said, interrupting what would have been a lecture.

"Right before they make us go mad," Jeremy added.

"I've never seen inanimate objects invested with psychonoetic energy, at least not on this scale." Arthur fingered the bubbly surface of the cairn. "Some human, or maybe a group of them, must be animating the stones. I don't believe those were ghosts you saw. Rather, I think they were memories of people, invested with energy by the living."

"Are you hurt, Emma?" Jeremy asked.

I shook my head. "No, I'm good. I can ride."

"I'll round Count up for you." Jeremy kicked his palomino to follow my horse.

Arthur walked over to stand beside me. His eyes were thoughtful as they rested on my face. "You're bruised."

"No worse for the wear."

"Serious bruises on your torso could indicate internal bleeding, Emma."

"I'm fine."

"Just let me take a look."

"Since when are you interested in looking at my body?" I retorted. "You do what you can to avoid looking at me or touching me—especially touching me."

"Emma—" Arthur began.

But Jeremy had Count by the reins and was leading him back toward us, so I turned on my heel and flounced off to my horse before Arthur could come up with an argument or excuse.

• • •

A FEW KILOMETERS later, a group of a few dozen riders loped toward us. Each had one white sleeve on his or her shirt. At about a half-kilometer's distance, they dismounted. Like statues or pillars, they were unnaturally motionless as they stood, holding their horses by their leads. They were a long, still line of people and horses blocking our path forward.

"What's this?" Arthur muttered. He touched his heel to Edgar's side, and the horse broke into a smooth, contained canter.

"I could never get that horse to work that hard," I mumbled, shaking my head.

Jeremy was riding in front of me, close enough that he could throw a grin back over his shoulder. "Arthur's a fine rider."

"That's a damn lazy horse."

"Sure. You're a good rider too," Jeremy said, winking impertinently.

So I wasn't the most skilled rider in what remained of the world. I had other good qualities. Still, I didn't have time to ruminate on them because Arthur had dismounted and was speaking to the centermost rider. I pressed Count forward at a quicker pace.

"We have no desire to take up your resources or your time," Arthur said. "We just want to pass through."

"Hospitality is our law, given to us by the Holy Voice," said the man, bowing slightly as he spoke the words.

"Thank you, but we have an objective to accomplish," Arthur said.

"You must come with us," the man said. "All are to be brought before the Holy Voice. That is His word." He bowed again. "It will be a great blessing for you to meet Him. He came to us recently. We heard Him in our minds for many months. Now He has joined us and given us new purpose. We are His acolytes."

"We don't want to trouble you folks. You must have pressing matters to tend to as acolytes," Arthur replied. "We'll just be on our way."

"You must come with us," the riders said in unison. "You must receive the blessing of the Holy Voice."

"Arthur, maybe we'd better go with them," Jeremy whispered.

Arthur swept him with a sour look, then nodded and mounted his horse. "Fine. Take us to your preacher."

"Preacher? He is far more than that. He is the Prophet!" exclaimed a woman at the end of the line, clearly insulted. "He went into the wilderness maimed and returned whole. He has been healed!"

A bolt of anxiety flashed through me.

Arthur nodded once.

The acolytes climbed atop their horses. The spokes-
man rode out in front, heading east at first but then veering
south. The others encircled us and made sure we followed.
We would have been hard pressed to break free, and the religious ones were well armed with bows and quivers full of
arrows, as well as a few handguns and rifles. Their prophet
was a practical man, whether or not he was as holy as they
claimed—and I had a sneaking suspicion he wasn't.

We rode back into the forest along the western bank of
Lake Koocanusa. After a couple kilometers, we saw people
fishing in the lake. Farther down, people swam and played.
The summer heat was intense enough that I felt a flash of envy.

We continued south until a small group of riders joined
us. They, too, wore one white sleeve.

Arthur, with his keen eyes, always discerned faces before I
did, and he whipped out his gun and aimed it.

"Wait!" I yelled. I touched my heels to Count's side, and
the animal sprang forth with such alacrity that I was nearly
unseated. I clamped my thighs around him and held on, and
Count galloped out ahead.

"Emma, welcome!" called a familiar voice. It was Dmitri,
the Russian doctor from Alexei's old camp in France. He had
greeted me at Alexei's Yellowstone camp, and now he was
standing in front of me again.

"Emma, get out of the way!" Arthur yelled in a tone of
pure fury.

Dmitri had halted his horse and was making a sympathetic
face. "I never expected to see Arthur whole again. You do
good work, old friend, and I applaud you."

"Arthur, don't shoot!" I hollered over my shoulder. I
turned to Dmitri. "I presume Alexei is here."

"The Holy Voice himself," Dmitri said without a trace of
mockery. "Your work is visible on him too."

"Emma, damn it, when I say move, you move!" Arthur had
reached us and was still aiming his gun at Dmitri.

"Arthur, I'm not your servant," I snapped. He had assumed a prerogative I would never again give away to anyone, and it was starting to annoy me.

"I don't blame you for hating me, Arthur," Dmitri said sadly. He was growing a salt-and-pepper beard that was bisected by the ropy red scar on his cheek. "What was done to you was so . . . terrible. For that, I am truly sorry."

"You didn't try to stop it," Arthur snarled.

"Would it have made a difference if I had?" Dmitri asked, the truth of the words hanging sorrowfully in his tone. He sighed. "But I suppose you are correct. I did not intervene. I did not try to stop Alexei, and for that, I am ashamed."

Arthur lowered his gun. "Is Alexei—"

"He is here, and he is expecting you."

"And what a happy reunion that will be," Arthur snapped. He kept his gun in his hand but wheeled his horse around to stand beside Dmitri.

"He is a changed man," Dmitri said.

"People like him don't change," Arthur snapped. He looked around, his head swinging about on his shoulders like a Doberman looking for prey.

"Maybe they do," I said, shrugging.

"Alexei is more than a person," Dmitri said. "He always was, even more so now."

· · ·

"YOU MAY SHOOT me, Arthur, but I wouldn't advise it," Alexei rumbled in his chewy Russian accent. With his back to us, he sat in a folding lawn chair on the sandy beach of McGillivray Campground. The beach extended into a lush green lawn that, in turn, was nestled in a dense forest.

"I've dreamt of this moment," Arthur said. He dismounted and walked toward his mortal enemy, then pointed his weapon squarely at the back of Alexei's head.

Alexei didn't bother to get up or to turn around.

The people around us fell silent and only observed, without intervening, as if they had great faith in their Holy Voice. The silence washed outward like concentric waves through the great multitude surrounding Alexei. Most of his followers were seated in prayerful postures. They spilled out over the beach, on the lawn, around trees, under the wooden shelter, and on the paved parking lot. Others moved about, distributing food or chatting or going about their business. All wore either one white sleeve or no sleeve on one side.

Wearing an expression of intense curiosity, Jeremy sat quietly on his palomino.

"You will need me, Arthur." Alexei was evidently communing with the lake and saw no need to interrupt that, so he continued talking with his back to us.

"I need to see you dead." Arthur cocked the gun, and his trigger finger tightened slightly.

"You will need me alive. I could have killed you before, but I did not. I spared you then, and you still live. If you do not believe me, ask Emma."

Arthur's eyes darted toward me.

Wordless, I gazed back at Arthur.

"There's every reason to blow a giant hole through your head," Arthur said, gritting his teeth. "What you did to me, the way you tortured me . . . it was inhuman."

Alexei rose slowly and stretched, drawing an ecstatic murmur from his congregated followers. "Vengeance is mine, saith the Lord." He gestured theatrically with both hands and turned to face us.

"You have a new hand," Arthur said numbly.

"You too," Alexei said. "You speak of inhuman, so we must discuss the mists. We must talk about the billions who are dead because of one man's dream to end war, as if such a thing is possible! God made us in His image, warlike. We cannot put asunder what God has made. After creation, God took vengeance for Himself."

"Vengeance is mine, saith the Lord," murmured the crowd around us. The words were taken up and repeated by the assembled masses, and the sentence rolled out and repeated and swelled like a vocal round.

"Arthur, we have each caused pain. Let us forgive each other. You will need me."

Now Arthur was pointing the weapon at Alexei's heart, or at least at the place where one should have existed. The gun did not tremble in his grasp, but suddenly he tossed it to me, then launched himself at Alexei, his fists flying.

Alexei shrieked with maniacal laughter and caught Arthur in a shattering left uppercut.

Arthur countered with a right hook, a left jab, and a right cross that rocked Alexei on his feet and left rivers of blood streaming out of his nose.

Then the two men were at it, as they must have wanted for so long, hammering relentlessly at each other. They knocked each other down and rolled around and then stood and pounded each other some more. They fought on the beach and on the lawn and up against trees. The acolytes rippled apart to give them space. The brawl was brutal and showed no sign of relenting.

"We've got to stop them before they kill each other," I called to Dmitri.

"I'm in," Jeremy said, jumping down from his horse.

"We go," Dmitri called.

He and Jeremy and I, along with some other men, ran toward Alexei and Arthur, both of whom were bruised and bloodied, their clothing in tatters. It took us several minutes to surround the two men, then another few minutes for me to wedge myself between them, while Dmitri and Jeremy wrestled Arthur away from Alexei and the other men held Alexei back.

"I will never forgive you, Alexei," Arthur swore.

Alexei laughed, low and throaty. "Let me serve you a feast. We will drink to God and to forgiveness, which you need as much as I, if not more. I have hurt few men, maybe 2,000, but never any children. You, on the other hand, have hurt and murdered billions. You have destroyed children and their mothers. That is your doing, little ones dead or in agony. That is your legacy, Arthur, what you've left in your selfish wake. Mothers dead in front of their sons. But I forgive you. You must accept my forgiveness by having dinner with us. I demand it."

"I never intended to hurt anyone," With an expression of raw pain, Arthur stopped struggling.

Still, Jeremy and Dmitri kept their grip on him.

"God is all intentions," Alexei proclaimed. He stood very erect, and the men around him released him.

The crowds intoned his sentence so it rang through the trees and hills.

Alexei's blue eyes turned to me, and they twinkled merrily, despite the cuts and swelling on his face. "Emma, you look well—beautiful, as always."

"Alexei, we're heading to Outpost City to meet our friends," I said tightly. "We haven't time for this."

"Stay and have dinner. Your friends are well," Alexei said.

"We're going now." Arthur jerked his arms away from Dmitri and Jeremy.

"Stay, Arthur. I demand it. If you do not, I will not help you when you come begging. And you will, for I have seen it," Alexei said as he wiped the blood off his face and Dmitri examined his nose.

"I would sooner feed myself to the mists than beg you for anything," Arthur grated.

Alexei shook his head. "You will come back, begging for my help. I tell you now that I will not give you help if you do not sit for this meal with me. That is the price, for you and I have much to talk over."

"You're lowlife scum, and I wouldn't ask you for a teaspoon of water if I was dying of thirst. I will never be back to see you unless it is to kill you. I vow this to you here and now." Arthur spat blood from his mouth, right at Alexei's feet. Then he spun around and strode back to Edgar.

"He will be sorry." Alexei shrugged, then pushed Dmitri away and came to clasp my hands to his heart, smearing me with blood in the process. "It is good to see you, Emma, my healer. I enjoyed our time together. It was . . . unforgettable."

"I was vulnerable and foolish. I never should have let you get close."

Alexei untucked my hand and kissed my palm. "I am happy when you are with me. Someday, you will come to stay with me."

"Alexei, what are you doing here, with these people?" I asked quietly, pulling my hands from his grasp, only to see that they were covered with the blood of both men.

"I give them direction, purpose. I found myself, my meaning when you healed me. I am to tell people that vengeance belongs to God." Alexei bent his head close to mine. "You did not tell Arthur, did you?"

"He's not stupid. He'll figure it out."

Alexei grinned and put his hands on my shoulders. "I forget how funny of a woman you are. Did the mists come to you after I left? When did Arthur stop being idiot?"

"The mists came ten days later. They woke Arthur up."

"Emma, get on your horse. We're leaving," Arthur barked.

Alexei sighed. "So impatient and still an idiot. I want to hold you again in my arms all night, Emma—in my two good arms."

"I have to go." I wriggled out of Alexei's grip and stepped away.

"Do you need anything, Emma?" Alexei asked as his eyes scanned my face closely.

"No. We're meeting our friends in Outpost City," I repeated.

Alexei took hold of one of my hands and escorted me to Count. "We are keepers of cairns now. People build them all over Earth. I feel their minds as they sanctify their memories. My acolytes are the keepers of the cairns."

"I had a weird experience with a cairn," I said.

Alexei held the stirrup for me. "That was how I knew you were here. The cairn told me." He winked at me, though his eye was grotesquely swollen and barely able to open or close. "Last chance, Arthur," he called. "Pay the toll for your future and stay for a meal. Listen and talk. I am here now, and this is a one-time special offer. Honor my religion. Vengeance belongs to God and God alone, and I will honor your request when you come for me. It's now or never."

"Go fuck yourself," Arthur snarled.

"You will be sorry, Arthur."

"Go to hell, Alexei!" Arthur yelled.

"I'll meet you there," Alexei yelled back. A vicious expression crossed his face, then disappeared.

Quaking internally, I swung myself up into my saddle. Arthur was staring with pure venom at Alexei and me, but I wanted to make sure Alexei would let us leave unmolested. "Your people will not hinder us?"

"No, Emma. If Arthur chooses to leave, you go. I give you my word." Alexei's craggy, damaged face took on an expression of offended innocence. Then the offense and the innocence slid away as easily as oil slicking over the surface of water, and I wondered how much he had really learned, how much he had really changed.

"Goodbye, Alexei."

"Until later, Emma, my love," he said lightly. He stepped away from my horse and crossed his arms over his chest. "Your friend, the pretty black woman . . . she had twins. You know that, Emma? She has two healthy babies. She is healthy too."

Twins? Is that even possible? I had not sensed two hearts, two minds, when I'd laid hands on Jeannie. But Alexei's madness was interwoven with strands of seeming omniscience, so I had to presume that maybe I had somehow missed a second heartbeat.

"Look lively," Jeremy said as I almost ran Count into his palomino.

"Oh! Sorry," I muttered.

Arthur trotted far ahead of us. The crowds parted like a sea to let him through, and another chant rose up: "The healing of God is many forms."

"Want to tell me what that was all about?" Jeremy asked. "And what did that Russian mean about Arthur hurting billions? What does Arthur have to do with the mists?"

For a few minutes, as we rode out through the campground, I said nothing. Finally I managed, "It's complicated."

"What the hell isn't these days?" Jeremy shot back.

He didn't press me, though, and for that I was grateful. Anyway, Arthur was cantering at a careen far ahead along the shores of Lake Koocanusa. I had no idea Edgar could run so fast, but Jeremy and I tightened the reins and set out after him.

13

A MASSIVE, UNMOVING WALL OF mists stood between us and Lethbridge, Alberta. It shed a toxic white luminosity over everything, as if an X-ray machine were zapping the plains. From the other side of the mists, a din sounded: a screaming, shrieking, rhythmic percussion. Clearly, the citizens of Lethbridge had employed their mist deflection system, but it wasn't working.

Arthur, Jeremy, and I sat astride our horses on a tallish hill on the prairie grasslands west of the city, just beyond a massive steel trestle bridge over the Oldman River. We'd traveled hard for ten days to get there, from early in the morning until late in the evening. Now, we stared down at what looked like a cloud bank that reached from the ground into the air, about fifteen stories high. It was several kilometers long, stretching out across the horizon, and it seemed to boil and pulse. The hot summer air around us was saturated with the scent of sulfur and flowers, but even the steady westerly breeze couldn't dissipate the mists' stink.

"It's not moving," Jeremy observed. "Do you think Lethbridge is even still there? And if it is, how far around the city do the mists extend?"

"All the way around," Arthur replied.

"Arthur . . ." I said.

"Lethbridge is still there," he replied somberly. "The mists didn't travel here over land. They floated, and they haven't moved since they arrived. They've been stationary. The mists surround the city like a bell jar, but they haven't moved through it."

"Why are they behaving this way?" I wondered aloud.

"Yeah, and how do you know all that, Arthur?" Jeremy asked softly but sharply.

Arthur didn't answer. He just dismounted and strode forward a few meters as the wall of mists inched toward us.

"It moves!" Jeremy exclaimed. "If they've been stationary like you said, why are they moving now?"

Arthur held up his hands, but nothing happened. "Emma?" he said.

"Yes?" I asked, as if I didn't know what he wanted me to do. During our last journey from Outpost City, our quest to save Beth, we'd encountered a huge embankment of mists, moving and wreaking destruction over a huge area. Arthur hadn't been able to dissipate them until I'd merged with him while pouring healing energy into him.

"Emma," he said again, swiveling around to give me a stare that was nothing short of truculent, one that looked particularly hostile coming from his black and blue face, which he hadn't let me heal with my hands.

"You could ask instead of always demanding," I responded. "What's the magic word?"

He inhaled deeply and faced the mists. "Emma, please. I need your help. A whole city is at stake." Two bright splashes of red stained his cheekbones.

What in the world is the matter with him? I wondered. *Is he really too proud to treat me as an equal after all I've done for him, all we've shared?* I shook my head. "Sure." I slid down off Count and stood next to Arthur.

The mass of mists pushed forward, a meter or so in our direction.

"It knows we're here," Arthur murmured, looking me in the eye and nodding.

I positioned myself at his side and took his hand in mine.

Arthur inhaled deeply, softening and sinking, just as I did whenever I wanted to invoke the healing energy, expanding and deepening his state of consciousness and summoning his greater being through intense focus. He released my hand and gently placed it on his shoulder, then held up his hands.

While he worked to change his state, I worked similarly with myself. I forced my breath and my heartbeat to slow. My body responded, as it had so often before, exactly as I asked it to: by becoming more peaceful. I cast my mind's gaze on Arthur and concentrated on him, lending my own consciousness to him so he could dissolve the mists.

The last time we had worked together in such a way, there had been a moment when my personal ego had dissolved. I became a river and ran into Arthur, filling him up, strengthening and empowering him.

This time, it was harder for me to let go. Some part of me didn't want to lose myself. I had to school myself fiercely to remember the task at hand, which was to save a city full of people. When I thought of mothers and fathers with children, all shreds of resistance vanished.

Arthur's, on the other hand, held onto his resistance. He was walled off from me; it was like hitting solid brick.

"Arthur," I said aloud, "let me in." I opened my eyes and noticed that he was steeling himself.

"I can do this," Arthur said, filling himself with breath and consciousness.

"You asked for my help," I murmured.

"Maybe I don't want or need it after all."

Under the bright sun, the mists shrank inward. Noise rushed out from within, the sounds of thousands of people dying, the swell of shrieks that had haunted my nightmares since the Day.

Beside me, Jeremy quailed. He, too, remembered the Day, that Christmas when the mists had risen from the oceans and swept over the Earth, scouring it clean of puny humans and their frail structures.

"Arthur, let me in. I can help. You asked me to."

"I can do this. I'm strong enough." He held his hands higher.

I placed both my hands on Arthur's shoulder. Once again, I went through the process of surrendering and dissolving so I could lend my energy to him. Once again, I met a wall of consciousness that kept me out.

Arthur was determined to do this on his own. "Got it!" he said.

I opened my eyes to slits and saw the mists rise above the plains. They lifted a few meters, high enough for us to see the foot of the cityscape. Dark balls rolled out from under the white embankment, shadows of people escaping the city. They fled in all directions on the rolling green prairie, like a flood of water.

"More!" Arthur commanded.

The mists lifted again, probably another meter, though it was hard to tell from that distance. More survivors poured out from under the curtain of the mists, flowing out like water bursting from a broken dam.

"Still more," Arthur breathed.

The mists rose another meter, and people continued to gush out from under the white clouds.

"Now!" Arthur said.

But this time, the mists did not rise again. Instead, they dropped halfway down. A wail sounded as a great mass was caught in the mists' maw. I knew, painfully, that they would die in great misery.

Arthur's jaw set. Veins bulged on his forehead, and a few crimson drops of blood trickled down from his nose. He was focusing with all of his mental abilities, and it was taking a physical toll on him.

"Please, Arthur! Let me help!" I begged. "It's not too late."

Arthur did not acknowledge my words, but the mists seemed to.

They expanded like the mushroom cloud from a detonated nuclear bomb, and then, with astounding speed—faster than lightning—they condensed. There was a moment of extreme, eardrum-shattering noise as the mists ripped through metal and concrete and pavement and wood and human flesh. They had never before worked with such lethal speed.

Then, there came the dreadful silence. The city was gone.

The mists condensed into a much smaller ball, perhaps the size of a Volkswagen Beetle, and floated up into the atmosphere.

Piles of yellow sand and the people who had escaped on foot were all that remained of Lethbridge. Fleeing survivors streamed out over the plains, like black dots on the prairie. A collective sob went up from them, such a loud choir of wails that we heard it ring out, even from as far away as we were.

"No!" Arthur cried, falling to his knees and clutching his chest. "No! This . . . it can't be!"

"So many people lost," Jeremy murmured. "How many got away? Maybe hundreds, a few thousand? Lethbridge was a big city, at least 100,000 or more, with all the survivors. It was a refugee center, never before touched by the mists."

I felt nauseous. Unable to speak, I walked back to my horse.

"I had them," Arthur muttered. "I had them in my control. I've always been able to disperse them before. They've always responded to me, obeyed. I-I can sense them, and they feel me and disperse. I can dissolve them. I—"

"The mists have grown," I said wearily as I mounted Count.

"I don't know what you folks were doing exactly," Jeremy drawled, "but maybe you should've let Emma do whatever she was trying to do to help you, Arthur."

"The mists are mine! I created them, and I can end them!"

Arthur howled. "This is my duty, and I will fulfill it. I have surmounted torture and death to destroy the mists. It's my purpose, my destiny—mine and mine alone! I will not fail!"

"Arthur, I don't know anymore if you can destroy the mists," I said numbly.

Arthur clutched his fists into his chest and curled around them.

Jeremy and I rode around him, and when I looked back, I saw him weeping.

Jeremy drew his horse up alongside mine. "So Arthur created the mists?" he said in a neutral tone of voice, exhibiting neither disbelief or anger. "That's what all that was about with the Russian?"

I nodded. "He was a military researcher and inventor. He created the mists to operate directly on the human biomind, to control the minds of enemy soldiers and to disintegrate the instruments of war. He meant to end war forever."

"That's arrogant, if you ask me," Jeremy commented. "What made him think he could do what God couldn't, not since He gave us all free will?"

We both glanced back. Far above him, directly in line with Arthur's head, the compact ball of mists hovered, as if taunting him.

Questions loomed in my mind: *What will we, as humanity, do now, if even Arthur can't control or destroy the mists? How long will our Safe Zones remain inviolable? Are our days as a species numbered on this planet? Will we finally be destroyed by our own creation?* A chill took me.

• • •

WE TOOK THE old Crowsnest Highway, passing riders and walkers to whom we waved or called greetings. Arthur was black-eyed, bruised, and distracted, refusing to eat or drink. We made camp each night.

The second night, Jeremy killed a deer, and I helped him dress it for roasting, something I'd had a lot of practice doing. At twilight, we sat by the fire with our saddlebags and tack near us. We turned the venison carcass on a makeshift spit while Arthur paced restlessly, gesticulating to himself.

"Do you think he's going mad?" Jeremy asked quietly.

"I don't think so," I said, but I wasn't as certain as my voice sounded. I watched Arthur, wondering if he was still the same man I had known in France. The man I had loved so deeply, the one for whom I'd given up my husband and children, was gone. Somehow, my Arthur, the one I knew, had vanished into the renewed body with its regenerated hand. It was a deep relief to see his body whole, after the way I'd found him at Alexei's, but his mind, his psyche, or some essential part of him, wasn't whole. *Am I supposed to heal his soul too? Can I?*

Jeremy's thoughts seemed to dance with my own. "You two have a relationship, right?"

"Used to would be a better way to put it."

"Nah, you still do. I see the way he looks at you sometimes, even if you don't notice."

"Yeah, well, whatever it was, it's different now," I said bitterly.

"What isn't?"

"I guess," I said, but I didn't want things to be different between Arthur and me. I longed for the old passion. Until I'd healed him, Arthur had wanted me deeply, completely, and without reservation. I had responded to his desire with my own. I had cherished the passion between us and had staked my life on it. I'd released everything else that mattered, all in the name of us. Of course, that had been my choice. Arthur had wanted me, but I had chosen him back of my own free will.

"Love is hard in the After," Jeremy noted.

I looked at him. "You think I ought to try to help him,

don't you? Even when he wouldn't let me help him save Lethbridge?"

"I think you knew he created the mists, so you must have always known he would break someday. How could he not? He's human." Jeremy used a stick to turn the deer on the fire. He gave it a quarter-turn, then used the stick as a strut to keep the carcass from turning anymore. "An even roast. That's good."

I lay back, cradling my head in my arms and staring up into the purpling sky and tiny, diamond-like stars. "It's starting to smell good."

"It'll be at least an hour, maybe two, before it's ready." Jeremy seated himself beside me. "You can't desert him in his time of need, Emma."

"But he deserted me."

"Remember that night in the boutique, at Bonner's Ferry, when I said your smile lights up a room? Arthur told me later, when you were asleep, that making you happy, making you smile, has always been one of his great accomplishments." Jeremy pulled out a pocket knife and scraped some crud from beneath his fingernails. Between fingers, he wiped the blade on the knee of his pants.

"That's nice, but he's frozen me out."

Jeremy smiled, a faint, pale glimmer of teeth by the light of the moon and stars. "A man like Arthur says something like that, he hasn't frozen you out."

I rolled myself upright and sighed. On the other side of the campfire, Arthur was pacing restlessly. I walked over and leaned against a tree near him. "Arthur . . ."

"I just don't understand," he said. He picked up his head and gazed at me without really seeing me at all. "I keep going over and over it in my head. I had the mists. I was holding them with my will, the way I always do. They were locked into my control. Then suddenly, the bond snapped. How, Emma? How could that happen?"

"The mists have evolved."

"But I had them! I was holding them with my will, the way I always do," he repeated. "Did something happen to me when Alexei tortured me? I think I remember dying a few times, but they brought me back. They . . . those bastards used a car battery and jumper cables to torture me, and they zapped me back when my heart stopped. Maybe that damaged my biomind, though near-death typically enhances it." He paused in his pacing and rubbed his hands through his ragged, black hair, making it stand up. His knuckles were swollen and mustard colored from his fight with Alexei. "They were locked in, I'm telling you. I had control, but then the bond broke. Why?"

"The mists have evolved," I said again.

"I keep going over and over it. I was holding them—" he repeated like a broken record.

"Arthur!" I snapped.

His head lifted, and he looked at me. Even in the dark, his eyes seemed foggy. "It wasn't supposed to happen that way. I had the mists. I had—"

"Arthur!" I said again. I gripped his shoulders hard and shook him.

"They were locked in," he said, his voice numb.

I was at a loss, so I did the only thing I could do I kissed him. I stretched up on my toes while dragging his head toward mine, and I thrust my mouth against his.

For a moment, he yielded, and he actually responded, his mouth warm and soft on mine. His cheeks and chin, no longer clean shaven, felt stubbly in my palms. Then he pushed me away and not gently. "Emma, what are you doing?" he asked coldly.

I stumbled back against a tree and scraped my arm against its rough bark. "You need me to explain a kiss to you?"

"Can't you see I've got other things on my mind?"

"Can't you see that you're spinning around in circles,

getting nowhere?" I cried. "You're not alone in this, Arthur. I'm with you. I'm here to help."

He recoiled as if I'd slapped him. "I don't need your help!" With that, he stalked off past the little stand of trees, into an overgrown sugar beet field.

I cast a look back at Jeremy, who poked the deer carcass and ignored me. It was only my pride, after all, and I'd long since discarded that; it was a useless affectation in the After. I followed Arthur. "Arthur, stop ignoring me. Sit still and let me heal your face."

"Keep your hands to yourself," he barked. "I don't want to do this right now."

"Do what?" I demanded.

Arthur picked up the pace.

I trotted fast after him, then finally sprinted to catch him. I laid my hand on his shoulder and swung him around to face me. "Arthur, talk to me. Why are you so angry? Why won't you let me in?"

He shook my hand off. "Damn it, Emma, what don't you understand? Do I really need to spell it out for you?"

"Spell what out?"

Arthur took an audible breath. "I don't want anything with you anymore."

"Why not? Because I took care of you while your mind was gone and you were an imbecile?" I was shouting, but I didn't care if Jeremy or anyone else left alive in the world heard me. "Because I healed you and fed you and cleaned you and wiped your ass and kept you alive until your mind returned? Is that why you don't want me now? Because I saved you?"

"I didn't need to be saved."

"Bullshit! You were burnt and broken into pieces like Humpty Dumpty," I snarled. "Of course you needed to be saved."

"Maybe I didn't want to be," he shouted back. "Maybe that was my fate, what I deserved for creating the mists in the first place. Do you really think I deserve to live after what my actions have cost everyone on this planet?"

I was shocked into silence. *So that's it. Arthur doesn't want to continue.*

"You should have left well enough alone, Emma, but you never do. I've never asked for you or for your interference in my life. You showed up in that little town in France wearing a goddamn sundress, offering free sex. What the hell were you thinking?" Arthur stepped toward me and tapped my head with his finger. In the night air, the sclera of his eyes were preternaturally shiny and white.

"I was just . . . I thought you had a safe camp, and I was in charge of seven children as well as my daughter, who needed to . . . I had to keep them safe," I stuttered, "no matter the cost."

"Did you even consider whether or not I'd want to take care of you and those kids? Did it ever occur to you that my camp and I didn't need the responsibility?"

"No! I was desperate, and they were *children*," I spat.

Arthur shook his head. "Not a good enough excuse. A band of armed men riding together were a clear and present threat to women and children."

"I knew you and the others weren't dangerous. Newt told us you had a safe camp, so I made a deal with you for the protection and safety of my kids. Don't worry though. I'd never make the same deal today, not with you or anyone else, because I'm not the same woman after all I've been through."

"I know you're not, but how do you think that makes me feel? I guess I was just an expedience to be dispensed with at will. And Newt was just one more innocent victim to add to my guilt," Arthur said hoarsely. "I'll never forget the look on your face when you returned to camp after she'd been killed. You were so heartbroken, and you looked at me with contempt and blame that I know I deserved."

"You're still the one person in the world who has a chance to stop the mists!"

"Apparently not. They're growing, evolving, as you say. They're stalking me just to prove that they can. They're toying with me. I couldn't keep them from consuming Lethbridge, and so many more people are dead! Dead because I'm useless, Emma! Why did you bother to save me?" He strode off again into the night.

Relentless, I followed him. "Arthur, don't you walk away from me, not after everything we've been through together, after everything we've shared!" I shouted. "Stop pushing me away and work through this with me. I deserve at least that!"

Arthur spun on his heel and faced me. Anger and the wounds from Alexei's fists distorted his beautiful, symmetrical face. "What about what I deserve from you?"

"I didn't ask you to leave Europe and come to Canada to find me!"

"You're right. I did that on my own initiative. But you threw yourself back into my arms all on your own, before running off with your husband yet again. Did I deserve that?"

"I owed Haywood! He's the father of my children, and he was taken prisoner rescuing our daughter. I couldn't let him rot in that cage. Once he was safe, I left him to get you. I left him despite the ultimatum he gave me. I chose you over him and my kids, under threats from him that I can never go back. I still wouldn't abandon you!"

"Your ultimatum, your problem." Arthur shrugged. "So that accounts for your husband, but what about Alexei? Did I deserve for you to fuck Alexei?"

I drew up short. "Wh-what?"

"You think I don't remember? It's the clearest image in my head from all the time my mind was gone, you lying naked under that Russian. You must have already healed him, because he had two arms. He was just a second from being hip deep inside you, and it was with your consent, because

I know that look of desire on your face. I know it well. You wanted him, Emma! You were hot and ready."

I felt stricken, and my gut churned. "I didn't sleep with Alexei."

"Really? Are you telling me I imagined that precious little scene? I don't think so."

"Almost, Arthur. Almost, but I didn't," I whispered. "It didn't happen."

"So you almost fucked the man who brutally tortured and nearly murdered me but not quite?" Arthur said. His mouth worked, and his throat made a sound of pure disgust. "Sweet."

"I was vulnerable and lonely." It sounded paltry, even to me. What had I been thinking?

"I don't know what hurts more, that you gave him back his arm after what he did to me or that you almost fucked him. Tell me, were needy children involved that time too? Is that your excuse again, Emma? Or were you just too turned on to turn him down?" He swept me with a withering look of scorn.

"I was just so lonely, so alone. I was scared all the time. I had so much to do, so much to deal with, and there was no one to help me. Everything depended on me. It was unbearable. First you were dying, and that was devastating, and then your mind was gone, and that was almost as bad. I didn't know how to help you. Don't you see, Arthur? No one person can do everything by themselves. Surely you understand the pressure I was under. I didn't know if your mind would ever return. You were like a child, and—"

"Go back to your husband and children, Emma. Then you won't be alone anymore. I'm done with you." With that, Arthur swung around and walked into the night.

I let him go, knowing words between us were useless. I walked back to the campsite with the wind whistling, crickets chirping, coyotes howling in the distance, and Arthur's accusations ringing in my ears. Part of me couldn't believe it was over, but the other part understood that my near dalliance with Alexei had been more than Arthur could forgive.

But what right does he have to judge me—or anyone, for that matter—after what he's done to the world? Furthermore, how could he allow himself to stay like this? He was paralyzed with guilt and rage, and he couldn't allow himself that luxury. He was still our last, best hope for eradicating the mists permanently, and if he couldn't pull it off, each and every one of us would eventually fall prey to the mists.

He had to rouse himself, and if he couldn't, someone else had to. Me. That someone had to be me, because I couldn't let him wallow in despair. *But how can I do it if he is so determined to end the relationship?* Luckily we'd soon be in Outpost City with the others, and they'd help me galvanize Arthur. If we couldn't do that soon, before the mists grew more powerful, humanity would soon be extinct.

14

PEOPLE WERE STREAMING OUT OF Outpost City through the south gate where Jeremy, Arthur, and I stood. We'd left our horses with the community in Cypress Hills, and I'd paid for their keep with more items from the mountain home: a can opener, some sharp and shiny kitchen knives, and a meat thermometer. We'd walked for about eighty kilometers, only to find Outpost City emptying itself through the gate. People walked out with their possessions on their backs or in their arms. Dogs, goats, and chickens flowed through as well, wending themselves around human legs. The barbed-wire fence had been cut out to create a wider gate. The stench of the sewer was almost unbearable, but I knew it wasn't the smell that was driving people out.

"Excuse me?" Arthur shouldered his way through the crowd to a guard standing on a wooden crate, with Jeremy and me close in tow.

"Yeah," the guard grunted. He was a young guy with Asian and European features, and he wore a leather aviator-style hat, despite the summer heat. He was focused on the crowd but finally turned and looked at Arthur. Something in Arthur's mien made him stand straighter. "What can I do for you, sir?"

Arthur seemed to straighten and broaden as well. "What's going on here?"

"There's a wall of mists at the north gate, just hovering

and not moving, but we heard about Lethbridge, so we're not taking chances. Outpost City is being evacuated."

"Darn. Who'll make Outpost Ale now?" I joked.

"I've heard about that stuff, but I've never tried it," Jeremy said.

"How long since the mists arrived?" Arthur asked, ignoring us, just as he'd ignored me since our fight in the sugar beet field.

"They showed up last night," the guard answered. His dark eyes perused the crowd, and he pulled his bow into position and aimed an arrow at someone in the horde. "You there! Is that woman going with you willingly?"

"Yeah, I'm okay. I just don't wanna go west," the woman's voice rang out. "I heard his mother's still alive in Calgary, and I can't stand the crazy bitch."

Some laughter and a few ribald suggestions trickled out among the masses.

The guard made a skeptical face and waved for everyone to keep moving.

"We have friends inside," Arthur said.

"Not likely. Most people have already left. No one wants to take a chance with those mists," the guard said sternly. "Do yourselves a favor and turn around and go back to wherever you came from."

"Not without our friends," Arthur said.

The guard examined him for a moment, then shrugged. "Your life, so you're free to gamble with it. Make way! Let these people through!" He gestured with his bow, and a path opened for us down the middle of the departing throngs.

Arthur motioned for us to follow him, and he went through without looking back.

"Outpost Ale tastes a bit like lighter fluid, but it isn't nearly as delicious," I said to Jeremy as we trailed Arthur. "Makes you blind and drunk quicker than wood alcohol."

"Hmm. Sounds good. I wish I could have sampled it," Jeremy said.

We wound our way through the labyrinth of the departing tide, and then Arthur drew me out of the crowd and pushed me back into a wall to talk to me.

"This isn't the first time you've thrown me up against a wall in Outpost City," I said. I deliberately made my voice husky and languorous and let my eyes rest pointedly on Arthur's mouth. "I was a brunette then, remember?"

Arthur reddened. "Where to now?"

"Norm's," I said. "Follow me." I slipped from his grasp and led them down a side alley. I remembered that part of town, the Badlands of Outpost City, from my time hiding from Arthur and the others there.

• • •

"WE'LL NOT BE leaving yet," Robert's voice sang through the closed door of Norm's red and blue modular home.

"Not asking you to," I hollered, then stepped aside so Arthur could be in front.

The door to the cube popped open, and Robert stood at the threshold for a moment, taking the three of us in. He launched himself at Arthur, wrapping him in a huge embrace. "Arthur!" he cried out, weeping and babbling. "You're all right! It was diabolical, but now you're here, and you're bang on!"

His words brought the others at a run. Laurette, Nwokocha, and Theo threw themselves out the door. In a tangle of arms and legs, they leapt onto Arthur and Robert, knocking them over onto the hard-packed dirt, raising a sheet of dust into the air.

Arthur lay on his back and laughed, the first time I'd heard him chuckle out loud since I'd held him in my arms in Outpost City, the night when I'd worn a dark wig and backless dress and had taken him to bed. We'd laughed in each other's arms that magical, unforgettable night. When we weren't making love, we'd laughed; it had been a joyous reunion.

"Hi, Emma," said Kangee from the door.

Donny, standing beside her, grinned widely at the puppy huddle on the ground.

Behind them, Gaff peeked out with a shy grin on his rakish face. "Hey, Emma. Good to see you."

Donny reached down and pulled me toward him for a kiss. "You did it, girl. You did it! Way to go! You brought Arthur back, safe and whole!"

"I knew you would," Kangee said. She spoke calmly, but her round face was wreathed in a huge grin. Even her long, black braid seemed to dance in the air with joy.

"Admit it. You all had your doubts," I said, smiling. I grabbed her head between my two hands and kissed both her cheeks. "Is that a new tracksuit?"

"It's Juicy Couture," she said a little defensively, as if I was questioning her taste.

"But it's not pink!" I teased. I was about to introduce Jeremy when a hand emerged from the scrum and yanked me down into the midst.

"Don't think we'll leave you standing, you beautiful bird!" Robert exclaimed.

There was no escaping; I was mashed on all sides in an exuberant, undignified huddle, with Laurette and Theo slobbering all over me. The six of us rolled around on the ground, and then Laurette pulled herself out of the mix.

I found myself lying, full length, atop Arthur. I looked him in the eyes and gave him our smile, the special one reserved for him alone, the very one with which I used to greet him at the door of his tent, back when we all lived in an ancient, Roman army-style camp in the south of France.

Arthur's gray eyes widened, and a spasm passed through him.

Another member of the pile moved, and I was shifted off him.

"Well, boyo," Robert laughed, "your cell phone in your pocket doesn't have to be that happy to see me!"

"It's not you it's happy to see. It's Theo," Arthur returned as we all chuckled and unraveled and returned to our feet.

Cell phones? Aren't those long gone?

Nwokocha steadied me as I rose, and then he hugged me. "Emma, things were dire when we saw you last. What a miracle you've accomplished, healing Arthur and reuniting us all!"

"Yes, Emma. We did not even have to rescue you from a gallows or a rogue band or the jaws of hell," Laurette said. She patted my face playfully before kissing both my cheeks. "Splendid work! Surely there were some disasters along the way though."

"Of course! You know me," I joked in a suffocated voice, because Theo had grabbed me and was squeezing me hard enough to shake out my stuffing. "God, Theo! Please."

"I thought I never see my Emmy again," he said tearfully.

"Where's Marco?" Arthur asked.

There was a brief lull before Laurette answered, "He is mad. It happened the same time you were taken."

Arthur's perfectly sculpted face drooped with sorrow, just for a moment. He couldn't stay glum when Robert and Nwokocha flanked him and clapped him on his shoulders. He grinned, then looked up the stairs at Donny and Kangee. "I haven't thanked you folks yet for all you've done." He reached up and shook Donny's hand.

"Glad to help," Kangee said. "Why don't we all go inside? Jeannie's dying to show you the babies."

"The babies!" I cried and scrambled through the door past her. I passed Susie en route and kissed her without slowing down.

Jeannie was sitting in the kitchen, with a baby on each arm. She looked up at me and whooped with joy.

I kissed her fiercely. "Twins!?"

"A boy and a girl," Jeannie said proudly, holding the infants up for me to see their faces. "You didn't tell me, Em. You didn't say it would be twins."

"I-I didn't know." Gingerly, I took the little girl in my arms, the child wrapped in a pink blanket. I hadn't felt her in her mother's womb, and I wondered how she had hidden her heartbeat from me.

"Robert says you came here to heal Jeannie, when she was ailing. You didn't sense two babies?" Arthur asked in a curious tone from over my shoulder.

"I guess there are still some mysteries left," Norm called from his place at the stove.

"I guess so," Arthur said. He laid his hand on Jeannie's shoulder and stared at the babies with admiration. "They are beautiful. Congratulations." He leaned past me and kissed Jeannie.

As the others bustled into the kitchen, Norm came over and patted my shoulder. "Good to see you, Emma. You too, Arthur. Quite a shiner you got there."

"Good to see you, Norm," I echoed. I opened the blanket a little and peeked at the baby's reddish hair. I held her down next to her brother in Jeannie's arms, comparing their plump, puckered faces. "Oh, Jeannie, I'm sorry to say it, they look just like Robert."

"Hey! Me mug's not so bad," Robert said. "It's fine enough to land a beautiful bird like me Jeannie!"

Jeannie rolled her eyes. "Black babies can be pale as infants. There's hope yet."

"Good to hear," I said. The tiny girl in my arms mewled, so I passed her back to her mother.

"Arthur, I'm happy to see you well," Jeannie said in a cooing voice meant to calm her infants.

"I'm lucky to be here," Arthur returned quietly. He sat down at a chair at the table. "I noticed your packed bags. Are you folks planning to leave soon?"

"We wanted to wait for you till the last possible moment, then get out fast and on the fly," Donny answered.

"I knew you'd show," Kangee added.

"What do you think, Arthur? Are we in a rush to leave?" Nwokocha asked.

Arthur cocked his head, and his expression went blank as he checked on the mists. "I don't think the mists are coming into the city. I sense that they're just poised there, by the north gate. They may leave in time, but I can't be sure. My power with the mists failed me recently."

"Failed?" Laurette asked in dismay.

"Lethbridge?" Nwokocha asked softly.

Arthur nodded and looked away.

"Then let's have dinner, and we'll plan to leave in the morning. It will give Jeannie and the babies one more night to rest," Nwokocha said.

"We want the babies to be as strong as possible before we ride out," Kangee said. "It was a hard delivery. The second birth was unexpected, and we almost lost little Emily."

"Good thing I was here with my midwife herbs," Laurette added.

"Emily?" I asked with pleasure.

"She's named after you, Emma," Susie said, smiling. She draped her arm around my shoulders and squeezed slightly.

I patted her gently, knowing how hard it was for her to express physical affection.

"Yes. The boy's name is Andrew, Andy for short," Robert said proudly. He scooped his wiggling son out of Jeannie's arms and laid him in Arthur's. "We took the first letter from your name, Arthur. Andrew is to honor you."

Arthur blinked, chuckled once, and shook his head. "I am honored and flattered. I've always wanted children." He looked at me for a moment, almost as if he couldn't help himself, then flinched and stared back at the baby.

Got you, I thought. *I've got you . . . still.*

"I'm Jeremy, by the way," Jeremy called, from the kitchen door. "Arthur, Emma, did you explain to your friends how fast the mists moved to destroy Lethbridge? I'm all for dinner, but will we have time to get out of here if the mists decide to attack?"

"Actually, the mists are leaving right now." Arthur looked Jeremy in the eye. "I can feel them. I know I couldn't save Lethbridge, and I will never forgive myself for that, but the mists are leaving. They've already moved away."

"Going for good?" challenged Jeremy.

Arthur raised his eyebrows. "No one can say that right now, but they're leaving Outpost City for the time being. This place has never been a Safe Zone."

"People will return to Outpost City if the mists depart," Nwokocha said. "There'll be a big turnabout on the plains and then a rush to get back."

"Unless they can't stand the stink," I drawled.

"You get used to it," Susie said. "Drink enough Outpost Ale, and everything smells good."

"That's because it burns out your olfactory sense," I said, smirking.

"I'm glad the mists left, and I'll be thrilled if people return. I didn't want to have to start my bakery business all over again," Norm said. "Amy and I have built something here. It's not much—hell, it's ugly as sin—but it's home to us."

"It's good for me if people come back. I'm looking for my brother, James. I traveled here with Arthur and Emma to find him. He looks like me. Have any of you folks seen him?" Jeremy asked.

"I know where you can look," called a voice from the door. Norm's wife Amy skipped in, her red curls bouncing around her shoulders. She grabbed me in a delighted embrace. "You guys look like you could use a drink. How about some Outpost Ale?"

• • •

DINNER WAS A loud, raucous affair. We had to speak up to be heard around the clamor of people returning to the city. We all got so loose with Outpost Ale while waiting for the food to cook that hollering at each other wasn't a problem. Jeannie kept shushing us because of the babies, but we just laughed at her and took turns rocking them back to sleep in our arms.

We were fifteen boisterous people crowded around two tables jammed together to accommodate us all: Donny, Kangee, Susie, Gaff, Theo, Nwokocha, Laurette, Robert, Jeannie, Arthur, Norm, Amy, Jeremy, James, and me. Amy had taken Jeremy to the Outpost City clinic, where James worked as an orderly, and the three of them had returned with their arms full of bread from Norm's bakery and an entire wooden barrel of Outpost Ale.

Robert and Theo cooked a leg of lamb, two chickens, and a buffalo roast. For sides, we had coleslaw, grilled zucchini, sugar snap peas, carrots, baked potatoes, and Norm's bread in every variety: whole wheat loaves, a sourdough boule, and several dozen of those little yellow dinner rolls drizzled with honey.

"This is some feast," I enthused.

"How you eat while travel?" Theo asked, passing the carrots.

"We had protein bars and found a church with meal replacement drink." I shuddered slightly. "We also killed a few deer, and we holed up in this wonderful house on a mountain. It had solar panels and a working refrigerator."

"A fridge!? Now that would be a sight for sad eyes," Robert said. "We have a little electricity here in Outpost City, but not enough for such a luxury."

"Stop eating this moment! We are not barbarians. We are civilized people with children present, and we must say grace," Jeannie admonished.

"After a few glasses of Outpost Ale, I'll be lucky not to pray to the porcelain god," I said playfully, gazing down at the carrot that was already perched on my fork.

"Yes, after the ale but before the meal is eaten," Jeannie said, smacking my hand with a wooden spoon.

"Ow!" I dropped the fork, and the carrot tumbled away.

"We represent several religions," Nwokocha said in his quiet way. "I don't know what kind of prayer would be appropriate."

"I'm Sioux," Kangee said. "My ancestors believed everything has a spirit, and that all are part of the Great Spirit."

"I'm Buddhist," Nwokocha said. "After college, I studied with a group of Tibetans and grew to love their ways."

"I'm Catholic," Robert said. "Religion's good for keeping people in order."

"Catholic? Me too," Laurette said.

"Baptist," Donny said.

"Methodist," Susie said.

"Serbian Orthodox," Theo said.

"Episcopalian," Arthur said.

"Druze," Norm said. "My mother was Lebanese."

"Jewish," Gaff said, then grimaced when we all looked at him. "What? There are a lot of blond Jews out of Poland, Austria, and Germany."

"It makes no difference. We'll say something proper. I ain't raising me babies to be brutes," Jeannie said firmly. "Arthur, you're the guest of honor. Would you please?"

Everyone fell silent and turned to look at Arthur.

Arthur's cheeks flushed faintly. His eyes flicked to mine and away quickly, before our gazes could catch. He waited a few beats, masterfully gathering our attention and focusing it on a reverent space. Then he bowed his head. "Let us honor all that is holy and sacred, as each one of us feels it in his or her heart. Let us give thanks to all that is holy and sacred for this meal before us. Let us give thanks for being together once again in the loving bonds of friendship. Amen."

"Ta, Arthur," Jeannie said, with great approval.

"That be lovely, Arthur," said Robert, misty-eyed. He rose with a baby burping on his shoulder and walked around the table to embrace Arthur.

"Please! Haven't you done enough of that? You're like a weepy girl," Arthur said gruffly, then submitted to Robert's affection as if under duress.

"No, I'm not done, and don't you be a wanker," Robert said. "We were all shittin' bricks, thinkin' you was dead. It was a powerful cursed time in our hearts."

"That was a sweet prayer, Arthur, if laconic," Nwokocha said. "Not like your wedding service for Robert and Jeannie. You had more to say on that occasion. You waxed eloquent then, as I recall."

Robert moved to sit next to Jeannie, and the couple clasped hands and beamed. Robert sniffed with sentiment. "I'll never forget me wedding day. What a feast! Vasily sang, and everyone cried like babies."

"You threaten to shoot me," Theo said. "Good times."

I squealed with laughter, recalling it all, and Outpost Ale snorted out of my nose. I held my nose and coughed while I laughed. "I remember that! You accused Marco of cheating at soccer."

"He cheat, the little brat," Theo said stoutly. Since he was sitting beside me, he slapped my back to help clear the cough. "But I not worry about Robert. He have bad aim."

"Not anymore, you ol' fart. You steal me groceries again, and I'll put a hole in your manly parts," Robert threatened, making the rest of us laugh and spit up our ale again.

A moment later, we were all reminiscing, all of us talking at once: the day the Japanese had joined us, the battle with the raiders, the notorious enmity between me and Cook—we had a hundred anecdotes to share over the meal.

"Remember when we almost amputated that Turkish woman's infected foot because James, the doctor, had gone with the men on a mission? And then Torsten arrived just in the very moment and did it for us?" Laurette asked. "I thought he was a crazy man with that bag of veterinary tools!"

"You were gonna chop him with the axe," I chimed in. "Lucky you waited, or we would have had to do the foot ourselves, and it was bad."

"You vomited more than I did," she said, pointing her finger at me, and both of us dissolved in laughter again.

"How could I forget?" I said. "You bring it up at every opportunity."

"Do not fear, Emma. I will not ever let you forget. You have the weaker stomach," she pronounced.

"I shot more raiders in the battle," I said.

"I cauterized more wounds afterward," she countered.

"Ladies, please dry your arses, you vixens," Robert said. "Remember when Arthur made showers for us, to please Emma?"

"I remember," Arthur said, his voice almost too low to be heard. He let his eyes meet mine and linger.

"The showers were awesome!" I exclaimed. "None of us had cleaned ourselves in months. It was all I could do to make the kids brush their teeth. Talk about being brutes."

"And the lice!" Laurette nodded. "Lucky I was there to help the camp through that."

"Yes, that was a serious crisis, much worse than the cannibal raiders," I mocked, drawing laughter from most of the table and a glance of high drama and contempt from Laurette.

"You only kept your long blonde mop because Arthur combed it out," Laurette said with a sniff of her trademark hauteur.

"I remember that too," Arthur said, looking a little more steadily into my eyes.

Everything in me quivered and began to melt under the power of his gaze. I was a little appalled with myself for responding to him that way. After everything that had happened, I wanted to hold a grudge. It seemed the only dignified course of action.

"You guys have done a lot together," Susie spoke for the first time.

Jeremy sat on my other side. He nodded and turned toward me but spoke loud enough for everyone to hear. "You certainly share some kind of history."

"That we do," Nwokocha said, suddenly looking chipper. "I've a mind to chronicle our time together. It may pass down in the folklore of our new community, like Homer's *Iliad* or *Odyssey*."

"Up the yard, perfessor," Robert sang. "I'm not listenin' to none of your lectures. I'll read your books when you make 'em, but no lectures at the table when I've cooked a bloody good meal!"

I leaned forward and looked down the table at Susie. "We've got new stories, that you're featured in, Susie. Remember when we interrogated that prisoner, a few days after the mists attacked, at the end of Nebraska National Forest?"

"When you rescued me from those awful raiders?" Susie said, a little shyly. "You gave me a new home."

"The way I remember it," Arthur interjected, "you demanded to be taken with us, in no uncertain terms. You had quite the mouth on you. Impressive, I'd say."

"I'll say!" Robert agreed. "That one swore like a bolloxed

sailor with pox on his pecker!" Robert laughed and ignored his wife's warning frown.

Susie flushed. "I had come out of a terrible situation."

"You were really angry back then." Gaff chuckled. "I know what Emma is referring to, those two raiders Arthur wanted to question. You said, 'We don't need this one,' and stabbed the poor bastard in the throat. Blood sprayed everywhere. It was like a fountain, and Arthur yelled at you about needing more humane behavior."

"Well, I——" Susie started.

I cut her off and shook a finger at Gaff. "You leave her be. So Susie's a little bloodthirsty. It comes in handy. I was about to be raped in the woods outside the Yosemite village, and she nailed the guy in the throat with an arrow. *Splash*!" I made a motion with my hands to demonstrate the blood splattering everywhere. "She got the other guy, too, a bull's-eye right in the center of his chest. You wouldn't believe her archer's aim."

"Our Susie's a fine thing, a welcome addition to our family," Robert said. "If she saved Emma's fanny, that's good enough for me. You're one of us now, Susie!" He lifted his mug of ale to her, and we all joined in, toasting Susie and her excellent aim.

"Here's to all of us," Laurette exclaimed, lifting her mug.

Everyone around the table cheered and repeated the toast.

"To us!" Arthur said. His eyes sought mine and locked in deliberately.

I started to palpitate; there would be no grudge-holding today. What was dignity, anyway?

Arthur lifted half of his mouth in a lazy, knowing grin, allowing himself to be drawn back into the reminiscing and storytelling.

• • •

AMY, SUSIE, AND I were clearing dishes when Gaff brought Marco down from the attic.

Arthur sprang to his feet, his arms wide for an embrace. "Marco!"

In response, Marco lunged, his teeth and fingernails snapping to tear Arthur's flesh.

Without even thinking, I dropped the dishes and leapt to interpose my body between the two of them.

Arthur laughed and put his arms around me, albeit loosely and only for a moment. "Emma, I don't need you to protect me. He wasn't going to get close." He released me and stepped toward Marco, then peered sadly into the young man's face. "Poor Marco. Has there been any glimmer of sanity?"

"Nope," Gaff said. "I oughtta know, 'cause I take him around a lot. He's just out of his mind."

"Poor mentaller," Robert said sympathetically. "There but for the grace of God—"

"He may have more going on than you think," Arthur said. He sat back in his chair, folded his arms, and stared thoughtfully at Marco, who growled and clawed the air. "Part of him may not be lost. If that's true, there may be a way to get him back."

• • •

IT WAS LATE, and Jeannie and Robert excused themselves with their infants and went to bed. Gaff waved goodnight and scooted off, with Marco on a leash. Theo tottered off, muttering something about too much ale.

"Let me show you to a room. You must be tired from all the traveling," Laurette said to Jeremy and James. She took a candle off the dinner table to light their way. "This crazy cube of a home has many rooms."

"Thanks," Jeremy said, jumping to his feet.

I rose as well and leaned close to Laurette, speaking

only loud enough for her to hear. "Show me to a room too please—and quietly. Don't say anything about it or draw any attention."

She raised a gamine eyebrow but didn't question me. She led us out of the dining room, through a cube, and up a staircase. She paused at a door, tilting her head. "Shall I send Arthur up?"

"If he asks," I said, "but only if he asks." He had to be the one to come to me.

"The vibe between you two is quite . . . strange," Laurette said.

I didn't say anything.

She shrugged. "Emma, that is your room. James and Jeremy, follow me."

I pushed open the door and found a small, square room with a low, double futon. It was open into a bed and made up with pillows, sheets, and a blanket. There was a nightstand with an oil lamp, a washbasin, and a pitcher, and a covered commode rested in the corner. An open window let in enough moonlight that I could see to pick up the book of matches on the nightstand. I lit the lamp, tucked my trusty backpack beside the bed, then brushed my teeth in the basin, with a little water from the pitcher. Then I sat down on the bed and waited, aching.

I wondered if Arthur would come to me. He had thawed some over dinner, but I wasn't sure it was enough. Because of his pride, he had to be the one to make the first move. All I could do was wait.

I sat and let myself relax completely for the first time since setting out from Carstairs. It was easy because I was well lubricated by Outpost Ale and the juicy companionship of my beloved mates. I let myself take in what I had accomplished: Arthur had been rescued and healed. He was whole and had been reunited with the people who mattered to him. Jeannie's babies had been born, and infants and mother were healthy. We were all together again, and, for the moment, we were all safe. Marco was mad; that was the one sour element. But still, so much was in place that it was a miracle.

For me, though, one crucial point remained: Arthur. *Does he want me? Did I leave my husband and children in vain?* I had sacrificed everything to rescue him, and I had succeeded, but I had to wonder if I'd lost Arthur—if I'd lost everything—in the process.

A light tapping sounded on my door.

"Come in," I said softly.

Arthur opened the door and closed it softly behind him.

I didn't speak.

He went to the window and looked out. "Jeannie's babies are cute."

"Adorable," I agreed.

"She looks well, remarkably strong."

"Healthy."

"Robert's great with the babies. He's happy and a good father."

"Delighted."

Arthur turned around and faced me directly. "I've been a jerk."

"Totally," I said, deadpan.

"Come on, Emma!" he exclaimed. Then he caught sight of my expression and burst out laughing.

I laughed too.

He grabbed me up into his arms and kissed me till I was crying and laughing at the same time. He used his body to push me down on the bed.

"Your breath smells like you at night, like mint toothpaste," he said as he pressed himself down into me.

"My toothbrush is beside the basin. You're welcome to use it." My body was opening to his weight, and I was tingling and softening all over, yearning for him.

He stilled. "You didn't sleep with Alexei?"

"No," I promised.

"But you came close."

I shrugged apologetically.

"I have to understand what you were going through, even if it doesn't make me happy," he murmured, peering into my eyes.

"That would be nice," I said wryly.

"You really left Haywood, despite an ultimatum?"

"Really, truly," I whispered. "Nothing in the world, not even my children, could keep me from trying to rescue you, Arthur. I had to do it or die trying."

He covered my face with rough kisses.

I kissed him back with all the passion in my being. I sucked his tongue into my mouth and thought I'd never tasted anything so delicious.

He winced a little from the pain leftover from his fight, but it didn't deter him. He kissed me more deeply and cupped my ass in his hands, squeezing as if he'd never let go.

Then we were rolling on the bed, our hands fumbling at each other's clothes. It was awkward and felt like we were all elbows and chins and knees knocking together. I couldn't get his shirt unbuttoned, and we ended up giggling like naughty teenagers making out in the back seat of a car.

Finally, we were both unclothed, and I lay on my back with Arthur kissing my neck. He ran his mouth down the midline of my sternum to kiss the soft rise of my belly around my navel.

"I've waited so long," I said, a little hoarsely. I stroked his erection, which was full and luscious and made me feel a hunger I'd forgotten I could feel. "I've wanted you so much."

He moaned. He knelt above me, then grabbed my wrists and pulled them together over my head, holding them captive with one large hand. He pressed himself on top of me. "I've wanted you so much I couldn't bear it." He nuzzled my neck.

"Coulda fooled me."

"Apparently I couldn't." He lifted his head and smiled. His gray eyes were all black, merry, intense, open, and warm all at once. "There's no way I could fool you, Emma. There are no boundaries between us. You've seen me at my worst, when I wasn't even human. You know me through and through. I know you that way too." He slid his thigh between mine to part my legs, and I was deliciously brimming with light as I lifted my hips to meet him. It was all radiance, and I was filled up.

Arthur was too. We shone with each other.

· · ·

I AWOKE THE next morning with my head against Arthur's broad, warm chest. We hadn't had much sleep, what with the ferocious lovemaking between bouts of elliptical conversation. My skin had been rubbed raw for almost the length of my body, from the scratch of his stubbly beard; there wasn't a square centimeter of me that Arthur hadn't consumed. It didn't hurt because of the sweet lassitude of bliss that still hung over my flesh. I'd given as well as taken, and Arthur was covered with scratches and bite marks, some in places that would have been hard to explain if anyone caught sight of them.

I slid upright and saw that Arthur was awake. His symmetrical face was set and serious, as if he hadn't slept even an hour. I kissed his mouth. "You didn't sleep."

He shook his head, then situated himself upright, with his back to the wall. He pulled me against him, cuddling my head and chest. He kissed my shoulder. "Emma, I think I know how to get rid of the mists. For good."

15

WHEN WE MADE OUR WAY DOWN to the kitchen, everyone was already seated around the table, except for Norm and Kangee, who must have been out, and Jeannie, who we assumed was probably in bed with the twins.

"There be the loud lovebirds," said Robert as he set a mug of tea down in front of each of us. "Heard the enchanting sounds of your frolicking all night. Quite the festival of fun going on up there."

"I considered throwing water on you like dogs in heat to get you to quiet down," Laurette said with a sniff.

"I'll remember that next time you and Nwokocha go at it," I retorted. I sipped the hot, sweet tea gratefully.

Amy giggled and gave me a roll wrapped in a cloth napkin. It was still warm, and cinnamon was oozing out of the soft, doughy interior.

I moaned with delight, nibbling the roll.

"That's it! The sound we hear all night," Theo said.

"Sheesh, you guys," Susie said. Blushing, she rose from the table and stalked out of the room.

"Someone's gonna have to tell her that sex can be fun," Gaff remarked. "Not me, because we hate each other. Not you, Emma, because she won't be able to look you in the eye for a while. But still, someone better talk to her about the birds and the bees."

"She'll figure it out for herself when she meets the right

guy," Arthur said. He squeezed my thigh gently and took a long swallow of tea.

"Hey, friends. Arthur has an idea," I said in a voice urgent enough for the others to straighten and look at us carefully.

"About the mists?" Nwokocha asked, raising an eyebrow. "That's positive news, because Norm heard this morning that the mists are returning to Outpost City. People are evacuating again. We were just about to rouse you two to tell you to pack your bags."

"The mists are returning," Arthur said with a nod, "but we want them to. In fact, for my plan to work, we need them to get close to us. Gaff, please bring Marco here. I want to try something."

When Gaff escorted the sleepy, daft Marco down, Arthur put him in the center of a circle of seven chairs. Gaff had to tie him to the chair to keep him from attacking anyone.

"I'll sit here," Arthur said, then seated himself to face Marco. "Donny, I need you here, on my right, and Emma, please sit on my left. Anyone else experiencing psychic gifts?" He looked around the room.

"I've been seeing auras around people," Jeremy admitted, shame-faced, then took the seat Arthur indicated.

"I hear the plants speaking to me," Laurette said and sat down beside Jeremy.

"I see lines of energy on Earth," Theo said, sitting.

"We need one more," Arthur said. "Any takers? Anything odd going on with anyone's perceptions? Intense dreams or anything?"

"Um . . . I've been having vivid nightmares, dreams that belong to another category of reality," Amy finally said, with an air of surrender. She took the last seat.

The others stood behind the circle, watching with interest.

"Donny, I hear you can influence minds," Arthur said.

"Yes, to some degree."

"Good. Do you think you can strengthen mine?"

"I think so," Donny said.

"Good man." Arthur smiled. "Emma, you'll do your healing thing, letting your healing energy flow into me. That good?"

"I'm happy to flow into you," I said flirtatiously. My eyes brushed into his, and we both smiled and looked away. We'd interpenetrated each other last night as if we'd never be extricated again.

"What do we do?" Laurette asked.

"Focus and concentrate. See what you feel and let yourselves be present in the space. See what you're called to do. You're here to support me and Marco."

"What are you going to do exactly?" Amy wondered.

"I'm going to interrupt the madness in Marco by connecting to the mists," Arthur explained. "Marco's madness is mist driven."

"Like all madness in the After," Nwokocha observed.

"Yes, and I was mad after Emma healed me, but it was the mists that drove the madness out of my mind," Alexei said. "They set up a resonance that acted as wave interference in my mind, and that set me to thinking. I want to try to set up the same conditions with Marco."

"But you have a special connection with the mists," Laurette said.

"That's true, and that special connection will be our way in. Donny will strengthen my connection. Once I'm connected to the mists, I'll exaggerate their resonance and direct it into Marco. Hopefully, it will act as wave pattern interference in Marco's mind, and let his sanity emerge."

"Like how mists are driven away by drumbeats?" Theo said. "Wave pattern interference?"

"Exactly," Arthur said. "I never thought about it before. Of course, it depends on my skill in manipulating the mists' resonance into Marco's mind."

"How close do the mists have to be for this to work?" Donny asked.

"The closer the better," Arthur said. "The physical proximity to the mists is what gives enough strength to the resonance to interrupt madness. At least that was how it worked for me. It holds true in theory, too, the theory by which we developed the mists. They were created to work via resonance. That resonance allows them to find and dissolve ordnance wherever it's hidden, and the resonance allows them to strategically and extemporaneously influence human thinking via control of the pineal gland. But, at the same time, the resonance is a back door into disrupting the mists. We've been using it that way crudely, with drumbeats and hooves."

"The theory sounds reasonable, but isn't it also dangerous?" Nwokocha asked in his thoughtful way. "If we let the mists approach us closely enough for you to direct the resonance into Marco's mind, will you then be able to dissolve them before they consume us?"

"That's the plan," Arthur said, a little grimly. "That's why I want everyone here, supporting me, lending me strength. This plan may be dangerous. I'm not certain it will work. I'm staking everything on my ability to connect into the mists, direct their resonance into Marco, and then dissolve them before we're exposed. If this works, Marco will be sane again, and the mists will leave this area. Outpost City will be the epicenter of a new Safe Zone."

"That would be good," Amy said. "I'd love to feel safe here! But why will Outpost City be safe now?"

"The wave pattern interrupt caused by the mists meeting the madness leaves behind an energetic residue that the mists avoid," Arthur explained. "I created them that way—well, my team and I did so they wouldn't return to a place where they could be destroyed."

We were all quiet for a moment, considering.

"Worth a try," Robert said in an upbeat voice. "I wish I had some psychic biomind gift to offer to strengthen your powers, Arthur."

Norm stood in the threshold. "Whatever you folks are doing, you'd better do it quick. The mists are at the north gate again, and they don't look like they're going anywhere."

"We want them to get close," Arthur said.

"What if you cannot dissolve them after bringing Marco back?" Robert asked. "Run like hell?"

Arthur nodded and gave an apologetic shrug.

"If that's the plan, I'll drag you out on my back if I have to, if they come to the house behind us," Norm stated. "Too close means dead."

Arthur nodded. He leaned forward and focused his gaze into Marco's mad eyes.

I laid my hands on Arthur's arm and let the healing current bubble up through me.

Donny leaned close to Arthur.

I felt it when Donny's mind became a bulwark for Arthur's; it was quite lovely, the combined strength that resulted. Then the healing current gushed out of me and into Arthur. This time, there was no wall. The healing current, along with the river of my own consciousness, ran directly into the Arthur-Donny unit, until we were all three merged.

I lost all sense of time and physical space. There was no "I" as I'd always before known there to be one; it was merely a single vibrational unit, Arthur-Donny-Emma, that streamed into the abyss. We were a conduit, a trail, moving outward.

In the abyss was something not quite alive but not quite inanimate, something intelligent, something with purpose.

Lines of fragrant white light arrowed back through the streaming unit, into a space I had known once before, when I'd gone mad, of my own volition, in France. When I had dropped into my inner chaos and taken three murderous raiders with me, in order to save Mandy and Alexei.

This time, though, the space of chaos wasn't Emma. It was Marco, and the lines of light, which I'd never before experienced nor imagined, were scalding, white hot. They smelled of lilacs and sulfur.

BOOM! There was an explosion. My consciousness was on fire, in agony. *Is it me who is screaming?*

A commotion erupted around me. Someone grabbed me by the arms. Painfully, I was jarred out of the merging with Donny and Arthur.

Robert held me upright and shook me. "Emma," he yelled, "we've gotta go! The mists are in the back yard! We only got two minutes to get the hell out."

Arthur was being stood up by Nwokocha. With blood streaming from his nose and tear ducts, he begged, "Just a few more minutes!"

"Can you dissolve the mists or not?" Jeremy yelled.

"A few more minutes," Arthur said. "Let me try!"

"We don't have a few more minutes," Gaff cried. He shoved my backpack at me and threw Arthur's messenger bag at him.

"We've got to go now!" Susie looped my arm around her shoulders and dragged me toward the stairs so Robert could haul Donny along. "The mists are here!"

Somehow, in the turmoil of people hollering at each other and scrambling to leave, a single, soft voice sounded above the melee. "Arthur?" said Marco, blinking and standing, with the chair still tied around him. His eyes were bright and clear, and he burrowed his head into Arthur's shoulder.

"Thank God," said Arthur in as prayerful a voice I'd ever heard him use. He sagged against slim Nwokocha, who struggled mightily to keep Arthur standing.

"Out now!" Norm bellowed, then helped Nwokocha drag the uncharacteristically weak Arthur along.

We were a rushing phalanx of people down the stairs and out of Norm's modular home.

Twenty meters away, the wall of mists hung and churned buildings into sand. The city behind the fleecy-white wall was erased. It was gone, as if it had never been. I could only hope, in a burst of anguish at the sight of all the destruction, that most people had been evacuated.

Nwokocha, Theo, and Gaff managed to keep us in tight formation as we raced, headlong, through the winding dirt streets of Outpost City and finally out through the south gate. When we reached the gate, Kangee strode up out of the ethers and hoisted Jeannie into her arms. Robert laid the baby he was holding on top of the other baby in his wife's arms.

"Hold tight, Jeannie," sturdy Kangee said, speaking loud to be heard over the babies' squalling. "See you guys in Cypress Hills." In an instant, she took off on a magical walk, then vanished back into the ethers with Jeannie and the tiny infants.

"Let me try now," Arthur said before we could disagree. He wheeled around to face the mists. He threw down his bag and held up his hands. I dived on him so I could lend the healing current to his own power, and Donny leaned into him with the same intention, hoping to use his psychic gift to support Arthur's.

The three of us merged again; it was easier this time, because we were still half-entangled.

The mists vanished.

Marco cheered, and the rest of us joined in.

"Finally!" Arthur said, then collapsed, unconscious.

• • •

OVER HALF OF Outpost City was gone. The remnant still stood, a reeking, shattered mess of buildings covered in fine, yellow grit; it had looked just as dilapidated before the mists, sans the yellow coating.

After we brought Arthur to and got him back on his feet, we welcomed Marco back to the land of the sane.

Arthur brought us up to speed on what our next move should be. "We have a task," Arthur said simply. "It's not here at Outpost City. It's at the ocean edge, where we sailed in, where the mists were reborn and erupted with lethal intent, where the true destruction began. That's where I—we—have to confront them. We have to retrieve the horses. We have a journey ahead."

Norm and Amy turned back, though. Norm said, "We'll stay and rebuild. They'll need us. I'm pretty sure two of my bakeries are still standing."

"Is this really a Safe Zone now?" Amy asked, her tearful eyes glued on Arthur's.

"About fifty kilometers in each direction. That was the original programming," Arthur said, swiping at his bloody nose with his arm.

I took my extra shirt from my backpack and blotted the blood on Arthur's face.

"You're bleeding too," Arthur said.

"I am?" I was shocked to feel the liquid draining from both nostrils.

"I have water. Give me that shirt, you fool," Laurette said. "Of course I am always the one to the rescue."

Laurette cleaned our faces as Norm and Amy hugged everyone goodbye.

"We'll rebuild Outpost City better than before," Norm swore. "This time, we'll put in plumbing from the get-go . . . and the ale will taste good!"

We all laughed, even as we ached, for we knew we'd never again see our generous baker friend and his lovely young wife.

Amy squeezed me in a tight embrace. "Thank you for everything, Emma," she whispered. "I never would have been reunited with Norm if it wasn't for you." She stood back and laid her hand gently on Susie's shoulder. "Susie, do you want to stay with us? I've come to love you like a sister."

Susie's eyes veiled over with unshed tears. "You're kind,

Amy, and I'm touched. But my place is with Arthur and Emma. If they have a journey ahead of them, so do I."

"Good, Susie. We need your arrows," Theo told her.

"Gaff, what about you?" Amy asked.

Gaff shook his head. "Nah, I've gotta catch Marco up, tell him everything that's happened since he went crazy."

"I'm *pazzo* for a few months. You are forever," Marco teased.

The two boys slugged one another in the arm.

After another round of farewells, we took our leave, setting off for Cypress Hills.

"It's only a day and a half on foot to reach our horses, as long as we skip a little sleep," I reminded everyone.

"We will sleep this time, oh pestiferous one," Nwokocha said wryly. "We have Arthur. We won't let you torture us anymore."

"You didn't sleep last time?" Arthur asked, mildly amused.

"None of us slept," Gaff said, groaning with the weight of the memory.

"You wouldn't believe what a pain in the ass Emma was when we set out to rescue you," Laurette said, almost hissing. "She would not let us rest and barely let us eat. My God."

"Trust me, I believe it wholeheartedly," Arthur said.

"Thanks a lot," I said sarcastically.

"Anytime." He wrapped his arm around my waist and let his gaze travel far out over the plains, into the convex purple line of the distant horizon. His beautiful face took on a calmness I'd never seen before.

I tried to sense the source of his assurance. We were still entwined, psychically, and he smiled and kissed the palm of my hand, without saying a word. "What are you thinking?" I asked.

"Not thinking." He smiled. "Remembering."

"Remembering what?"

He touched my cheek gently. "Do you even know what a

pain in the ass you can be?" When he saw my expression, he grinned. "It's not what you think. It's good. We're traveling to the ocean. Our camp is on the other side of the Atlantic." He raised his eyebrows and perused my face. "On the far shore of memory is love and hope. That's what I'm thinking."

"So once we get the horses, we ride east to the ocean?" Susie asked, curiosity written all over her pretty face.

"Yes. We'll get some help along the way," Arthur said. "We need some old friends before we face the mists once and for all. Emma, we need Haywood. He sees possible futures. We could use such a gift."

"Tough sell," I muttered. "Mandy might be useful too. She can create and amplify sounds in the air. Resonance, right?"

"Yes, very useful," Arthur said. "We'll persuade them to join us."

I shrugged. "We can try."

"Then we go to the ocean?" Susie asked insistently. "I've always wanted to see it. We can sail to your camp in France, the one I've heard so much about. I want to see it and meet all the others, Vasily, Torsten, James, Tara, and Bojana. I remember all their names."

"We have to pick up another old friend along the way," Arthur said. "We're going to need him. He's the missing link who'll make it all work. He's the final piece in the puzzle to help us rid the world of mists and bring people back from madness at the same time."

"Who?" asked Nwokocha.

Arthur's expression remained serene. "Alexei."

ACKNOWLEDGEMENTS

MANY THANKS TO Lori Stone Handelman, for her brilliantly insightful editing and kind support.

Thank you to Autumn Conley for meticulous, thoughtful copy-editing.

Thank you to Drew Stevens for his beautiful book designs, and for being great to chat with.

Thank you to Gwyn Kennedy Snider for her fabulous book covers.

Thank you to Michelle Czernin von Chudenitz, for too many reasons to enumerate.

Many thanks and much love to Gerda and Mark Swearengen, Stuart Gartner, Linda Hillebrand, Komilla Sutton, Lynn Bell, Paul Brodeur, and Don Steelman for the warm support. Thank you to Tom Farina and Phil Kanter.

I offer heartfelt gratitude to Sarah Miniaci for the best blog tour support ever.

All of my love and the deepest gratitude to Julia and Madeleine Howard and to my husband Sabin Howard.

TRACI L. SLATTON is a graduate of Yale and Columbia. She lives in Manhattan, and her love for Renaissance Italy inspired her historical novel *Immortal* (BantamDell). Also the author of novels *The Botticelli Affair*, *Fallen*, *Cold Light*, *Far Shore*, and *The Love of My (Other) Life*, Slatton has published *The Art of Life*, a photo essay about figurative sculpture; *Dancing in the Tabernacle*, a book of poetry; and *Piercing Time & Space*, a non-fiction title on science and spirituality.